A labor of love . . .

Seraphina Fawkes is ready to make her mark on the Little Rock design industry as Gallagher Interiors' new lead on Tanbee House—a coveted historic restoration project. But the job's biggest perk might be her handsome boss, Grant Gallagher. Grant shares Seraphina's straightforward, no-nonsense demeanor, so she's surprised when he hires an old adversary who was suspected of involvement in a drug ring. Though Grant seems intent on giving him a chance, she'll keep a close watch on anything that could jeopardize the project—or her growing partnership with Grant.

Getting what he wants—even at others' expense—never used to be difficult for Grant, but sexy, stubborn Seraphina tests his resolve. Though deception is necessary to maintain his covert investigation into the crime syndicate plaguing the city, Grant knows that the longer he hides the truth, the more destructive it will be when revealed. Will Seraphina still trust Grant, and their intense connection, after she finds out their foundation is built on secrets?

Visit us at www.kensingtonbooks.com

Books by Roxanne Smith

Long Shot Romance
Men Like This
Relapse In Paradise
Running the Numbers

Bound By Design
To the Studs
Love On the Vine
From the Top

Published by Kensington Publishing Corporation

From the Top

Bound By Design

Roxanne Smith

LYRICAL PRESS
Kensington Publishing Corp.
www.kensingtonbooks.com

First Electronic Edition: December 2017
eISBN-13: 978-1-5161-0084-2
eISBN-10: 1-5161-0084-0

First Print Edition: December 2017
ISBN-13: 978-1-5161-0087-3
ISBN-10: 1-5161-0087-5

Printed in the United States of America

This one is for Granny Dot.
I still want to be you when I grow up.

Acknowledgments

My deepest appreciation to my favorite cheerleader, Spencer. Once again, your boundless urgings worked to push me forward when I might've otherwise been content to linger in one place for a time.

Marci Clark, my favorite editor in the world.

And Dawn Dowdle. I'd wish every author an agent like you in their corner.

Author's Foreword

Please forgive any liberties I've taken with Little Rock's Governor's Mansion and the surrounding area. Sometimes, reality works. Sometimes, it takes a strong dose of fiction to pull a story together.

Chapter 1

Seraphina Fawkes ran her fingernail down the list of appointment times. Once again, her meeting had been pushed back, and Roper McLeod had taken her time slot. She'd give anything to hate him, but not only was he kind, he was also talented, helpful, and outgoing. All things the mighty and imposing Grant Gallagher prized in his designers. Seraphina wondered, not for the first time, how on earth she'd ever been hired. She didn't seem to fit in very well at Gallagher Interiors. And yet, here she was.

Annie Lester blinked up at her expectantly through Coke bottle lenses, and a small smile stretched tight on thin lips. She was ninety if she was a day, with thin, gray-streaked hair pulled into a too-tight ponytail. Not a lick of style, but sweet down to her bones.

Seraphina gave Grant's secretary her most winsome smile, which wasn't much of a smile she'd been told. More of a smirk, but Seraphina tried her best. It wasn't her fault if grinning ear-to-ear felt unnatural. "Ten-thirty works fine for me. Thanks, Annie." The false brightness in her own voice made her cringe internally, but she kept her face composed and walked with purpose, her head high, back into the small waiting area.

Some waiting area. Just a few chairs lining the hallway outside Annie's reception area. The line of chairs ended at a small table, like the caboose of a train, that held a tacky fake flower arrangement weirdly out of place at Gallagher Interiors but just right for Annie's style, and a spread of magazines, which were mercifully up-to-date. Seraphina eyed the cover of one, enjoying the view of a shirtless Orlando Bloom on a tropical beach somewhere, but she wasn't in the mood to browse. She was too wired.

The tablet she tightly grasped was searing her hands like a hot stone. She'd joined Gallagher Interiors just in time. Grant's firm had won the bid to create a new business office on a piece of property annexed to Little

Rock's historic Governor's Mansion. Tanbee House. Originally the project had been slated for Cupper Cottage, but the city, in a move that surprised some city officials and most of the local Historical Society, switched the site to Tanbee House, once the large home of a farming family.

Today, she'd present her personal designs. She was lucky to have been included, new as she was to the company. But she'd joined Gallagher Interiors for this very reason. She wanted to make her mark, and the chance to get her hands on one of the protected historic buildings of downtown Little Rock probably wouldn't come again anytime soon.

Unfortunately, she had Roper McLeod to contend with. There were a couple of other designers in Grant's firm who were putting forth ideas for his consideration. But Roper was the one to beat. Between him and Grant, Seraphina had her work of breaking up the boys' club cut out for her.

Her nerves refused to settle, so she paced the hallway. The hiring process she'd endured had been almost overkill, like she'd applied to work for NASA or the FBI. She'd undergone several interviews, but none with the man himself—Grant Gallagher. He'd hired her sight unseen. For the first time, Seraphina would meet the man behind the curtain. He had a reputation spanning a wealth of creative descriptions—terrifying, intimidating, cold, uncompromising—none of which frightened Seraphina terribly; she'd been accused of some of them herself. But meeting him the same day she had to hand over her maiden assignment for his company, well, even she wasn't immune to that level of scrutiny.

Had she played it too safe, too conservative? She could be as creative and innovative as the next guy, but this was different. She'd chosen to keep her designs true to the original concepts of the building they were renovating, with little deviation. Her draft maybe lacked flavor, some spice and fun, but surely this was a special case.

She'd settled into a meditative wait when the soft scuff of shoes brushed the carpet. By the time Roper rounded the corner into the hallway, Seraphina was on her feet, balanced comfortably on the stilettos she'd purchased just for this meeting, and smoothing the soft fabric of her dress pants. They were pleated so perfectly, no one would ever guess she did her own dry cleaning at home. The idea, always, was to hide the effort. Make it look easy. Never let them see you sweat. That was a lesson from her father Seraphina would never forget, because it was one of the few worth remembering.

Roper's lips parted into an easy grin. It took nothing for the man to smile. He bowed slightly, dark brown eyes merry behind square lenses in nearly invisible frames. "Apologies on taking your time slot. I realize my boon came at your expense, even if he doesn't."

She smiled back. Roper's disposition had that effect. Her smile might be vague to anyone who didn't know her well, but Roper was catching on. "It gave me plenty of time to sit out here and build myself up."

"Into a ball of nerves, I bet," he shot back agreeably. "I know you're nervous, but I think you and Grant will find you've got a thing or two in common."

So she'd already suspected. It didn't make the heaviness in the pit of her stomach go away. "Thanks, Roper. I hope your presentation went well."

He shrugged and waved his tablet carelessly. His was the exact same make and model as Seraphina's, which didn't surprise her in the least. Any more, part of succeeding was staying on top of the constantly shifting world of next-level technology. He probably had many of the same software programs installed, as well. "Okay, I suppose. I guess we'll see. I'll be in the lounge if you want to compare notes after your presentation."

Actually, she wouldn't mind seeing what the great Roper McLeod had come up with. Once they'd pitched their ideas to Grant, proprietary concerns went out the window. "Sure. I'm certain I'll be in dire need of an espresso by then."

"If not something stronger." Roper winked, gave her another merry smile, and left her.

Part of her wanted to scurry after him. Seraphina sighed and let her shoulders droop. Five seconds. She gave herself five seconds to doubt, tremble, and be afraid. Then, on a forced exhale, she squared her shoulders, hitched her chin, and cleared her mind of every negative thought and emotion. Easier attempted than achieved.

Annie waved her through without looking up. Seraphina was glad to avoid another round of uncomfortable small talk. Grant's office was behind a set of double doors. They weren't any more special or impressive than the flower arrangement in the waiting area—outdated and out of place. She'd imagined someone like Grant Gallagher inhabited the most sleek, high-end, state of the art office in the city.

Once she stepped through the doors, she was satisfied to see she hadn't been too far off the mark. In here, the design changed so drastically, it was jarring to her finely tuned sense of style. To call the square room austere wouldn't quite do it justice. For one, there were some elements of warmth. The desk faced her, and was backlit by morning light beaming through a checkerboard wall of windows. The side walls were paneled in aged, mellow wood, utterly unembellished. No photographs or shelves. The only thing to break up the monotony was an unremarkable door off to her left, only noticeable because of the black iron door handle. The desk was perhaps a shade or two darker than the walls and just as blank.

And there, so still she'd missed him at first glance, sat the imposing figure of Grant Gallagher.

He stood as her gaze alighted on him, straightening his jacket and smoothing his tie. He wore an expensive suit, cut perfectly, the color of wet sand. His hair nearly matched it, a beige blond he wore close cut. It suited the angular planes of his face—razor sharp cheekbones and a wide, stubborn jaw, both coated with a fine stubble of blond hairs. He came around the desk swiftly and offered Seraphina a long, narrow hand. He moved with a brisk industry; not the type to tap his foot or drum his fingers restlessly across a surface. Seraphina could almost sense the reserves of energy coiled inside him, as if he were poising himself to strike the moment it became necessary.

"Seraphina." His greeting was brusque but not unkind. He didn't waste effort on a false or weak smile, only nodded slightly.

She grasped his hand firmly, suddenly certain they would get along famously, even as the energy he exuded made her nerves tingle. "Mr. Gallagher. A pleasure."

The color scheme of the room, combined with Grant's likewise suit, hadn't prepared her for when their gazes locked. His eyes mirrored the startling blue of her own. They were perhaps a little brighter, even, all the more intense for how they contrasted so sharply against so much brown and beige. She blinked as the unmistakable burn of desire whispered through her, stoking fires low in her belly.

"All mine." If Grant was having a similar attack of sudden attraction, he showed no signs. He indicated one of two empty chairs, both light brown tweed, for Seraphina to sit, and went back to sitting at his desk like a statue.

Not a statue. A lion. The thought came unbidden. And indeed, as still as Mr. Gallagher was, there was simply no ignoring the power he radiated, even as he sat back in his chair deceptively relaxed. Perhaps some others wouldn't notice there wasn't an at-ease bone in his body, but Seraphina did. But she was a special case. Deciphering body language and reading facial expressions were part of her skill set—an ability cultivated from a childhood spent trying to read her dad's moods—but Grant offered no physical clues for scrutiny. Not a man who wore his emotions.

Another thing they had in common. Seraphina took the chair and settled with her back straight. She smothered the flare of sexual tension that had snaked through her. She wasn't embarrassed or chagrined. The body wanted what the body wanted, and it was pretty obvious why hers might want

Grant Gallagher. Besides being lean and tall, his air of self-contained power spoke of a fierce discipline that was her personal kryptonite. She was a sucker for a man with an iron will and a masterful grip on his self-control.

But her mind was focused elsewhere. Currently, it was engaged in keeping her hands from shaking from nerves. Her career at Gallagher Interiors began—and possibly ended—here in this room, today.

* * * *

Seraphina was almost exactly what Grant had expected her to be, given her résumé and the reports he'd read on her hiring interviews. Her answers had been so picture-perfect, he'd rejected her offhand. Roper had intervened. He'd said there was more to Ms. Fawkes than could be put on paper. Trusting the opinion of his most highly regarded designer, Grant hired Seraphina sight unseen. Now, he had some small idea of what had impressed Roper about this particular candidate.

Seraphina carried a peculiar energy he found both unsettling and familiar. She was earnest yet guarded, sincere yet rigid. She shared little of herself, but what she shared was true. A good thing, since duplicity was Grant's pet peeve. He'd take an honest sinner over a lying saint every time.

All this, he thought wryly, perceived from a handful of exchanged words. Ah, but those were instances of the truest communication. Without saying much at all, he guessed he and Seraphina had taken one another's measure and found a commonality in how they approached the world.

He settled into his desk and peered at her, enjoying being on the receiving end of a piercing gaze from such interesting, nearly ethereal, eyes for once. His eye color was a nuisance most of the time. Men were more likely to feel intimidated by a steady gaze, and women more likely to find him attractive. Seraphina didn't appear to suffer from such a malady. If she thought him handsome, she hid her thoughts well behind her stark, measuring gaze. Maybe the direct stare threw people off, he mused. He wasn't prone to intimidation, but Seraphina looked as though she could pull it off if she wanted, and with minimal effort.

A delicate patrician nose sat perfectly on her heart-shaped face between wide, high cheeks. Her blue eyes were ice against the fire of her brilliant red hair, which she wore to her shoulders, sleek and straight like she'd had it dry-cleaned and pressed alongside her suit, and bangs that fringed over delicate eyebrows the same vivid shade of red.

She was beautiful. And waiting for him to say something, he realized.

Grant cleared his throat, sat up straighter, and held out his hand for the tablet Seraphina held clutched in her hands. It was the only trace of nervousness she betrayed. "May I?"

"Yes, of course." She relinquished the device with a slight smile.

The folder icon was labeled clearly as soon as he turned on the device, and he spent twenty minutes of complete silence pouring over Seraphina's drawings and calculations. She'd gone a step further than Roper had. Grant's go-to guy had included plans for Tanbee House once the bottom-line renovations were complete. Seraphina had considered that in her notes, flagging dates, materials, potential resources, and additional permits required for things like the electrical and the plumbing.

Grant raised his eyebrows. "You're thorough."

She seemed almost confused by the compliment. "I assumed the remodel included all aspects, not just the fun stuff."

"No, you're absolutely correct. This is so detailed, I could hand it off to the renovation team tomorrow. However." He paused, then glanced up and matched her stare. "I don't need a designer to replace drywall, repair the original hardwood flooring, or tell plumbers and electricians how to do their jobs. What I need my designer to do is design. Your job is the fun stuff, as you call it. As I said, I appreciate that you're thorough—"

"You didn't actually."

He'd looked down, but the edge to her voice caught his attention, and he glanced up sharply. "Pardon me?"

"You remarked on my thoroughness, but there was no mention that you appreciated it. You can tell me you don't like my plans without insulting me at the same time. I'm a big girl, Mr. Gallagher. And an experienced one. I'm well aware of my job title and what my part entails. However, you asked for plans for a decrepit building, and seeing as I've worked for you all of three weeks, I daresay you'll have to excuse my efforts to consider drywall replacement, a stable foundation, and running water in my calculations."

His mouth opened. He shut it quickly, irritated to find himself slack-jawed. He inhaled deeply and set Seraphina's tablet on his desk. "I apologize if I was rude. You're right. You're new here, and someone should've explained that we have a special team that handles what we call 'cleanup' before a big remodel. We do this so that our designers can focus on style and function without worrying about the basic garden variety needs of every job. If your idea is greenlighted, your plans are handed off to the cleanup crew, who run power and water lines where they're needed. By the time you're on-site, it's stick and paste."

Seraphina glanced around his office with a thoughtful expression. "Thanks for clearing that up. Are you going to tell me what you think of my designs, or is there some other company procedure I'm unaware of?"

He wanted to sigh. Her defensiveness was tiresome. "Ms. Fawkes, I don't apologize unless I mean it. In fact, that goes for anything I say to you. Rest assured, I will never pander to your feelings. I said I'm sorry. I won't say it again. If you wish to hold it against me, you'll find the coming weeks unpleasant."

Finally, something like chagrin crept onto her face. She looked at her lap demurely for the span of a few seconds before her chin came back up. But the chill had left her, at least. "I'm not usually so prickly. It's nerves, I suppose. This is difficult. I'm new, and you give very little away. I spoke facetiously, but the question was fair. And I'd still like to know what to expect."

He studied her. Her hands were pulled into tight little fists on her lap, but her face was open and questioning, waiting for his answer. "I'll take some time. If you'll wait here a moment, I'll transfer your files from the company cloud."

She nodded, and he left the desk and slipped through the door that led to his inner sanctum. His secret office, he sometimes thought of it, where he could let papers pile up, blueprint rolls bunch into corners, and coffee cups sit forgotten. Quickly, he opened the necessary file from the company server but didn't bother to save a copy on his personal device. He would only keep a copy of the plans he intended to use. He left Seraphina's files open on his desktop, so they'd be ready when he returned to pore over them. Then he hooked a finger at Ophelia, his assistant, so to speak, and beckoned her to follow him into the outer office.

She rose immediately, so instantly obedient he almost rolled his eyes. But for the sake of appearances, he gave away nothing.

Seraphina's eyebrows drew in confusion when she noticed Ophelia behind him. He stopped near her chair and nodded toward Ophelia. "Ms. Fawkes, meet Ophelia Quenby. I asked her to wait in the inner office for our interview to pass until I introduced her. I judge she'll be an asset to you as you learn your way here. Ophelia, this is Ms. Fawkes."

Seraphina stood up and offered her hand to Ophelia, but did not smile. "A pleasure," she said. "Please, call me Seraphina." She turned an inquiring look at him. "I'm being assigned a helper?"

She appeared dismayed, although Grant couldn't credit why. "Ophelia is something of a catch-all assistant. She's been working with me lately, on a recently completed proposal. Roper likes to work alone, and most of my staff already have assistants, so she is currently untasked. Even if I choose Roper's design for Tanbee House, you won't be long without a new assignment. We turn down more work than we accept."

"I prefer to work solo myself."

"When you've been with me as long as Roper has, perhaps you may." She pressed her lips together. "So, not an assistant so much as a babysitter."

Ophelia looked away, toward the square windows and their broken view of the downtown skyline. Her dark brown eyes glittered, but she said nothing. Grant guessed she wasn't admiring the picturesque scenery. Seraphina had taken a swipe at the young woman's pride; spoken as if Ophelia wasn't standing right next to them. That alone was enough to invite his ire.

He kept his expression carefully neutral, which made the stinging words all the more effective. "I prefer to call her a guide. She knows what I like, what I expect, and makes better coffee than most baristas in Little Rock. But if insulting her by likening her work to that of an inexperienced child taking care of a toddler makes you feel better about letting her tag along, then sure. Babysitter it is."

Seraphina's vivid blue eyes widened and a crimson tide rose from her neck and stole over her cheeks in a deep flush. Her first exhibition of real and deep emotion.

He was sorry the emotion was mortification. He would've preferred not to take her to task with an audience—or at all, if he could help it—but lopping off big heads was often necessary. Disrespect of any of his employees, from his dowdy secretary down to the janitor who swept the floors and emptied the trash bins in the evenings, was dealt with swiftly and harshly.

More importantly, he considered it good business practice to discourage his employees from questioning his authority before they developed a habit. He had a reputation, after all, and not for being a nice guy. Fair, yes. But not nice.

He analyzed his watch grimly, aware of the lunch hour creeping ever closer. "Ladies, I apologize if I'm cutting this short, but I have an appointment elsewhere. Ophelia, I'll need you this afternoon. Report to Seraphina first thing tomorrow morning. Ms. Fawkes, it's been…interesting. Expect my decision before the end of the day."

Seraphina's face registered relief. Well, that didn't surprise him. He hadn't given her any reasons to relish his company. Ophelia only nodded knowingly. She'd probably surmised by now where he spent his hour-long lunch breaks most days, even if he'd never said it out loud to a single soul. She had an underrated intelligence, but he didn't try explaining that to Seraphina. She'd figure it out on her own. Or she wouldn't, and be all the poorer for it.

Chapter 2

Grant signed in with a friendly nod at Emma, the longtime front desk aide. Her scrubs were a cheerful pink today, scattered with yellow daisies with happy faces drawn inside the center of their petals. For him, it only made the contrast between her bright outfit and the gloomy atmosphere of the home all the more noticeable. But he'd been told he was the only person who found Heritage Acres gloomy.

Maybe that was so. His mother liked the place well enough. She claimed the orderlies treated her well, the doctors and nurses took careful note of her penned complaints, and the other seniors who called the place home were happy. Content as they could be, at any rate, living in a nursing home, even if it was an incredibly nice nursing home.

That his mother had to live in such a place at all, chafed badly. But Grant had stopped being able to care for her once he'd started college. By then, Kathleen Gallagher was sixty years old. Grant had done his best, but there were limits to what a kid could do for a mute old woman with a club foot. She couldn't talk, couldn't walk without a walker, couldn't work, cook, or communicate easily. They'd been on their own as long as he could remember, so there was no one to call when he simply couldn't do it any longer. Certainly not the dad who'd abandoned Grant to Kathleen's care as a child. She wasn't even his real mother.

Still, he hated it. He hated coming here, visiting his mom, chatting with coat-clad doctors who were always in a rush, nurses who were too kind. Mostly, he hated the relief he felt that he no longer carried the burden of taking care of Kathleen. At this point, he wouldn't know what to do with a seventy-seven-year-old woman.

He waved at Emma as he passed by the nurse's station. She smiled so sweetly the apples of her cheeks were like bulbs stuck to her face, then scurried away. He reached Kathleen's door and knocked before entering. As usual, she waited patiently at a pop-up table. There was a cafeteria, but in-room lunches were arranged on request. Grant could remember a time when they hadn't enjoyed such a luxury. It had taken him a long time to earn the kind of money that kept Kathleen at a place like Heritage Acres. As much as he disliked the home for being what it was, he'd never forget there were far worse places for Kathleen to be.

For their meal, she sat in a wheelchair, even though she hated it. She preferred getting around with her walker. She'd said to Grant once, in a letter, that the exercise is what kept her alive. She wouldn't give in to the chair until it was the only option left to her. She smiled warmly at him. Her eyes were sunken into folds of wrinkles, but the effect made her look merry and amused. On the table, their meal was ready. He never could complain about the food. He knew the staff tried extra hard for his sake, and a few other regular visitors who came for meals and didn't want the gooey oatmeal or boiled vegetables their elderly parents or grandparents usually ate.

Today, it was sautéed mushrooms and mashed potatoes for Kathleen, who still had a hearty appetite—thanks to all that exercise, she'd say—and chopped steak and mushrooms, with the same potatoes and a side of steamed broccoli for Grant. In the center of the table, next to a small vase of dead dried flowers, sat a bowl of banana pudding. Not his favorite, but Kathleen loved it, so he was pleased the kitchen had whipped it up. He took his seat and reached his hand across the table to hold Kathleen's for a brief moment, their customary wordless greeting.

No matter how often he visited, he never felt quite right. He did his best to seem at ease. But always, the room felt too small. He felt like a big, lumbering idiot. Like he were the burden now. Kathleen insisted on seeing him, but she happily accepted his absence on the days he couldn't make it. Maybe she looked at him and saw the man who'd dumped a child on her doorstep thirty years ago.

Kathleen squeezed his hand and patted it, as if she read his thoughts and wanted to offer comfort. Her smile never waved. She rubbed her belly and lifted her spoon.

Grant couldn't help grinning in return. Yes, he was hungry, too. He picked up his fork and made a mock bow. "I've had an interesting morning," he told her. He never knew what to talk about, so he always talked about work.

Kathleen was as much a therapist as anything, listening silently, nodding or shaking her head depending on her opinion of one thing or another. Occasionally, she'd scratch out a note or a question on the pad she kept in the pocket of her long cardigan.

"I met with a new designer this morning. Her name is Seraphina, and I think you'd like her. She has a direct way about her. Not unlike me," he added, wondering at the involuntary smile on his face.

His mom's thin eyebrows rose slowly, but rise they did. She ferried a spoonful of fragrant, garlic-rich mushrooms into her mouth, then tidied herself with a cloth napkin, and retrieved her notepad. It took her some time to write out her words, and Grant busied himself with eating. Begrudgingly, he admitted the food was excellent. The mushrooms were buttery and garlicky, the steak tender, and the broccoli not overdone.

Finally, Kathleen slid the pad across the table.

Grant wiped his mouth on his napkin, then picked it up. He almost choked on his last bite of broccoli. He coughed, finished chewing, and swallowed. If he took his time, it was because he wasn't sure what to say.

If you think I'd like her, you must like her already. Is she very pretty?

She'd never let it be if he admitted he liked a pretty woman, but Grant had a hard time lying to Kathleen, even remotely. They'd withstood too many rough storms together for the niceties of polite nonsense to stand. "She's not ugly," he admitted reluctantly.

Kathleen's eyes twinkled merrily but she said no more on the subject.

Surprisingly, Grant wished she would. He'd brought up Seraphina because he wanted to discuss her, and there was no better confidant than his mother, even if she gave him sly, amused glances from beneath her lashes.

He smiled, opening himself up to the conversation, so Kathleen wouldn't feel uncomfortable asking more questions if she wished. "The most arresting thing about her, and why I mention her, is because she's the first designer I've hired that could take my company from under me, if she chose. She's like steel. And I can't help but wonder if she's like me in that she never turns it off."

His mother rolled her eyes and spooned mushrooms and gravy into her mashed potatoes.

Reading her unspoken sentiment was easy. "Well, sure, I can relax around you. But only you. I wonder if Seraphina lets her guard down for anyone."

Kathleen paused in eating to scrawl another note. Then find out. She sounds like a perfect apprentice.

Hm. He hadn't considered taking on an apprentice for months now. He'd first had the idea last year, but there were no likely candidates. Roper, despite all his talent, didn't dedicate himself as completely as Grant did. Grant's work was his life. Well, and Kathleen. Kathleen's comfort and his business, they were the two pillars of his existence. If he was going to take on an apprentice, someone who would eventually rise to be his equal and partner in his enterprise, they had to be nothing short of perfect.

"I fear my standards are set too high," he said regretfully. "But as usual, your advice gives me something to think about."

Kathleen nodded somberly, as if she were a queen merely accepting her due, but Grant did not miss the pleased touch to her slight grin.

* * * *

Roper was altogether too amused for Seraphina's taste. Almost smug as she joined him at the little round table. Steam rose from the thick white mug he held. "You could move to Bali. Change your identity. Bleach your hair, get some contacts," he said. "Killing yourself should be last resort, that's all I'm saying." He sipped the scalding contents of his mug tentatively, watching her with dancing eyes.

"I said I wanted to die," she pointed out. "Not kill myself."

"Come on, Seraphina. Your meeting couldn't have gone that poorly." Roper's voice changed to hold a plaintive note. He really disliked her mood, apparently.

Well, that was his problem. Not everyone could walk around in a haze of simpleminded contentment, Roper's apparent default personality setting. Normally, she was cool as a cucumber, but the meeting with Grant this morning had flustered her. She'd hidden in her office, and only just convinced herself to duck into the lounge for a pick-me-up coffee. The lounge was a glorified breakroom for the employees. An expensive gourmet coffeemaker and espresso machine sat on a gold-flecked granite counter. A stainless steel fridge held take-out containers, Tupperware marked with names, and a million flavors of creamer. Several small round tables dotted the room, made of a smooth dark wood. Seraphina ran her hand over the surface, appreciating the satiny finish. It soothed her, for some reason, but it wasn't enough to kill her anxiety.

They were expecting Grant's decision any moment now. He'd seen both their plans, and it was merely a matter of choosing his favorite. What were her chances against Roper? They both had their tablets sitting on the table, physical reminders of the one thing they did not discuss.

She held in a long-suffering sigh. Sighs and groans were signs of weakness; displays of tired emotions she'd long ago trained herself to forgo in professional company. But then again, she was whining in front of a coworker. She wasn't exactly in top form, and couldn't resist sharing her burden with someone who might understand and help her assuage some of her complicated feelings. "I made a fool of myself twice. I insulted a valued member of Mr. Gallagher's team. I don't even know why I'm still here."

Roper shrugged, took another sip of coffee. His eyebrows rose in a hopeful expression. "You're an up-and-comer. A lot of people heard your name when Sweetclover made a splash several months ago. You're here because you're a promising talent. You're lucky the head designer at Free Leaf Concepts gave you so much credit. Not everyone in her position would have. Besides, Grant understands we're human, even if he isn't. He makes people nervous and knows it. Don't let one off meeting eat you up." Some doubt crept into his gaze. "I mean, how bad could it have been?"

"Well." Seraphina paused and sipped from her own mug. The contents had gone cold. "First there was this weird staring contest. Like confronting a bear. Like all sorts of stuff was being said, but without any words." Roper was nodding as if he weren't surprised. Perhaps Grant routinely engaged in stare-downs with his employees. "We hardly spoke until he introduced Ophelia. And poor Ophelia. I'm such an idiot. If she hates me, I'll deserve it."

"Ophelia can't hate you." Roper assured her with a light laugh. He relaxed, like the whole thing was suddenly all better. "She's too nice from what I've seen. Besides, you're hardly the first designer to disdain her help. You'll notice I didn't get saddled with an assistant. Seniority does have its perks." He gave her a brilliant smile.

She answered with a wry grin. "Doesn't make me feel better. Actually, can you tell me a little more about Ophelia? I need to apologize, or I won't be able to focus on working with her. It'll be this big, fat, terrible thing between us."

Roper shrugged lightly and readjusted his glasses. His dark hair was ruffled, and he'd undone the top button of his soft blue dress shirt. Even so, it had the effect of making him seem busy and important rather than harried and unkempt. His expressive eyes were open and guileless. The man was charmed, no doubt. "Ophelia is new, actually. She hasn't been here long at all, but she didn't waste any time. Dove right in. Replaced the old satellite assistant with hardly a hitch in operations. I've worked with her on one project, more or less as a favor to Grant. He wanted Ophelia to get a feel for what we need from her, the type of help we expect. She was on the ball, I tell you. She's, uh…" Roper paused, and his eyes narrowed thoughtfully as he hunted for the right word. "Self-possessed, I guess. Not in a bad way. She's one of those people you can't imagine has a life outside of her job, that's all. I can't see her as someone's mother or significant other." He smiled and cocked his head to the side. "Not unlike you, actually."

Seraphina's first reaction was discomfort. She didn't enjoy being analyzed, and yet couldn't deny it wasn't at all far-fetched for Roper to see her that way—elusive, private, contained. What made the statement particularly unnerving was that she wasn't a mother or a significant other. She lived her work.

At least she had some good friends. Kay Bing was the head designer at Free Leaf Concepts, who'd given Seraphina her dues for Sweetclover, Little Rock's newest spa, which was making waves among the young and moneyed set as the hot new place to go. And recently, Seraphina had begun making some headway as a friend of Neve Harper's, one of Grant Gallagher's most famous contemporaries. In fact, Seraphina hoped the two of them never met. It would be like stars colliding, and the universe would implode from the impact. As for romance, who had time to go chasing fairy tales?

She studied her manicure and nibbled her lip, hating the nervous tics even as she couldn't help herself. "Married to our jobs." She smiled humorlessly, hoping it worked to put distance between Roper and herself. She didn't like when people became too familiar. "Families are needy distractions, and plenty of men in high performance industries forgo them without any ill effects. Perhaps Ophelia and I will find some common ground, after all."

The lack of warmth in her reply had the desired effect. Roper cast her an uncertain glance, laced with a tinge of regret, and pointed to her tablet. "May I?"

She cocked an eyebrow. "If I can, as well."

The glow returned to his smile. He handed his own tablet to Seraphina. "Doesn't matter now, does it?"

They each settled back to peruse the other's work. Roper laughed out loud. "We even named the file similarly. You labeled yours 'GovMan,' and I named mine 'GovsMan.'" He tapped his temple. "Great minds. Too bad we're competing. We'd make excellent partners."

After that, they fell silent. Seraphina snuck glances over the rim of the tablet she held in front of her, curious if Roper's expression gave anything away. It didn't, although he wore an intent look she'd seen only once or twice before. When he worked, he devoted his whole mind to the task.

Seraphina shuttered away her curiosity—self-possessed, indeed—and focused on Roper's file. She scanned through his measurements, noting differences in sizes and dimensions of certain rooms. He wanted to do away with the still-standing fireplace, and install a carousel closet. The original fireplace remained in her plans, and she'd tackled the question of storage by converting the old canning shed attached to the back of the house.

Her puzzlement grew the deeper she delved. Roper's design lacked integrity. Imagination, even. Everything seemed so modern. He wanted glass and steel and plastic and nylon, where she'd opted for locally sourced wood and other natural materials. She desired to compliment the history of the old building. Roper wanted to rewrite it.

Had Seraphina presented a strong enough portfolio to win Grant over, to convince him to bank his trust on her vision? She nibbled her lip. Perhaps she had played it too safe, but surely class and harmony would win over... over...whatever Roper had done. His vision wasn't strictly modern, she realized, poking further. Brass hardware? Linoleum in the back entryway? Stark white walls in nearly every room?

His ideas were terrible. A flutter of delight beat in her chest like a tiny butterfly. The tendril of hope ignited an equally fierce measure of guilt—she liked Roper. She wished they weren't competing, but all the same, she wanted to win. And she was almost certain she was holding proof that she had won.

She didn't get the chance to ponder further. Her cell phone buzzed in the pocket of her fitted black coat at the same time Roper's chimed softly from the pocket of his slacks. They met one another's eyes for a fraction of a second. She and Roper set their tablets down on the table simultaneously. Doing her best to appear completely unaffected by whatever came next, because she had no doubt this was an e-mail from Grant announcing the lead designer on Tanbee House, Seraphina pulled her phone from her hip and checked the incoming message. Yes, an e-mail. And yes, it was from Grant.

But the words made no sense at all.

I appreciate your waiting for my decision. I don't count it among easy ones to make. After deliberation with several other designers, Gallagher Interiors will be moving forward on the Governor's Mansion expansion with the design proposed by Roper McLeod. My heartfelt congratulations, Mr. McLeod. To those of you who submitted plans, I thank you for your effort and your many excellent ideas. The one thing we do not lack here at Gallagher Interiors is talent.

Best Regards,
Grant Gallagher

Her heart fell. Well, there was the cost of confidence when she dared have any. Roper's designs were atrocious. Grant had to see that. She shook her head at herself.

She gave Roper a cursory farewell, pausing only to issue the briefest of congratulations as she swiped her tablet from the table and all but fled. She didn't swing by her office, but headed straight for the exit, deciding no one would miss her for one afternoon.

She arrived at her small studio apartment a little while later. The bottle of wine she grasped seemed like a glowing promise, and she could hardly work out the stubborn cork fast enough. If she were truly as wise as her friends believed, she'd call someone and get her feelings off her chest instead of indulging in an expensive pinot noir. But tonight, she felt like a failure, and couldn't bear to face anyone.

Her whole life was about maintaining an image of control, of power over herself, because it was all she had the ability to manipulate. She couldn't tell her father that his criticisms and his neglect seared her from the inside out, or she'd be mocked for her weakness. She couldn't take those deep hurts to other friends and family, because they were all ghosts. And she couldn't escape one parent for the refuge of another, because her mother had left them behind before Seraphina learned to say her name.

And always, those criticisms were the demon she battled constantly. They'd held her back from pursuing her dream when she was younger. She'd floated around the university for years after graduating, helping kids like Kay Bing realize theirs instead. She and Neve Harper were nearly the same age, but Neve rivaled Grant Gallagher's esteem all over Arkansas, in both business and reputation.

While Seraphina was still struggling to make a dent. She thought she had with Sweetclover. Kay's acknowledgment had given Seraphina's career the small boost it needed—just the thing to catch Grant Gallagher's attention and secure her position as the newest member of his company. Yet still she failed. Every time she started to think she had some innate talent, she failed.

Tomorrow was another day, of course. She'd do what she always did—grab the fresh start with everything she had. She'd call Kay and let her coo and cluck, she'd call Neve and let her dish out stark advice, and then she'd go to work and do her best to live up to the potential she'd been struggling to realize her entire life.

An ancient pain filled her. No, she couldn't handle her well-meaning friends tonight. Tonight, she'd drink too much wine and feel sorry for herself. She'd delete every scrap of the Tanbee House plans from her tablet and the company cloud. Not for the sake of self-pity, though she was practically drowning in it, but because she'd keep coming back to them over and over again. She'd tweak, and change, and turn it upside down and sideways looking for the fatal flaw in her designs. One day, she'd learn to fail without needing to know why or how.

Today was not that day.

Chapter 3

Seraphina's skull was too tight for her brain. Her throat was the kind of dry that water couldn't soothe. Concealer couldn't quite hide the purple half-moons under her eyes. The elevator made her stomach pitch, and the lights along the corridor were bright enough to shine through the dark lenses of her Ray Bans.

Red wine hangovers were the worst.

She groaned and ignored the few strange looks from coworkers. Gallagher Interiors was an industrious place. Designers, assistants, couriers, engineers—a veritable hive of people buzzed and flitted around. Grant's firm was huge, and despite being Arkansas's Wal-Mart of interior design, at least in terms of output and popularity, managed to maintain a superbly high degree of quality and exclusivity. He managed a productivity that seemed at odds with the elite nature of his reputation.

Seraphina could only envy the hectic energy. She kept her dark sunglasses on until she finally escaped to her small office. Small, but functional and warm. The wallpaper danced with a subtle silver design on a faded golden background, and the lush carpet was a deep brown that complimented the honey-hued furniture.

Her personal touches were few. A small potted cactus she kept on her desk for the sake of having something green and difficult to kill nearby. A few framed photographs of family, none of whom she was particularly close to. But it seemed strange not to display them, like she was ashamed or something. Besides, it was a reminder she did, in fact, have family, even if their connections were tenuous at best.

She picked up the photograph of her father that sat on the shelf next to the printer. She recognized the shape of her own face in his, but that was where their likeness ended. Daniel Fawkes carried his mother's Greek heritage heavily, from the olive tone of his skin, the deep green of his eyes, and his long, hooked nose to his thick wave of black hair, worn long and unruly. Seraphina had few photos of her mother, and sometimes wondered why she kept any at all, except for that the mystery of the desertion tugged at her. Certainly none of those pictures were on display, not even at home. Her fair Irish skin, dramatic red hair, and striking blue eyes were all courtesy of her mom.

At least she gave me one thing I can appreciate, Seraphina told herself dryly. She set her father's picture down. He was smiling, and it seemed that she was the only person in the world who saw the cutting edge on that happy, carefree grin.

She was waiting for her computer to boot up when Roper knocked on her doorframe, greeting her with a wide smile. She'd say he was an insufferable morning person, but he was in the same mood regardless of the time of day. She didn't even try to match it. She grunted a hello and downed a big gulp of coffee. She also had a Sprite and a sleeve of saltine crackers near at hand. If Roper noticed the ingredients for a recipe against a hangover strewn across her workspace, he didn't mention it. In fact, he seemed distracted.

Roper approached her desk, looked down, and spotted her tablet. "Ah. There it is. We accidently mixed them up yesterday. You left in such a hurry, I didn't realize the swap until this morning. Grant's waiting, so I'd better jet." He snatched up one tablet, traded for the other.

Seraphina's jaw unhinged. Her mind emptied of everything expect a loud roar of utter disbelief. She froze, unable to respond. Roper didn't notice. In his hurry, he hardly glanced at her while making the swap, and rushed from her office before the words and their horrifying implications settled onto her brain.

She was awash in paralyzing fire. Her scalp tingled and she couldn't swallow past a hard knot in her throat. She stared blankly ahead at the empty doorway, trying fruitlessly to convince herself it wasn't true.

No. No, of course not. She'd been drunk and pitiful, but surely…surely she hadn't actually deleted the files for the Governor's Mansion project.

Oh, God. Was it 'GovMan' or 'GovsMan'?

She pressed her palms to her temples. The throbbing had nothing to do with last night's indulgence. She closed her eyes, forced herself to work through her faded memories from the night before. There'd been some crying. Smeared mascara on her fingers this morning. A little nausea, if the Pepto on her nightstand was any indication. She'd definitely done some stuff on her tablet—on Roper's tablet. It had been laying on the pillow this morning when she'd woken up with her tongue thick in her mouth and her eyes on fire from bad sleep.

It just wasn't possible. Oh, shit. But it is. It's totally possible...

Her palms were sweating, and she swayed on her feet as she stood. She felt stone-cold sober now. The shock of what she'd done broke through what remained of her fogginess. Her stomach clenched painfully against on onslaught of nerves that zapped like lightning. When had she last felt this incredibly bad and frightened?

Fear tried to root her to the spot, but she forced herself to move. She couldn't keep silent. Whatever the fallout, she wouldn't, couldn't, be that person. Once, back at the university, when she'd been a teaching assistant, she'd screwed up big time. A student had accidently taken credit for her mishap. She finally came clean, and the professor had been a good sport about the whole thing, but she'd never forget how slimy and hollow it made her feel.

Shaking, she made her way to the elevator and pressed the button for Grant's floor. How would she ever look Roper in the face after this? Shit, how would she look Grant in the face? They'd suspect sabotage. They'd think her capable of a graceless act of spite that was, in reality, beyond her. Her mind raced through possible explanations like a magician whipping through a deck of cards, scattering them like confetti. Somehow, I got wasted last night and meant to delete my own plans didn't sound all that believable. But, really, who could make that crap up.

This morning, she'd slapped on her least favorite outfit—a black dress that fit like a traffic cone. Tight at the neck and flowing out in a tulip skirt, like some sixties tunic dress. The only good thing was that it was a single piece of stretchy fabric. There were no buttons, ties, or clasps. She wore it only on her laziest days, when the thought of dealing with skirt zippers and dress shirt buttons was beyond her. She was regretting the decision now. The worse thing about the dress, besides being utterly unflattering to every body shape known to man, was how it made her feel like a blob. She wished now she had picked an outfit that might've given her the illusion of some backbone. Not only did she feel like death, she also looked like something a street paver had rolled over.

It was a strange time to care about her wardrobe, but early in life she'd discovered the power of clothing. The right packaging made all the difference in the world.

Her knees were weak when she stepped out of the elevator. She had to force herself forward. Apprehension settled over her like a cloud, making the air thick with tension. She swallowed hard outside Grant's office, then strode around the corner like she'd been summoned.

"Hi, Annie. I know Mr. Gallagher is seeing Roper, but I have something, uh…something related to Tanbee House I need to tell them, before it's too late." Technically true.

The older woman blinked up at Seraphina with her mouth slightly open. Probably this type of thing didn't happen too often. Or maybe, Seraphina mused, she looked worse than she realized, and Annie was just soaking it in. Her eyes still pinned to Seraphina, Annie picked up the phone on her desk, punched a button, mentioned Seraphina's name, and then hung up. "You can go back."

"Thanks, Annie." Seraphina forced a grateful smile.

The coffee from this morning sloshed around in her stomach, a hint of threat in the roiling discomfort. She prayed she wouldn't be sick, but stepping through the door and under the tense, expectant gazes of Grant and Roper, Seraphina's stomach turned over. She swallowed past the awkward lump in her throat and forced a deep breath, exhaling with as much control as possible through her nostrils. She couldn't even hide her nervousness. Between her hangover, the awful dress, and emotions she couldn't button down for once, she felt like a fraying rope, dangerously close to coming completely undone.

"Seraphina," Grant greeted her, standing briefly behind his desk. "You said this is about Tanbee House? I was actually about to ask Annie to schedule a meeting with you later. It's just as well you're here now, though. Roper showed up with some unfortunate news."

"Oh." Her throat was painfully dry. She noticed she was wringing her hands together, and forced them down at her sides. "Um. Yes. I-I came to tell you, Roper and I, we—"

"Looked at each other's designs yesterday," Roper cut in, smiling widely at Seraphina, but with an open warning in his gaze. He shrugged and looked back at Grant. "I know, we shouldn't have. And I can't blame Seraphina for wanting to admit the breach in the unspoken rule among us. Frowned upon, of course, due to the proprietary nature of a designer's personal ideas, which in turn encourages an environment free of 'borrowing.' But I trusted Seraphina not to steal any ideas of mine for future use." He sent her a brief smile. It still didn't quite reach his eyes. Then he stood, and put a hand out to shake Grant's. "Again, I can't tell you how sorry I am about the mix up. I really did think I'd deleted an older version of the file, not the final blueprint."

Seraphina's mouth fell open. "You—"

Roper swiveled toward her, his hands tucked easily into the pocket of his slacks. He looked, as unlikely as it seemed, completely relaxed. "Word to the wise, Grant deletes our plans once he's gone over them."

Grant's blond eyebrows came together in a pained expression. "I open files from the cloud, but I only save the ones greenlighted for use on my personal device. If I kept them all, I'd run out of hard drive storage twice a year. Perhaps I should consider changing tactics."

"But the cloud—"

Grant gave a humorless grin. "The files were deleted there, as well, it seems."

"I'll be more careful cleaning out my files in the future," Roper assured him. "Seraphina, I believe congratulations are in order." His grin this time was the genuine article. "Grant tried to talk me into drawing up my designs again, but after seeing yours, I respectfully bow out of the running. Besides, I have my eye on a few other projects."

He bobbed his head in farewell, and his easy stride carried him out of the office.

Seraphina's mouth was still agape, and she closed it with an abrupt snap. She had no idea what had just happened. Okay, well, the what was pretty easy to figure—Roper had taken the blame for his deleted files. The why escaped her entirely. She itched to run after him and get answers, but part of her was relieved he was gone. Not that dealing with Grant Gallagher was any balm to the situation, but she had no idea how to right such a grievous wrong. For all his easy demeanor, Roper was probably fuming on the inside, and simply too nice of a guy to let Seraphina accept responsibility. She swallowed thickly. Would Grant fire her if he knew the truth? Just how much had Roper's false confession rescued her from?

Grant's pale blue eyes alighted on her. "Interesting turn of events." His tone was clipped, his expression unreadable. He sat down and motioned for Seraphina to join him.

Wanting nothing more than to run away, she sat, beyond ill-prepared for the meeting. She thought it'd be a long while before she dealt with Grant face-to-face again. Maybe it was because she felt so hideous and gross, but he seemed even better looking than before. So neat and together in a crisp pale gray suit that complimented his lightning gaze.

Inside of her, something deeply buried and sentimental sighed wistfully. She'd made herself into a creature of poise and care and thoughtfulness—a bright, intelligent person with tight control. Grant Gallagher impressed and attracted her, because all of those traits she held so dear appeared to ooze off him with a natural ease she could only dream of possessing herself.

He'd be perfect for her in another life. But not this one. In this life, he was her boss, and didn't seem equally impressed by her. Not even a little.

In fact, there was repressed regret in the lines around his mouth as he offered her congratulations. "As you've heard, Roper accidentally deleted all of his files for the Tanbee House project, supposedly thinking he was deleting older versions. What you may not have realized is that you had the runner-up spot. Your ideas were a little run-of-the-mill. I'd like to work with you on putting a few unorthodox touches on the final plans. That is, of course, if you haven't also deleted your files?" His tone was dry, with little evidence of humor despite the joke.

"No." She was all but drowning in guilt. She'd figured yesterday she had to be a contender for Tanbee House, but having Grant confirm it only made everything worse. Oh, God. Did Roper think she'd deleted his plans on purpose to steal his place? The churning in her stomach increased.

Grant peered at her, suddenly seeming to take in her pallor and nerves. His gaze scoured her, and she felt the heat of it on her skin. "Are you all right?"

"Totally fine." The lie came out in a voice much higher than her normal tone, but she also managed to squeeze in a small reassuring smile for Grant's sake. She doubted it was the most convincing thing in the world. For now, she'd go along, but she needed to find Roper as soon as possible and try to fix this. Even if his plans were gone, it didn't mean he shouldn't lead the team in charge of one of the firm's biggest projects. Maybe he had time to start over. She could offer to help. She could—

Grant cleared his throat, wrenching Seraphina back into the present moment. "Don't feel bad," he said. He must've read the guilt on her face. "Roper is a big boy. There are consequences for being careless. If I'm honest, I was going to suggest he partner up with you, anyway. If you saw his layout, then you'll know there were places for improvement."

And then some. She bit her lip. Guilty or not, Roper's plans were bad. And if Grant was going to suggest another designer present changes, then he had to know it, too. "You said you were going to call for me? Before Roper came in?" Something that had nothing to do with the deleted files, then. Their initial meeting hadn't been a smooth one, by any definition of the word. Maybe Roper had taken a bullet for her because she was already screwed.

Grant nodded slowly. He had a considering air, like he were thinking hard on whether or not he wanted to say anything at all. "I know you're an established designer in your own right. And I imagine you have grand plans to strike out on your own, which will certainly be easy for you to do once you've earned accolades doing something that will have as much media coverage as the new expansion to the Governor's Mansion property. Your name will be known in conjunction with mine. And I always give credit where it is due. I may request changes, force my own ideas into the final plans, but I always give my head designers the recognition they deserve. All that being said, I'd like to make you an offer."

It was the last thing in the world she could've expected. She didn't even believe he liked her very much, and her designs were only second-best. Why he'd want to offer her anything at all was unfathomable. "Oh?"

He smiled, and the whole room seemed to shift. He had a brilliant smile that transformed everything about him. Something moved in her stomach, but this time for completely different reasons. A lick of desire made her breath hitch. Grant quirked a brow at her, his grin less intense but still present. He looked amused, and not a little sexy…a lot sexy. "No need to sound so surprised. You made an impact on me yesterday. I think it's fairly evident we have many common traits, and we both strive for a certain level of…well, I guess you'd call it distance. I work very hard not to allow my emotions to rule me. It's important to be impartial. On the surface, it's at odds with our profession. We're artists at the end of the day. But there's more to running this firm than the art. Art is also business. And business requires a different kind of mentality."

Seraphina fought the urge to squirm in her seat and held perfectly still. Grant had become more somber as he spoke. His smile faded into an earnest expression, and his gaze crystallized. The softness his quick laugh had brought disappeared. Something big was coming. A new kind of apprehension filled her.

Grant folded his hands neatly on top of his desk. "Seraphina, I'd like you to consider becoming my apprentice. You're advanced for the position. But I've been waiting a long time for someone like you—someone I could one day trust as a partner at Gallagher Interiors."

* * * *

A million doubts assailed Grant the moment the question went from a mere thought to a voiced statement. Out loud, it grew arms and legs and potential. Once said, he couldn't take it back or change his mind. Well, he could, but not until he gave Seraphina a fair shake. And although she seemed a little off this morning, he still had a certain surety in his breast. He'd just met the woman, but it felt right. As always, he went with his gut. "Your thoughts?"

At the moment, she didn't appear to have any. She stared at him, her vivid eyes like pools of ice, perfectly blank-faced. Her surprise was only evident in the small o of her mouth. Finally, she blinked. "Are you sure?"

Not what he expected. "Is there some reason I'd ask if I weren't certain you were a good fit for the future vision I have of this company?"

"No, I..." She cleared her throat, then gave a low, throaty chuckle. "Honestly, I'm shocked. I wouldn't say our interview yesterday went well enough for you to make this sort of offer. You haven't even seen me at work yet."

"I've seen your blueprints." He paused, unsure of how to convince her without heaping on praise and coming across like an idiot. "Seraphina, I know I gave you a hard time yesterday, but the truth is your plans encompassed much more of the process than most of my staffers stop to consider, and that says a lot about how you approach tasks. That's the way I think, but it's not how I expect my designers to think. They take a white space and fill it with their vision. You worked backward from the white space, detailing how to achieve it in the first place. Besides that, we seem to have the same approach to work. I like Roper. He's a good guy, works hard, and is superbly creative."

A doubtful expression flitted across Seraphina's face. Grant almost sighed. Eventually, they'd have to broach the subject. Roper's plans were a huge let-down, but Grant would get to the bottom of why before he discussed the issue with anyone else.

"But," he continued, ignoring the elephant in the room for the time being, "Roper also has an artist's temperament. You seem more grounded. It wouldn't be permanent unless you decide it's what you want for certain. It's a very big leap, and a lot of responsibility, and my expectations are exquisitely high." Again, Roper's poor designs made him feel like a liar. He pushed them from his mind.

Seraphina's gaze settled onto a spot between him and his desk. She nibbled her lip, the only motion that gave any hint as to what she was thinking or feeling—nervous? Excited?

"From here, I'll keep a close eye on how you bring your vision for Tanbee House to life. I have other items on the agenda that demand my attention, but we'll work together near the end of the process. I'm sure by the time we wrap up this project and put a bow on it for the city, you and I will have a pretty good idea if we're a good fit to move forward as partners."

She nodded slowly. "Kind of like one really long job interview."

"Yes. If you're interested."

"Well, yeah. I mean, of course."

For the first time since she whirled into his office that morning, she seemed to relax a little. Her face opened up, and something not unlike a smile crept over her lips. Her face was flushed, and she looked tired, but it didn't diminish her beauty so much as give it a haunting effect. The black dress, the somber gaze. He wanted to wrap her in a flannel blanket and give her some cocoa.

"You're right." She shrugged slightly. "I would love my own firm one day. It's a dream I got a late start on, because…well, because. Doesn't matter now. You're offering me an opportunity to make up for lost time. My biggest worry"—her gaze rose quickly, locking onto to his with a sudden intensity—"is that we may be too alike. But that's a chance I'm willing to take, if you're willing to take one on me. You don't even know me." She gave another one of those low chuckles, like she couldn't believe her luck, that Grant could almost feel moving over his skin.

Belatedly, he recognized the tingle of attraction. Well, damn. There was a complication he hadn't accounted for. He straightened his back and wiped whatever answering smile lingered on his own lips. "Well, then I'd better start. Dinner tonight at Rosa Rita's. I'll send a car at eight, if you'll leave Annie your address." At her wide eyes, he held up a palm. "Not a date, Ms. Fawkes. Just an expenditure I can write off. I don't have time during the day to sit and chat about what makes us tick. We need to get to know one another, however, and it's worth putting in the time before we break ground. I prefer to do so over food and good wine if it's all the same to you."

Maybe he imagined the disappointment that came and went from Seraphina's face like a shadow. Maybe it was just wishful thinking, and he should kick himself or call a halt to the whole thing before he got himself in trouble.

Seraphina transitioned smoothly into her usual poised countenance, and nodded. "Eight o'clock."

She left, and much to his chagrin, he watched her leave beneath his lashes. A funny little dress, but the fabric swayed neatly from side-to-side, giving him a pretty good idea of the curves underneath. Then he shook his head and lamented his bad fortune. He'd finally met someone who might be worthy of putting their name alongside his on the company letterhead, and he was going to screw it up. Grant Gallagher's love life would forever take a backseat to his company, and Seraphina was too important to the future of Gallagher Interiors for him to risk the chance with her.

Chapter 4

The moment Seraphina stepped inside the restaurant, Grant regretted everything—the offer of apprenticeship and the acceptance of her plans for Tanbee House. Hell, even giving in to Roper's insistence to hire her in the first place.

Gone were the bags under her eyes and the tiredness she'd carried around at work all day. She sloughed them off like an old layer of skin, revealing fresh, flawless perfection underneath. Grant swallowed around a sudden dryness in his throat as the head waiter led her through the throng of tables toward him.

The red cocktail dress was like a candy wrapper, fun and enticing. The strapless top flowed seamless into a red skirt, overlaid with black lace. Her black heels were towering. Her brilliant red hair was twisted up into a loose bun, and the straight ends stuck up and to the side in some punk rock version of a fancy up-do. Her eyes were lined in kohl and zeroed in on him from across the room.

His heart did a rapid thump-thump as their gazes locked. He stared the whole while she worked her way toward him, and he knew he wasn't the only man—or woman, for that matter—to stop and stare. At some point, he wasn't watching her eyes anymore, but the way her legs' long strides made the silky fabric of her dress slide over her thighs and waist.

Seraphina thanked the waiter and lowered into her seat across from Grant. She settled herself, taking several seconds before she deigned to meet his eyes again and smile demurely.

Grant took a long swallow of lemon water. Whatever had been bothering Seraphina this morning, she had not only recovered, but came back swinging. "You certainly make an entrance."

She shrugged lightly and glanced around the room. Her gaze took in the glittering chandelier overhead, one of many scattered around the dining room. "I had a rough morning. Needed a boost. I tried to dress for the occasion. Rosa Rita's has a waiting list months long."

"We could've postponed if you weren't feeling well." Maybe then she wouldn't have dressed like they had definite plans to have sex later. Every person in the restaurant had to be thinking it. And he'd be totally okay with that if it weren't for all the bad ways that might end. Seraphina couldn't be his partner if they had baggage, and she was probably right—they could very well be too alike to get along.

He wryly admitted he hadn't exactly dressed down. His suit was one of the finest in his closet, a deep black with a silver gray shirt underneath. On some subconscious level, he saw this as more than a simple discussion over dinner and drinks. He wanted to get to know Seraphina. He couldn't help but wonder if they had similar pasts that made them both so standoffish. He adjusted his tie for the second time and realized he was nervous. In the unspoken—yet very real—arena where he and Seraphina faced each other, she had the upper hand for once. What unsaid thing between them had encouraged this battle of wills?

Grant cleared his throat and relaxed as the waiter came and poured their wine, a white he'd chosen before Seraphina arrived. One of them had to give. And though it wasn't in his nature to be the one to cave first, he knew he wouldn't get any closer to Seraphina if he didn't let down a few of his own barriers.

He looked around at the restaurant, dismayed. He'd chosen the most pretentious restaurant in the city. They'd never be at ease enough to do any more than swap niceties. He nodded to himself. "Maybe I should've chosen someplace less...well, less. I really didn't think this through." He tossed down his napkin across his plate. "We haven't ordered yet. Do you want to leave? We can go someplace..."

"Less?" she ventured carefully. Seraphina's head was cocked to one side as if waiting for him to spring a trap. They made each other wary, which only intrigued him more.

"Way less. Like a taco truck."

Seraphina sputtered on her first sip of wine. Hey, ho, how about that. He'd surprised her by showing off a personality. Deeply buried under the exterior of his professional demeanor, but there nonetheless. She dabbed hurriedly at her mouth before wine could dribble down her chin, blue eyes wide and glittering with mirth. The touch of caution was still there. She recovered and glanced up at him through her lashes, but a small smile stole across her lips. "I'm pretty overdressed for a taco truck."

Grant shrugged and answered her smile with a tentative one of his own. A bit of the wall between them crumbled, but not enough. He could feel the reserve like a stone fence, thick and low. It was as if they peered over, both curious, but neither willing to let down their guard. "I'm not wearing holy Levi's and tennis shoes," he said, glancing down at himself for good measure. "Besides, you're going to receive some looks no matter where you go."

Seraphina blushed prettily but didn't look away. "A dress like this one doesn't need much from the wearer."

He gave her a sardonic smile. False modesty didn't look good on her. "I enjoy giving a beautiful woman a compliment as much as the next man, but I'm not one for empty flattery. Even here, in a place full of women dressed likewise, you command the room's attention. I think it's safe to say it's not the dress. It's how you wear it." He took the chance, standing and offering his arm. He dared her with an arched brow.

Seraphina stared up at him, blinking as if astonished. He read the uncertainty in her gaze and the gleam of excitement beneath it. She took his arm, telling him more than she perhaps realized about herself. For one, Ms. Fawkes was a risk taker. Secondly, she looked good on his arm. Excitement thrummed along his nerves as he led Seraphina back through the crowded restaurant. He'd meant what he said. People stared. Women conspicuously, men more furtively, mindful of their own companions, but at nearly every table, eyes followed their path toward the front entrance.

Grant was surprised by the flash of possessive pride he felt. Hardly anyone made him edgy and self-conscience, and the fact that Seraphina made his nerves hum only made their strange chemistry all the more interesting. Unfortunately, he wouldn't know if their combustible energy would lead to success or ruin until he got to know Seraphina better. Suddenly, glancing at her profile and noting the tug of a smile on her lips, it struck Grant he'd find the task enjoyable, regardless. Hell, fireworks were entertaining, even when there was the risk of fire. That only added to the thrill.

Grant hailed a cab. Once they were folded inside, silence reigned, but it was a comfortable span of quiet that held the subtle hint of promise. They weren't sure where they were going, and Seraphina didn't seem to mind the mystery any more than he did. He grinned and caught his reflection in the car window, surprised at himself. He looked...different.

He instructed the driver to take them to a well-known area of downtown, where the best food trucks congregated, vying for the attention of evening strollers and the bar-hopping crowd. Even on week nights, downtown Little Rock had plenty going on. They were let out on a busy corner under a yellow streetlamp. Grant surreptitiously took possession of Seraphina's hand as they walked through a jumble of eight or nine loud college students as they poured out of a sports bar. The red and blue neon signs in the window reflected onto Seraphina's red dress until she glowed purple, like something out of a comic book.

Finally, the next block down, Grant found his quarry. Like the maître d' at Rosa Rita's, he held his arm aloft and bowed slightly, keeping his face perfectly straight. "Madame, I give you El Taco Loco, and the absolute height of Tex-Mex delicacy. At least as good as you can hope to get in Arkansas, anyway."

To his delight, Seraphina laughed. Loud at first, then she covered her mouth and looked contrite. "I never imagined in a million years you'd be funny," she confessed.

The apology in her voice made him smile, and he nodded. "I'm not. Not usually. Not out loud."

Her smile faded, but her gaze became understanding. "So, what would you recommend?"

Together, they perused the menu next to a line of people. Two couples who appeared older and one scraggly kid, way too young for the bar circuit, waited ahead of them. Grant pointed at the hand-painted sign displaying their choices. "The loaded smothered burrito. It's a steak and fried potato burrito smothered in sour cream sauce, chives, bacon, and cheddar. It's amazing. I never eat it in public, though, because I always need a bath afterward. Very messy. I have an image to maintain, after all. The goat cheese nachos are pretty incredible, too, and not a bad substitution if you're not up to ruining your dress."

As slowly as the rising sun, and nearly as majestic, an ominously mischievous smile took over Seraphina's mouth. For a moment, he stared, caught by her beauty. "I dare you."

He placed his hand on his chest. "I'm sorry, you dare me? Do I strike you as the type to play it safe?"

Her grin widened. "I know people who think I'm insane to want to work for you. You're a scary guy. But I really want to try the burrito, and I'm not going in alone. So, yeah. I dare you."

Part of him was tempted to balk just because she was forcing his hand. Another small part of him was pleased to know his reputation still worked for him. And yet another part didn't give a damn about any of that, because Seraphina was probably the first woman he'd met in the last decade who wasn't all that impressed with him. His silence was intimidating, his forthrightness a turn off. He was her boss. He was Grant Gallagher, who regularly terrified veteran designers and interns alike. And she dared him to eat a messy burrito in a three-hundred-dollar suit.

"You're on," he said, showing all his teeth in his smile. "But I've got one for you."

She placed her hands on her hips. It was outrageously sexy, but she didn't seem to realize the striking figure she produced—hip jutted, fingers curled over the fabric, and her back slightly arched. His mouth went dry. She was too bent on copping a daring attitude, narrowing her eyes and trying to fight off the big grin on her face to notice. "I'm not scared of you."

He laughed. "So I've noticed." He pointed behind her, waited while she turned, read the sign, and looked back at him with wide eyes.

She hooked her thumb over her shoulder, toward the flashing sign inside the bar window behind them, and stared at Grant incredulously. "You want to go dancing after we wreck our clothes with sloppy burritos?"

"Smothered, not sloppy. And yeah. Why not? Maybe there's something in the air, but I'm having a good time." He shrugged. A small pill of awkwardness began to form in his gut at trying to put what he felt into words. He glanced at his shoes. Maybe he was just crazy. "Ah, you're probably right. We have work in the morning. Probably just let the wine go to my head. I had a glass before you—"

"Okay."

He met her eyes. "Okay? Okay, yes, or okay, we have to work—"

"You already asked me. You can't change your mind now. You're at the whim of my answer. And yeah. Okay. Yes. Let's do it."

They shuffled forward as the line to the taco truck moved. "For the record, I didn't change my mind. I was being a gentleman, giving you an easy out."

She met his eyes. Her gaze was almost solemn, completely at odds with the giddy sense of anticipation between them. "Maybe I don't want out." She blinked, and the levity returned to her vibrant blue eyes. "At least not until you buy me dinner."

Feeling very much like he was walking out onto a shaky limb, Grant caught Seraphina's fingers with his own. She didn't acknowledge his touch, but she didn't pull away, either. "I should've guessed you were only in it for the burrito."

* * * *

Before Seraphina could come up with a suitably entertaining reply, the couple who'd just received their food from the truck's next window breezed past. The man accidently jostled Seraphina's shoulder. Their gazes caught, and Seraphina's breath hitched.

"Seraphina, hey. Hi. How are you?"

"Brendan Berkley," she replied coolly. "Fine. You?"

She was ignored as Brendan recognized Grant. "Oh, hi. Um, wow. Sir. Grant. Mr. Sorry, Mr. Gallagher." He gave a short laugh and cleared his throat. "So weird, running into to you. This is Maria, my date." The woman beside him smiled wanly, seemingly unimpressed with running into Brendan's friends. Seraphina remembered the dress she was wearing and didn't blame Maria for her cool greeting. Brendan cleared his throat again. "It was nice to, uh, see you...Mr. Gallagher."

Grant raised an eyebrow at Brendan, exuding both curiosity and a certain unspoken assessment. Seraphina was caught off guard by the jolt of attraction she felt. He exuded such a quiet power. He said everything while saying nothing at all, and when he did deign to speak, he never wasted a word, so she found she hung onto every one.

"We look forward to seeing you at the office Monday, Brendan." Grant's voice held the clear note of dismissal. Polite, but an unmistakable end to the impromptu gathering.

Brendan looked relieved, and nodded another acknowledgment at Seraphina. "Have a good evening."

"Whoa. Wait. What?" She snapped out of it when she realized Grant seemed to know Brendan, as well. It was one thing for someone in the design industry to recognize Grant. He was as well-known as Neve Harper, and both had reputations all around the state. They were homegrown celebrities, in their worlds, no different from locally celebrated chefs or authors.

Brendan and his date waved and took off into the night, Seraphina gaping after them like an idiot. She turned to Grant. "I'm sorry, did you say we'd see him Monday at the office? Why would Brendan Berkley be coming to the office on Monday?"

Grant's brow gathered. "I'd forgotten the two of you worked together briefly."

"We passed in the hallways of Free Leaf Concepts once or twice. I wouldn't call it working together." Not by a long shot. And besides, Brendan Berkley had been far more than a high-level assistant. "Look, I know you're aware of the arrests made at Free Leaf. The receptionist and the manager of their greenhouses were growing illegal genetically altered magic mushrooms. Brendan was a person of interest in the case. He was questioned—"

"Twice," Grant easily supplied. "I know. But he was never arrested, let alone tried and convicted. Annie is retiring next year, and Brendan has the best résumé I've seen. I can't judge him by what almost happened, Seraphina. Would you expect me to?"

She bit her lip and peered down the vaguely lit sidewalk at Brendan and his date's retreating forms. They were shadows in the distance now. "I suppose not. It's just that I was there. And I know Oliver Pierce personally. Oliver was the undercover agent who brought down the whole arm operating inside Free Leaf Concepts. With Kay's help, of course. Both of them are certain Brendan got away with something. They just can't prove it."

Grant looked down at her with a wry, knowing smile. He tugged her forward, as the line moved again. "I do stay abreast of the local news. As well as those things that don't make headlines in the paper. And I'm well aware Oliver Pierce overstepped and can no longer investigate Brendan. In fact, I hear he's been removed from the case altogether."

Kind of… Seraphina glanced away so Grant couldn't read her expression. Oliver, now Kay's boyfriend, had moved, but not to another case. Oliver was merely working a different angle. One most likely to keep him as far from Brendan Berkley as possible. But he definitely hadn't given up on nailing the guy down once and for all.

"It's true," she admitted. "Oliver got a little carried away. Kay tried to warn him, but…well, he's got amazing instincts. All he needed was something concrete to take to a judge. He didn't break any laws, but it doesn't take much for a civilian to claim harassment after so much time passes without any new evidence coming to light. Either Oliver is way off, which isn't likely, or Brendan is playing a very deep game."

Grant was silent. He approached the truck, gave their orders to a happy-go-lucky guy behind the counter, and moved on to wait for their burritos to come through the next window. While they waited, he retook possession of her hand.

It was something she might've expected from a boy at a junior high dance, the tentative mingling of their fingers. Not exactly holding hands, but compelled to have contact, to touch. Her skin warmed at the small connection, even as her mind struggled to wrangle her feelings into tangible terms she could understand. Something really was in the air tonight.

Grant received their food, handing one laden container to Seraphina. The burrito was huge. Like a swaddled baby.

"Jeez," she breathed. "It's a monster."

"I should've warned you." He shrugged, then used his spork to scoop a huge bite of the topping—sauce, bacon, chives, and cheddar—into his mouth. He grinned at her, his cheeks full. "S'good."

She laughed and balanced her container carefully in her hands. "We need a table."

Grant shook his head and sat on the curb behind the truck. "As long as the taco truck driver doesn't reverse, we're safe."

Seraphina looked from the pavement to her dress and back again. She thanked the stars she had a spectacular dry cleaner and sat next to Grant. Their shoulders and knees knocked companionably while they ate. Seraphina experienced a small thrill each time. There was ease between them that made the contact seem intimate and loaded with potential.

When was the last time she'd felt sparks like this? High school? Her first date, with all the forbidden touches, so new and exciting and exhilarating. She knew indulging with Grant Gallagher like this was a bad idea. A train wreck waiting to happen. But at the same time, she didn't have it in herself to deny them both the pleasure. It was odd and so obviously unwise, but it felt…amazing, if she were honest. Amazing, and liberating, and electrifying. She didn't know where the hell they were going, but she wasn't jumping off the ride until they hit the end of the line.

She hated to ruin the moment, but she couldn't let go. "You're sure about Brendan? You're not worried? You know, in case Oliver Pierce is right about him. Could bring trouble down on the firm."

She didn't miss the slightly impatient gleam in Grant's gaze. He clearly didn't want to talk about Brendan Berkley anymore. "If anything, I imagine doing Annie's job will keep him too busy to cause trouble, should that be on his agenda. The truth is Annie does a fraction of what her job should require from her. I'll miss her, but I look forward to having someone who can keep up with the demands of the position." He paused a beat. "And who might update that awful waiting area."

Seraphina laughed out loud, then covered her mouth. "I'm sorry," she mumbled. "I wondered why it was so outdated. It's so unexpected. You keep it that way for Annie's sake?"

Grant sighed and eyed his burrito. "This spork just isn't up to the task, you know it?" He aimed, tossed, and the utensil sailed unerringly into a nearby trashcan. He grinned. "I played point in college."

He was certainly tall enough to have been a basketball star. He picked up the massive burrito. Seraphina cringed and snorted at the same time as sauce ran over his fingers, then watched with wide eyes while he quickly licked his thumb. It wasn't just men who fixated on women's mouths. Watching a man do things with his lips and tongue could be just as much fun.

Seraphina inhaled and eyed the giant burrito in her lap. In for a penny, in for a pound. She grimaced and laughed as sauce oozed over her fingers. She took a dainty bite, ended up with nothing but tortilla, and went back again. This time she came away with a mouthful of perfectly tender steak that dripped juices down her chin. She squealed and leaned over her container so she wouldn't drip on her dress.

"Wow. That's just tasty," she said, with feeling, once she swallowed.

He wasn't much better off. He'd given up trying to eat it in one piece, and tore pieces apart with his fingers, using the tortilla shreds to swipe up the meat and potatoes, then running through a pile of toppings before popping the big bite into his mouth.

She realized she was watching him, but he was fascinating to watch. So together. Fastidious, controlled, and careful. But he ate with a man's single-mindedness, taking huge bites and occasionally grunting his appreciation.

When he'd eaten all he could, leaving only a few corners of tortilla behind, he grabbed extra napkins from the guy inside the taco truck and wiped his hands while Seraphina kept picking at hers, and rejoined her. "Annie is my mother's old friend," he said suddenly. "When I first started out, she came to work for me, accepting the paltry amount I could afford to pay her back then. Mostly, just to be helpful. When I moved the business into the building I'm in now, I gave Annie free rein. I let her choose the furniture, the finishes, and the décor. Money isn't always the best way to show gratitude."

"And you certainly couldn't replace her," Seraphina said around a chunk of potato. They'd been delicate and crunchy, but were turning to mush from the sauce. Delicious, delicious mush.

"God, no. I wouldn't want to. I owe Kathleen. She took me in as a kid."

Seraphina paused in licking her fingers. "You're adopted?"

Grant's gaze was ponderous as it roamed over her face, as if gauging what he wanted to tell her. "I barely remember my dad, and don't know anything at all about my mom."

Seraphina blinked. For a minute, she considered their eyes, so strikingly similar. Shit. Was it possible? Because that would be weird as hell. "I didn't know my mom, either." She swallowed. "You don't suppose…"

Grant's eyes opened wide, and he burst into laughter. His wrists rested on his knees, and he shook his head. "No, no. I don't think we have to worry about that. You born and raised here?"

Seraphina nodded, wiped her hands one last time, and pushed away the remainder of her burrito. If she didn't stop now, she'd bust a seam on her dress.

Grant smiled at her. "I was born in New York City. Kathleen moved us here a little while after she realized my dad wasn't coming back for me. She had a few cousins she'd lost touch with, and it seemed Little Rock was a better place to raise a boy like me."

"I sense there's a story there."

"Maybe. Maybe not." He stood and brushed off his slacks as best he could. Then, he offered Seraphina his hand, and helped her stand. "Another time. For now, I'd desperately like to recapture the vibe we had going before Brendan Berkley showed up out of nowhere and put a sour taste in our mouths."

"Oh?" She brushed off her dress, especially around her bottom, where she'd been sitting on the pavement, careful to make sure there was no grime or cigarette butts clinging to the lace fabric. "I admit, I haven't met many men who like to dance. Consider me officially intrigued."

"Oh, I'm a terrible dancer. Don't set your expectations too high." He was looking down at her, a pensive expression on his face and a smile in his eyes. Quickly, as if on a dare, he lowered his head and pressed his lips against hers.

Warmth spread out from her belly, into every limb until her whole body buzzed. She opened her mouth and moved her tongue along his in a lazy glide. She snuck a peek at Grant to find his eyes already wide open and watching her. She pulled away and grinned. "I'm good enough for both of us." She grabbed his hand and pulled him after her, toward the lights and the music and the glimmering promise of the night.

Chapter 5

Seraphina stifled a giggle as she tittered out of the elevator after Grant. He waited just outside the doors to offer his arm. "Did you see how that woman looked at me? Do you know her?"

"She looked terrified. You're not quite steady on those towering heels. But even without the shoes, the dress makes a hell of an impression."

"Want to see if you can do better after...well, after more than a couple of beers. I lost count somewhere in between 'Gimme Three Steps' and 'Mary Jane's Last Dance.'"

"Nope," he replied, with an easy smile. "I wouldn't look nearly as amazing wearing them. And I'd probably have to crawl to my front door. It would un-man me, and you'd probably change your mind." He paused and looked at her. "You can, you know. Change your mind."

Seraphina admired the gold wall paper and intricate crown molding. Grant's apartment was in one of the most expensive buildings in the city. Even the hallways were swank. "I wouldn't have agreed to..." Come home with you was too on-the-nose for her to say out loud, even with a head full of hoppy beer. Besides, he'd invited her in for a nightcap. Things between them didn't have to go any further than that, but she knew she wanted it to. And guessed Grant wanted the same. Once again, he was being the gentleman, giving her an out.

She watched him studying her. She already had ahold of his arm, so it was easy to grab ahold of the other and pull him toward her. She reached up to circle his neck and leaned into him. From dancing, she'd already learned a thing or two about the hard planes of his body. He'd rolled up the sleeves of his dress shirt to reveal muscled forearms with a sprinkling of golden blond hairs. They came around her, his hands not quite daring to grab her ass, but close enough to make her smile at his reticence. All night, besides several stolen kisses, he'd skirted the edge of taking it to the next step. Apparently, he'd leave that to her.

Seraphina took the reins gladly. Tomorrow, he'd be her boss again, and the liberties would no longer be hers to take. Thinking about tomorrow morning—facing Grant after whatever happened between them tonight, and the hellacious hangover she'd likely suffer—put a black cloud over this otherwise pristine, carefree night. So, she brushed her concerns away from her mind like no more than a wispy tendril of smoke, and went up on her tip-toes to kiss Grant.

Not a sweet kiss or a fun kiss, or a playful one like those they'd shared on the dance floor, while laughing at their clumsiness and outdated moves. Not this time. She drank him in possessively, owning him like some craven cave woman staking her claim. For a wild moment, there was only the heat and desperation of the kiss, two bodies fighting to get closer, and go deeper.

Grant broke away first, pulling out of her embrace. He ran his thumb along her swollen bottom lip. "I'm officially indecent for public." He kissed her again, roughly. His adroit hands finally found their courage and smoothed over the fabric that hugged the curve of her ass, until his fingers brushed the sensitive skin of the back of her thighs.

She made a small noise in her throat and felt herself melt. She was going to end up naked in the hallway if they didn't move it along soon. This time, she pulled away. She gripped the front of his dress shirt. "I appreciate a gentleman as much as the next lady, but I'm not feeling very ladylike at the moment. So, whenever you're ready to stop playing nice…"

A feral grin overcame his face, morphed it into something predatory that sent a shiver down Seraphina's spine. One hand gripped her waist, while the fingers of the other trailed the hem of her dress. His light touch ran along her thigh until he reached the front of her dress. He kept his gaze locked on hers as his fingers continued their walk, pausing only briefly before disappearing beneath her skirt. His thumb brushed across the tiny bud at her center.

She moaned softly and leaned into him. She pressed her hips forward, silently begging for more than the light teasing taste he offered.

He said nothing as he rubbed her one last time, hard enough to make her gasp and feel the spread of warmth between her legs, and stepped away. He cupped her cheek and kissed her sweetly. Then he took her by the hand and led her down the hallway to his apartment. A true gentleman, he gave her exactly what she asked for.

* * * *

Seraphina squinted at her watch as she stumbled into her apartment. She was tipsy enough to make telling the time difficult, but not so drunk she had to search out the digital clock on her stove. With one eye squinted, she ignored the dread at realizing it was nearly four in the morning. She made a beeline for her bedroom, collapsed onto her bed, and stared blearily up at the ceiling. She was still buzzing from the most extraordinary couple of hours with Grant Gallagher.

She'd come so very close to staying the night. But they had work in the morning, and she'd be damned if, at her mature age, she'd take a cab in the morning wearing last night's dress. No walk of shame for her.

She had an important task to handle before she could strip to nothing, take a searing hot shower, pop some Advil, and get some sleep. She stared at her phone, realized she could have simply turned on the screen to get the time, and chuckled at herself. Drunk people were stupid.

Kay answered on Seraphina's second try. "Sera?" she asked, her voice fuzzy with sleep. "Everything okay?"

Seraphina heard husky murmurs in the background and guessed she'd managed to wake Oliver, as well. Couldn't be helped. This was important. In fact, she guessed Oliver would be wide-awake soon. "Brendan Berkley," Seraphina said, careful to enunciate around her thick tongue. Her mouth was uncomfortably dry.

"Um. Sera, it's very late. No, actually. It's very early. Very, very early."

"Brendan Berkley," she repeated, then sighed and made herself sit up. She swung her legs over the side of the bed, blinked away the sleepiness, and forced herself to wake up some. "Listen, it's important. I know it's late, and if it weren't for the drinks I had tonight, this could totally wait. I was out with Grant tonight—"

"Whoa. Stop there." Kay paused a beat. "You went out with your boss? Specifically, you went out and had drinks with Grant Gallagher? The Mr. Gallagher? Scary dude who's designed half the buildings in this city constructed in the last decade? Drinks? Really?"

She'd shared a little more than that with Grant, but that was a conversation she'd happily postpone indefinitely. "Kay." Seraphina tried to muster some of her usual control. It was a tone thing, though, and her buzz was really killing her ability to ring the necessary chords. "Just listen, then we can gossip all you want. We ran into Brendan Berkley. Apparently, he's coming to work for Grant, to replace his secretary who's retiring soon. It can't be coincidence, can it? First, Brendan is at Free Leaf Concepts, where you guys have greenhouses that can produce the modified magic mushrooms, and now, he's going to work for one of the most influential people on the city council."

More murmurs in the background as Kay filled Oliver in. His voice was stronger now, even though Seraphina still couldn't quite make out what he said. "Hm. Oliver thinks not. But, Sera, his hands are tied, you know that. One more misstep with Brendan Berkley, and Oliver's going to be looking at stalking charges."

Oliver made a rude snort and mumbled some more.

Kay giggled. "He says I'm exaggerating, but I'm totally not. Seriously, we can't go anywhere near this. But Oliver can do the next best thing." A pause while Oliver murmured some more. "He says he'll call Cappy Don in the morning."

Cappy Don was Captain Donald Cappricci, Oliver's boss. He led the investigation that busted up the arm of the drug ring running out of Free Leaf Concepts. A hard ass with out-of-control eyebrows, but as thorough as they came. Seraphina relaxed. Then she stiffened again, considering Grant's role in all this. "You guys looked into Grant already, right? Nothing sketchy going on?"

"He was cleared. While he does have political dealings, his business practices are all on the up and up. Cappy Don's team didn't uncover a single bribe, or otherwise shady deal. The city contracts he always seems to win are legitimate. Simply, Gallagher Interiors has a reputation for competence and quality," Kay assured her. "But you know, with Brendan popping up out of nowhere, couldn't hurt to keep your eyes open, Sera. Did you say anything to Grant?"

"Of course. I can't believe he'd hire someone questioned in a drug sting, but Grant said Brendan is the best applicant for the job, and it's unethical to hold that against him since he was never arrested or accused of anything, let alone convicted. It's a noble, if somewhat naïve, approach. Surprising, really, for a guy so business-minded." The last of Seraphina's energy was seeping from her pores. She rubbed her hand over her face and frowned at the black smears of mascara. She groaned. "Ugh. I need to go. Tomorrow is going to be pure hell. Kay, why don't you come over tomorrow for a dinner, and we'll talk some more."

Kay chuckled, her voice turning sleepy. "You bet your ass we're going to talk some more. You went on a freaking date with Grant freaking Gallagher."

And then some. Seraphina smiled to herself, tossed her phone onto the bed, and dropped like a sack of potatoes onto her pillow. She'd shower in the morning.

* * * *

Grant paced, convinced he was wearing a groove into his carpet. He checked the wall clock again, exhaling loudly in an attempt to keep his impatience in check. He'd had a late night, too. It was no excuse to waltz into the office well after nine in the morning. He'd left her a text, a voicemail, and a terse memo on her desk. If she didn't show soon, he'd go looking for her, and neither one of them would enjoy the encounter.

Finally, Annie announced Seraphina's arrival. Grant leaned against the desk, with his arms crossed, and waited.

Seraphina walked into the room and sat down. She didn't wear any evidence of their night together, and he'd never have guessed she was hungover if it weren't for the fact that she was an hour late. She wore trim, sharply creased gray slacks and a bright red silk top, with generous sleeves, and a fitted bodice. The color had visions of last night flashing through his head—that damned red dress. On her body, half off her body, pushed up over her hips, and finally, in a heap on his bedroom floor. He coughed, suddenly uncomfortable. He fumbled with his greeting, starting and stopping.

Seraphina simply waited, poised and so together it was annoying. He had a raging headache, while she looked completely untouched. "You're late," he finally managed.

They stared at each other. Seraphina cocked a brow. "I thought maybe that might annoy you. But one of us didn't have the luxury of merely passing out. One of us had to track down a cab, make small talk with a guy from Zimbabwe on the way home, and worry about things like hair and makeup. Trust me, you didn't want me walking around this place an hour ago. My hair was a rat's nest and my face looked like someone had taken a crayon to it. Smeared red lipstick, brown eyeshadow, and black eyeliner. Also…" She paused and glanced up at him from beneath her lashes before quickly looking away. A subtle flush of pink crept over the apples of her cheeks. "One of us was a little…tender this morning. I needed a long hot shower, and not just to wash off the sour smell of beer."

He hadn't expected her to discuss last night so brazenly. He'd actually been looking forward to teasing a few blushes out of her. He almost smiled but held fast. He met her challenging glare with one of his own. "Hey, I showered. And who says I passed out after you left? Who says I didn't call a twenty-four-hour flower service and order a dozen pink roses for a certain woman? And who says I didn't toss and turn long after that, because a certain red dress wouldn't stay out of my head?"

She sat back in the chair and looked at him uncertainly. She narrowed her gaze and nibbled her lip. "Trying to convince me you were good for a second round?"

This time, Grant couldn't stop his smile. "You mean third? You could've stayed to find out."

"Would I have been excused for being late, then?"

"No. I would've made sure you were awake in time. Offered you coffee and a hot shower. Maybe a hot shower with benefits. I'm a gentleman, after all."

Her grin slowly grew into a full smile that dimpled her cheeks and made her blue eyes dance. "Except for when you're not."

"Except for when I'm not," he agreed quietly.

This time there was something else in the air as they stared at each other. Seraphina watched him like a wary rabbit eyeballing a fox. "You really got me roses?"

He nodded. Suddenly, he had all the patience in the world. "They'll be delivered at ten. Is that weird? I just wanted to acknowledge last night, somehow. I laid awake thinking about you, guessing things would be different today, but not knowing how. I've never had the pleasure of seducing someone who works for me before."

Seraphina stood up and approached him, her arms crossed. "You seduced me, is that what I heard?"

He leaned back, already fantasies of christening his desk playing out in his head. If only she'd worn another dress. "It's possible I'm wrong. But then, that means you must have seduced me." He gave her his brightest smile. "I'm flattered."

Her mouth opened, then closed. She gave a little snort of laughter and shook her head as if she couldn't believe him. "It's a boon to mankind you're not a lawyer. And maybe no one was seduced. Maybe things just… happened." She bit her lip and gazed at him, considering.

Grant would have given anything in his possession to know what was behind her thoughtful expression. More importantly, he would've liked to know if she were having the same reaction he was to their sudden closeness. She was near enough to wrap his hands around her hips and tug her close. Near enough to notice her breathing grow shallower. Near enough to smell her. Lilacs and mint. He had a momentary flashback to last night, when those scents, mingled with her body's own alluring essence, had intoxicated him.

When he finally dared himself to reach out and touch her, it was like someone else guided his hand. His conscious mind hovered nearby, appreciating his bravery and daring, because at any minute, Annie or

Ophelia might walk in. Those small potential problems couldn't seem to reach him, though. His fingers smoothed over Seraphina's hips. The fabric of her slacks was thin and soft. He inhaled sharply as she stepped closer, her body moving beneath his hands in a swift, sure motion.

She blinked up at him, seemed to weigh something in her mind. Then her mouth was on his, open and pliant and demanding. Her hands traveled up his chest and back down.

They stayed that way, locked together, exploring with desperate mouths and curious hands until they were forced to break apart at the sound of footsteps approaching the door.

Grant smoothed his shirt and tie and gave Seraphina his most genuine smile, then quickly kissed the tip of her nose. "I can relax about one thing. We're definitely compatible."

She stared at him haughtily. "Don't jinx our juju."

She left a minute later, after Ophelia entered and made small talk. Ophelia was so smooth, Grant wouldn't have guessed at her impatience if it weren't for the text messages they'd exchanged earlier that morning. She had a masterful grip on her self-control. He was quite in awe every time he watched her balance her character with her personal interests.

Once they were alone, she dropped into a chair, in a most undignified position, and groaned. She pinched the bridge of her nose. "Being Ophelia Quenby is no one's idea of a good time. And you." She narrowed her eyes at him over her fingers. "You're really complicating things here, Grant."

"What's going on with me doesn't have anything to do with what's going on with you."

"The hell," she shot back, sitting up. "I report to Seraphina starting today. Her relationship with you changes everything. You know, you didn't have to offer to give her an audition to be a partner in your firm to get in bed with her. You could have gone about it like a normal person. Asked her out for dinner and a movie. That sort of thing."

Grant's good humor faded. He moved around to sit at his desk properly. He had business with Ophelia, but she'd do well to remember their alliance could end as swiftly as he'd agreed to form it. "You misunderstand." He let his tone convey his displeasure. "Seraphina is convenient for you. But I didn't hire her for your convenience. Nor does how I operate within my business concern you. I will facilitate your needs when and where possible, but do not mistake me as working for you. In the end, I'll serve my own prerogative, Ophelia."

She sighed, accepting his point with a small nod of apology. Her hair was not unlike Seraphina's, a sleek curtain that fell straight to her shoulders.

They had very little in common besides that, physical or otherwise. Ophelia's hair was so dark it was almost black, her eyes were a deep brown, and her personality didn't have the polished finish of Seraphina's. She was crude, sometimes humorously so. Grant had to admit she put on a hell of a show for his employees. To everyone else, she was soft-spoken and exceptionally helpful.

"Very well," she relented. "I'm rude sometimes, aren't I? I assumed. You're a powerful man, she's a lonely woman—"

"She's not lonely." Grant had no idea how he could know such a thing. It just didn't fit. Seraphina was self-possessed and contained, but she didn't strike him as lonely. "She keeps to herself. We can't all be babbling social butterflies."

"You think I babble?" She seemed genuinely curious. Not offended in the least.

"Certainly in my company."

"Well, that's a relief. I'd hate to think I was breaking cover without realizing it. Now, listen, I think you're underestimating how this might blow up in our faces. You're right, Seraphina is convenient. She's a blind conduit, and I couldn't have arranged it better if I'd had to. If things go sour between you two, and she quits, we wouldn't be entirely screwed, but it would certainly put a kink in the program." She was silent as she chewed the inside of her lip thoughtfully. Then her dark eyes zeroed in on Grant with a calculating gleam. "But then, we must use what tools we have. You can at least report what she says, so we know for sure the system is working as we hoped it would."

He stared dubiously. "You want me to spy on Seraphina?"

"No. More like confirm our hopes. Mention what she mentions. Being her assistant gets me close, but you've swooped in, and there you are, already closer to Seraphina than I can probably get in my limited capacity. Between the two of us, we can put together whether or not the information is moving in the direction we'd like it to."

Grant shook his head slowly to display his aversion to the plan, but didn't disagree. Not yet. After all, he'd accepted the terms from Ophelia and her cohorts, and he understood sacrifice for the greater good. Only now, he had some doubts about what constituted "greater." If relaying information behind Seraphina's back put a cold stop to their budding relationship, could he still say he'd done the right thing?

"It's a lot of cloak and dagger," he finally said, committing to nothing for the time being.

Ophelia's expression grew somber and her gaze fierce. "I've told you what we're up against, Grant. When Brendan Berkley walks into this office Monday morning, we'd better know what we're about. And you gave your word to do everything you could."

"Yes," he replied in a clipped tone. "I did. Fine. I'll report on Seraphina. But keep in mind, doing so could just as easily be the thing that ruins your game plan. I don't think she'd continue to work for me, or with me, if she were to find out I was spying—yes, spying, let's not mince words here, Ms. Quenby—and I still think it's not a bad idea to simply involve her."

Ophelia smiled thinly and rose from the chair, signaling an end to their strained meeting. "You'll just have to make sure she never finds out. And in the dark is where she will stay, because everything happening here is strictly need-to-know."

"That's absurd." Grant could feel himself losing patience.

"Maybe. Maybe not. But I don't follow my intuition, I follow orders. Seraphina is an unknown player. Gathering information is one thing, giving a civilian detailed information in an ongoing case is quite another. I'm not Oliver Pierce. I don't act on whims or flights of fancy. I plan and execute."

"Even if you know that civilian is trustworthy?"

"Orders, Mr. Gallagher. Orders." She said nothing else as she strode out of his office.

Chapter 6

Seraphina's hands shook slightly. She balled them into fists. Her office door was closed. She'd meditated, checked her e-mails for anything of dire consequence, and mentally run through her grocery list, but still couldn't shake the internal signals telling her it was time.

She needed to call her dad. She glanced his photo, her lips pressed tightly together. She hated the spiral of emotions he encouraged. Since the dawn of time, she was stuck in the embarrassingly stereotypical rut of craving Daniel Fawkes's approval.

His love had a sting to it, and his approval never seemed to come, no matter what Seraphina achieved. If she told him about her accomplishments, he playfully accused her of bragging. But halting communication also backfired. When she didn't keep him in the loop, he caustically labeled her ungrateful and "too good" for her less than successful gay father, and it must be because she was ashamed of him, because what else.

At thirty-one years old, she still did not possess the courage to tell him her reticence had nothing to do with his sexual orientation, and everything to do with him. Just him. His personality, his corrosive judgment, and his barbed compliments.

At the same time, she wasn't sure he even realized what he did. His hurtful comments were usually made in an off-hand manner, and the burrs that stuck to her pride were tossed carelessly her way. He loved her. He showed that love in small ways. Sometimes, even in big ways. Despite herself, she lived for these moments. And it wasn't like she had another parent to turn to for simple affection or advice that didn't begin with a piercing insult. So she'd learned early and quickly to not need these things. Or at least, to not show she needed them.

She calmed herself, erected her emotional barriers, and dialed her father. It would be news that Grant Gallagher was taking on an apprentice to eventually—potentially—become partner in his firm. If her dad heard about the apprenticeship through the grapevine before she had a chance to tell him, it didn't bode well. But making the announcement without coming across as a braggart also weighed on her, and she considered her words carefully when Daniel finally answered the phone.

"Hi, darling. I was thinking of you this morning. Looks like I was on your mind, too. Did you need something?"

"Um, no, Dad, I just—"

"Because I can't help you, Sera. Please, I can barely help myself. I'm thinking of moving out of town. What do you think of that? Nuts. But I'm running out of work, and Little Rock is a small town. Too small for me."

She'd often wondered why he'd hung around as long as he had. Community theater wasn't non-existent, but it was a pretty small niche in a place like Little Rock. Her dad had been complaining about the lack of culture in the theater scene her entire life. The other totally unsurprising thing was leap of relief her heart made at the mention of him moving away. She loved Daniel and craved his affection and approval like nothing else on earth. But it was a heavy load to bear.

"I don't need help, Dad."

"I know, I know." He sounded amused and indulgent, like she were a small child denying she'd gone to the potty in her big girl undies. "You're a big deal now, aren't you? Working for Grant Gallagher. I don't know shit about designing stuff, but I know that name. He always pops up in the political section of the paper, for this or that fundraiser. Swell guy. I don't trust him. He never smiles. But he donates to all the right places. Don't be embarrassed to tell him about me, he gave a pretty penny to the LGBT charity they ran last year."

She'd roll her eyes if she weren't convinced Daniel would somehow hear it over the line and accuse her of having no respect. "Actually, I am kind of calling about my job. I know you hate to find stuff out from the paper, so I thought I'd better tell you myself. Grant has taken me on as his apprentice, with the idea that I might become a partner eventually. We're going to be working together on the Governor's Mansion project the city greenlighted earlier this year. If things goes well, I suppose, I'll...um, well, I guess I'll get quite the promotion." She ended on a light laugh. She hadn't realized it, but she'd been counting on him interrupting her before she got to the end of her spiel. So much for considering her words carefully.

"You know you don't have to impress me, Sera." Her father's tone was dry, but he didn't sound particularly annoyed. "All the same, good for you."

"Sorry, I don't mean to gloat or anything. It's just every time you learn something before I have time to tell you myself, you feel like I'm avoiding you."

He took a deep breath and turned complacent, as if she were the unreasonable one. "You're right, you're right. I know you don't mean to gloat. You just have that way about you. I have no idea if you inherited the trait genetically from your mother, or if she had time to teach it to you before she ran off, but that's one-hundred percent Rebecca Fawkes, I tell ya."

Seraphina bit off a nasty reply. Of course, her dad would never take credit for the parts of Seraphina he didn't like. The bad stuff came from her mother, and if ever there were anything about her Daniel deemed worthy of his pride or praise, it surely will have come from the Fawkes side of the family, ensuring the credit was more Daniel's than Seraphina's.

"Sweetheart, I have to go. Whatever all that means, I'm happy for you, good luck, or whatever, okay? Sorry, some of that crap just goes over my head. But listen, if I do leave town, I'll call first. I wasn't yanking your chain, girlie, I'm really considering getting the hell out of this place. You could come with me. Fresh start, all that. I'm thinking L.A. or New Orleans, maybe New York City. Somewhere that's alive. I'm drowning in this dusty place."

She wanted to bang her head on the desk. She didn't need a fresh start. If her dad paid any attention at all to anything besides his own chaotic emotional state, he'd understand she'd made an incredibly important leap in her career. She'd be insane to walk away. Becoming Grant Gallagher's partner would make up for the years she'd spent at the university tutoring other hopefuls instead of working toward her own goals.

"This is home for me. But I wish you luck, Dad, if you decide to go through with the move."

"You say that like it's a tough decision." His derision was potent, but Seraphina tuned it out. "And hey, I could do without the condescension, thanks. I'm amped about making a big change in my life, and I got doubts a-plenty. Don't need your help."

"Sorry, Dad, I—"

"Yep, gotta go, hon. Like I said, I'll be in touch."

Seraphina let her phone drop onto her desk. She groaned, slumped back in her chair, and rubbed her face. How did she keep convincing herself the next phone call would be better than the last? At least he never wanted to do lunch or see a movie together. She didn't think she could survive more than a few minutes. He isn't obligated to understand me, just because it's my desire to be understood.

A long time ago, she'd sought therapy to work through her tough relationship with her father. That mantra was the thing she still carried with her, years later, and made the exorbitant fees wholly worth it. Her dad raised her. Beyond keeping her alive, healthy, and reasonably happy, he didn't owe her anything as an individual. She was entitled to be herself, and so was Daniel. Dealing with the fact that he was a self-centered tool was just part of the package. Everyone had flaws.

She laid her head on her desk and waited for her headache to ebb, which it stubbornly refused to do. Her head sprung up at the light tap on her door. "Come in," she called, straightening herself behind the desk. She could feel like crap, so long as she didn't look like crap.

Roper smiled sheepishly as he stepped inside.

"Hi." Seraphina recalled suddenly the last time they'd seen each other, and felt her face drain of color. She'd swear in a court of law, she blanched to her toes. Not that anyone would notice on her pale skin, but she could feel the blood draining away like it were going into hiding. Which is what she wished she could do. "I looked for you yesterday."

Roper closed the door, and the quiet snick sounded like a gunshot in the loaded silence between them. He moved slowly, finally sitting in one of the extra chairs Seraphina had shoved against the wall opposite her desk. "I took the day," he replied easily.

She didn't wait for him to ask for his due explanation. "Roper, it's going to sound like complete and utter bullshit when I tell you what happened. I don't even know how to go about convincing you it was an accident. And I have no idea why you would cover for me."

Roper grinned. Not in a nasty, malicious, or unkind way. The genuine article. In fact, he smiled like a man released from indentured servitude. "I came by to thank you."

Seraphina sat back, stunned. "What?"

"Quietly," he added, his smile still firmly rooted to the spot. Unflinching. "I don't want Grant to know this, so if you wouldn't mind keeping it between you and I. In fact, I almost didn't say anything at all, but you look so mortified and guilty. I can't leave you hanging. Hell, I probably can't pretend to be all that upset. I told Grant I think it should've gone to you, anyway, to sort of explain away why I'm not all broken up about not getting the spot."

She shook her head. "What?"

"Seraphina, come on. You saw the crap I turned in. You think I'm Grant Gallagher's secret weapon because I suck that bad? I tried to throw the contest. I underestimated Grant. I don't doubt he would've changed my blueprints. Yours will be tweaked and refined, too. But I really thought he wouldn't have the nerve to choose those awful designs."

Seraphina raised her hands to put a stop to Roper's explanation. "First of all, why? Why put anything on the table you weren't prepared to back?"

Roper shrugged lightly. "It was expected, ever since Gallagher Interiors won the bid for Tanbee House. I knew if we did, I'd get the assignment. It was my idea for Grant to give some other players a shot at the spotlight. He probably had me figured out, even then. See, I'm looking to move on from working for Grant. Grant and I haven't said a word to each other, but I suspect he's figured me out. I tried my best to get out of Tanbee House. So, deleting those files was more than I could have hoped for. Accident or not, I extend to you my heartiest of thanks."

"So, that's the real reason you refused to recreate your design for Grant?"

His smile deepened. "Yes. It's also why I lied about not having any other copies saved, although I immediately deleted all of my backup files after I left Grant's office."

He meant every word. She could hardly believe it. "But...but he's looking for a partner. You're the likeliest candidate." Despite what Grant may have said, Seraphina still believed it. The two of them had worked together for ages. Maybe she had the better temperament, but Roper had earned his place at the top.

"Me and Grant, we go way back, sure. He's a fair man to work for. I'm good at my job. But we're different people, with different ideals. I don't want to work for Grant Gallagher. I want to work for Roper McLeod. But the market here is flooded. Between Grant, Neve Harper, and places like Free Leaf Concepts cornering the spa and outlet mall markets, I'm going nowhere if I stay in Little Rock. And I've got bigger plans for myself than merely designing. See, I want to create. I've been taking classes. I'm going to finish my degree in architecture, and take it to the next level." He relaxed into the chair, settling in as if they were going to sit and chat indefinitely. "Besides, I'm aware he offered the apprenticeship to you. We discussed it, and I agree wholeheartedly. Running a place like this is about more than talent, of which you have plenty. It requires a certain aplomb. Grant moves in some important circles. He needs someone who can be taken seriously. I love my job, but I don't want to deal with any of that crap."

Seraphina did. She wanted all of it. "So, Grant didn't choose your designs because they were better?"

Roper stared at her plaintively. "Come on. You saw them for yourself. He'd have gotten around it somehow. My best guess is he's just trying to keep me on. He doesn't want me to go. And you can't pick up the slack, because if you're to work one-on-one with Grant, you won't have time for my workload."

Red flashed across her vision. So, she had won. Roper's suspicions were her only proof, but she'd bet her studio apartment he was right. A tight ball of indignant anger formed in her chest. "That weasel jerk—"

"You can't tell him." Roper squinted at her in a pained expression of apology. "You can't. I mean, you can, obviously, but I really wish you wouldn't. Look, Grant knows I'm fading away, but he doesn't realize how far I've gone. I'm only waiting for a few small things to align, and I'm out of here. I want to tell Grant on my own terms, because it's all going to end rather abruptly. I owe the man more than he's gonna get."

"But why? You won't even give him proper notice?" She berated herself for caring how Grant might react to the news of his star designer suddenly ducking out. She shouldn't care. Not after he'd deliberately chosen plans that weren't as good as hers. She ended up with the job all the same, but still. There were principles to consider.

Roper's smiled faded into something sadder. "Because if anyone could talk me into sticking around, it's Grant Gallagher. He'll offer to pay for my education. He'll give me bonuses and incentives. Not as bribes, but because he wants his people to be happy. And it'll just make it that much harder. I don't just want to move on from his company, I want to get the hell out of Arkansas."

Seraphina tapped her fingernails on her desk and wondered why everyone suddenly had a strong desire to move away. She'd better check in with her few friends, make sure they weren't planning anything drastic. "Where do you think you might go?"

"Denver. I've got a cousin out there. He's military, can't say enough good stuff about Colorado. Figure why not? I could use a break from this humidity."

Pfft. Seraphina had been to the deserts of Arizona and the wastelands of Nevada. Whoever coined "well, at least it's a dry heat!" was out of his ever-loving mind. Before she could rattle off something witty, there was another tap at the door.

Ophelia poked her head in, saw Roper, and apologized.

He waved her in as he rose from the chair with an exaggerated groan. "She's all yours, Ophelia. Seraphina, thanks for giving me your two-cents on the Coulter Bridge. Appreciate the tip." He winked and left them with a jaunty little wave. The guy could be a real goof.

Seraphina's new assistant smiled guilelessly, lowered her voice, and gave a slight nod toward the doorway, where Roper had passed seconds ago. "Can you believe he accidently deleted his files on Tanbee House?"

Seraphina swallowed past a weird lump of guilt lodged in her throat. Even with Roper's blessing, she felt stupid and awful. What had she been thinking, anyway, deleting files like some child throwing a temper tantrum? Only she hadn't been angry, then, only mournful. Now she was angry. And as per usual, could do nothing about it. She gave her best version of a smile to Ophelia. It wasn't much. "I suppose you're checking in."

"Yes." Ophelia rubbed her hands together and looked around Seraphina's small office. "I'd love to jump right in, if you don't mind. It's Friday. Mind if I download a set of your blueprint files to my tablet and get started over the weekend? I do my best work at home, wearing holy cotton pants with a cat curled into my side."

She decided she liked Ophelia. "Sure. That'd be great. I have a list of materials I'd like to use. They are all available through local sources. If you want, you can start making calls. I'd rather have suppliers lined up than have to hunt them down at the last moment. At least reach out. Maybe get with the contractor Grant assigned to Tanbee House and ask for his estimation on demolition so I can work out a tighter schedule."

Ophelia nodded enthusiastically. "You bet. I'll get started right away."

The woman bustled from Seraphina's office at the same time her phone buzzed. It was Grant. She inhaled deeply and answered, taking care with her tone. She was mad. But she'd told Roper she wouldn't give him away, and if Grant started asking questions about her sudden change in attitude, well, it wouldn't take much for her to slip up and spill her guts. She didn't enjoy confrontation. But she didn't shy away from it, either.

"Can I take you to dinner again?" he asked. "Maybe something in between the two extremes of fine dining and a taco truck."

She grinned despite herself. "I have plans with a friend." It was true, and Seraphina was glad, because she needed some time away from Grant and her job. "I think I'm going to take the weekend to relax. I'll see you Monday, Grant."

She noted the disappointment in his voice, but he recovered smoothly. "Yeah. Of course. See you Monday."

* * * *

Emma's scrubs had pink elephants on them today. Grant thought there was something rather inappropriate about that, but wisely kept the quip to himself. Kathleen's nursing home was probably not the best place for jokes about drunken hallucinations. He doubted Emma would appreciate it, even if it earned him a small chuckle from Kathleen. She'd always had an edgy sense of humor.

And a keen sense of intuition. Lunch today was roasted squash medley over brown rice, soft wheat rolls, and baked beans. For Grant, there was the addition of a tough pork chop seasoned liberally with lemon pepper. He scraped some of the seasoning from the top with the side of his fork and cut off a corner where the fat had sizzled into a crispy edge, just the thing to ease down the dry meat.

Kathleen pushed her food around her plate. There was a pronounced lethargy in her movements.

Grant frowned and set his fork to the side. His appetite hadn't exactly been rampant to start with. Some lunches were better than others at Heritage Acres. "Are you not feeling well?"

She shrugged and didn't meet his eyes.

"Mom, come on." He put a hand over hers, until she finally glanced up. She had rings beneath her eyes. "You don't look like you slept. What's going on?"

He didn't wait for her. He snagged the pen from his breast pocket and handed it over. Kathleen eyed the pen tiredly before taking it from his grasp, sighing, and digging her pad of paper from the pocket of her robe. Until then, Grant hadn't even noticed she wasn't dressed as she usually was. "Mom, you could've canceled, you know that. I'd completely understand if you wanted to rest for a day. Since when are we toeing around each other, huh?"

She sighed again and began to write. Slow, methodical strokes of the pen, but her hand shook slightly.

Unease coiled around Grant's stomach as he watched Kathleen's knuckle-y grip on the pen. Seventy-seven was too old. He couldn't deceive himself and blow off her fatigue like it meant nothing. Because it could very well mean something. He wasn't ready for that, but he'd face what came regardless. Denial and a blind eye had never been his coping behavior of choice. Several moments of heavy silence passed. Finally, Kathleen passed him the pad of paper, but kept the pen, an indication she expected to have more to say.

Only tired. Don't worry, please. Not sleeping right. Muscle spasm keeping me up. Nothing I can do. Doc said take some pills, and maybe I will tonight. Just to help me sleep. You were smiling before you noticed me. I'd rather hear about you than complain about me.

Grant glanced up and responded to her watery smile with a wry one of his own. "That's only part of the answer, I suspect." But he resigned himself to accept her privacy. If fatigue and some muscle pains were the worst of it, there was little he could do for her. Still, he'd have a word with her physician before he went back to the office. Then he smiled at Kathleen, because he knew she wanted him to relax and not worry. She'd only feel bad.

He handed her back the paper. "Was I smiling? Hmm. Maybe I was."

It was Kathleen's turn to look skeptical. She scribbled another note and held it up for him to see. Don't be coy.

His laugh was genuine. "Fine, fine. You know the woman I mentioned. Seraphina. We, uh, kind of went on a date." Even to himself, he sounded surprised. Dating had been so far from his radar for so long. "I don't think we meant to. Things just kind of happened. I took your advice. You were right, naturally. She made a definite impression on me. So, I've decided we'll work together on the Governor's Mansion project, and if that goes well, she'll apprentice with me."

Kathleen grinned and returned to her paper. The pen scratched along rapidly. Don't care about work. Tell me the good stuff. I can't recall you've been on a date in years.

"Years?" Had it really been years? No, no, there was the flight attendant a year and a half ago, but maybe he'd never mentioned that to Kathleen. A strictly casual affair, not something to discuss with one's mother, who'd once expressed concern she would die before seeing him married. Grant didn't like to consider that she may be right.

Kathleen merely shrugged, as if allowing for the fact that there may have been dalliances he'd neglected to mention.

"I guess," he conceded, unwilling to change his story now. "The good stuff. Okay, well, the night started out as a working dinner. I suppose I can admit to you, should you swear yourself to secrecy, that maybe I was trying to impress Seraphina. A little bit. I squeezed in a reservation at Rosa Rita's last night."

Kathleen's eyebrows rose at the swanky restaurant. Everyone knew about Rosa Rita's, but not everyone had the pleasure of getting last-minute reservations. If Grant hadn't been responsible for their remodel a couple of years ago, he doubted even he could have pulled it off.

"Anyway, Seraphina dressed for the occasion. As did I. But the restaurant was so formal and stuffy, I didn't think we'd ever get around to a genuine discussion. As swell as the food is, Rosa Rita's atmosphere can be a little on the oppressive side."

His mom held up a finger, bidding him to wait, and scribbled on her pad. Tell me what she wore. Was it beautiful? You mentioned it, so it must be important.

Grant shook his head but smiled in spite of himself. Kathleen had a way of getting down the bones of a thing. He supposed when speaking was as painstaking as penning down each word, you probably learned to key in on important details. Naturally, he'd mentioned the dress, probably because he could still remember vividly pushing the lacy material up over Seraphina's hips, to find an equally lacy thong awaiting his eager hands. He cleared his throat and ruthlessly shoved the image from his mind so he could look Kathleen in the face without turning beet red.

"It was a stunning dress," he admitted, nodding. "A little racy, if I'm honest. Strapless and short. Brilliant red, and the skirt had a black lace overlay. If Seraphina was a hair less polished and poised, the dress would've been too much. But she loaned it some class."

Kathleen's smile was wide. Grant had no idea what she must be thinking, but it made him nervous. She bobbed her head as she penned yet another note. She took her time. I'd like to meet her. She sounds like someone worth meeting.

Her expression was so hopeful, Grant didn't hesitate. "Absolutely. It's only natural for you to be curious. She may very well end up as my business partner, if things go as planned. I meant to thank you for suggesting her as an apprentice. Sometimes, your insight convinces me you could run my company better than I do."

His mom's smile turned coy. Once again, she hovered over her notepad, then her pen moved quickly across the top. I bet you'd have ended up on that date, all the same. I just gave you a handy excuse.

Kathleen winked at him, and at least for the time being, Grant's concerns about her health faded from his mind. And he couldn't think of a single reason Seraphina would object.

Chapter 7

Seraphina checked the broiler again. The cheese wasn't bubbling, like the recipe said it was supposed to, but turning a deep black. Quickly, she shut the oven off and removed the sheet pan. It clanged loudly onto the glass stovetop, and the pieces of toast bounced like pebbles, a couple flying off completely and landing with small thwacks a few inches away.

She blew out a plume of breath that fluttered her bangs and stared at the mess. Cheese toasties, the recipe said. So easy, anyone could do it. Anyone but her, apparently. For once, she wanted to serve her friends something more than tap water and trail mix. She picked one of the toast triangles and took a tentative bite. She grimaced at the charred flavor. Not the tasty "blackened" version, either. Just plain burned.

Her doorbell chimed. She tossed down the dish towel she'd had tucked into the waistband of her plaid pajama bottoms and padded to the door. She opened it wide. Kay Bing's smile could contend with the sun for sheer brightness. Behind Kay, Neve Harper looked like a bored teenager, dragged along with her mother to a church fundraiser.

Seraphina stepped back and let them inside. A huge sigh of relief escaped her when she spotted the takeout containers. "You're a damn lifesaver, Kay."

"Not my idea," she said over her shoulder, placing the bags of containers on the island that served as a kind of border between the kitchen and the small living area. Her studio apartment didn't allow for a real dining table, but it did have a two-seater bar that did the trick. More often than not she ended up on the sofa. Kay tossed her chin toward Neve. "I was willing to give your cooking skills the benefit of the doubt. Neve's idea to bring a back-up plan."

Neve had wandered over to the stove, where Seraphina's failure with the toast was on display. "Looks like I was right, too. We're artists, not members of the Betty Crocker army." She picked up a slice of toast, grimaced, and tossed it back onto the pan. It hit like a stone.

"So glad you could come, Neve," Seraphina said drily. She hadn't invited Neve, but Kay had called to request a special invite at the last minute. She and Neve were new friends, still feeling each other out, and Kay was absolutely determined that they would come to love each other as much as she loved each of them. Seraphina wanted to tell Kay not to hold her breath, but couldn't bring herself to quash the young woman's dreams. She was a genuinely endearing, bright person in a world full of sarcastic pessimists like Neve Harper. Seraphina fancied herself something in between. Meanwhile, Kay couldn't get enough of Neve's awful abrasiveness. Something about opposites attracting. Probably despite herself, Neve was likewise drawn to Kay's bubbly personality.

It was good to see Kay back in true form. Back when Seraphina had been helping her out at Free Leaf Concepts, Kay had been going through a rough patch. An identity crisis of sorts, after making a few bad decisions. She was better now. Probably thanks in no small part to Oliver Pierce, Kay's adoring boyfriend.

Both of these women were in happy, stable relationships, a fact not at all lost on Seraphina. At thirty-one, she was starting to lose hope. But then again, if someone like Neve Harper had found happily ever after, surely Seraphina had a decent shot at any age.

Kay and Neve unloaded food while Seraphina hunted through kitchen cabinets for plates and silverware. She brought out a pitcher of tea, the kind that steeped in cold water on the countertop, and three tall glasses she then loaded with ice. Finally, the three of them were settled around the coffee table with full glasses and plates heaped high with food.

If Neve weren't there, Seraphina would've launched into an explanation. Instead, she waited for Kay to begin the interrogation, which she did after a single bite of beef and broccoli.

"Okay, Sera, time to spill like BP."

Neve's eyebrows went up. "Stealing my lines again."

Kay smiled helplessly at Seraphina. "She's a really terrible influence. Anyway, I'm so serious." Her round hazel eyes unerringly found the red dress Seraphina had put inside a clear zippered bag for a trip to the drycleaner, hanging on the backside of her bedroom door. "I'm absorbing at least half the story through osmosis just by seeing the dress you obviously wore on your date with Grant Gallagher."

Neve whistled. "Look, I know Duke is manly and delicious, but I'm a little jealous, because me plus Grant Gallagher equals a new world order."

Seraphina didn't doubt it. She also wasn't so sure she wouldn't turn down a trade. Neve's husband, Duke, was about as sexy as they came; a long-haired, leather jacket clad hottie with a heart of gold. No one had any idea how the hell he'd ended up falling for Neve. "Grant definitely has a strong personality," Seraphina agreed. She bowed slightly to Kay, confirming her guess. "And yes, I wore the dress."

"So, you had an idea of where things were headed from the get-go?"

"No." Seraphina almost rolled her eyes at Neve's annoying question but changed her mind. She'd only come across as defensive and lose credibility. "It's just that Grant was a little rude about the whole thing. Asked me to this amazing restaurant. He could've at least pretended the non-date was for my sake, you know. Woo me a little. But he made this little dig about it being a company write-off. Maybe I wanted to see him swallow some of that pride."

"And I bet he almost swallowed his own tongue right along with it. That is a hell of a dress. I'd look like a prostitute," Neve said sadly.

"I'd look like a teenager who raided a prostitute's wardrobe," Kay lamented.

They both looked longingly at the dress. "But you." Neve pointed a chopstick at Seraphina's face. "I bet you looked like vamped up royalty. It's not even how you look. It's how you carry yourself. If I could command respect without opening my mouth, I wouldn't have to be such a bitch."

"Yeah, but you would anyway, because you enjoy it."

Neve nodded to Kay's matter-of-fact remark. "It is fun." She swung her vivid, amber gaze to Seraphina. Whether she realized it or not, the granite behind those honey-colored eyes had a lot to do with Neve's intimidating countenance. "Did you sleep with him?" she asked bluntly.

"Yes. More than once, if you want the detailed version." What the hell? No sense keeping secrets from her friends. She regretted it, though, once she caught on to Kay's worried expression. "What? How else did you expect last night ended, Kay?"

She worried her lip and set her plate aside. "Seems really unlike you, Sera."

"How so?" She pushed a floret of broccoli around her plate and wondered whether she actually wanted Kay to answer the question.

"I don't know. You're careful. This is risky."

"Eh. She's kind of right," Neve chimed in. "It's one thing to, say, get involved with a coworker. Another designer. An equal. A hot carpenter."

Kay rolled her eyes at the obvious reference to her previous disastrous relationship.

"But Grant Gallagher is something else altogether. He's a visible figure. A quickie affair with a guy like that is news in certain circles. I know you want to get your name out there, Seraphina, but you might get more than you bargained for if it comes linked to a casual fling."

Seraphina realized with a start that those implications had never even entered her mind. And, Jesus, they were right. She ran a hand through her hair. "It was just so…hell, I don't know. Like some dreamy high school musical sequence or something. I wasn't really thinking of the future. I don't think Grant was, either."

She still wasn't. She eyed the red dress. Last night had been one of the most fun nights of her life. Regret just wouldn't come. Whether it was fairy dust in the air, certain stars aligning, or plain chemistry, she couldn't say, but she'd be glad for the evening she spent with Grant regardless of what came next. If the make-out session in his office this morning was any kind of clue, she had a good idea. But maybe she'd better wise up before it was too late. She was Seraphina Fawkes, known by friends, family, and acquaintances alike for her cool head. She nodded. "He wants to take me on as an apprentice. An affair would be—"

"Oh, la-la. So scandalous." Kay grinned mischievously, then grew serious with almost comical quickness. "Fun, probably. But maybe not great for your long-term career goals. After all, only men can be slutty without it negatively affecting their jobs."

Neve quirked a brow and mumbled around a bite of brown rice. "Preach it, girl."

Well, shit. Kay was right about that, too. If her little office romance with Grant did end up getting attention, she'd be accused of sleeping her way to the top. Seducing a powerful rich man. Yeah, because that was totally every woman's goal in life. Why be good at stuff when putting out could pay the bills? She snorted at her own joke, then sighed heavily. "I'm not sure letting what others might think about me dictate my actions is any better. I'm grown. He's grown. And if I'm working with him no matter what, then I don't see the harm."

"Sure." Neve shrugged, but it was one of those shrugs that heralded some smart-ass remark. She didn't disappoint. "No harm in sleeping with the guy signing your paycheck. That never backfired for any woman ever."

The comment snagged Kay's attention, and she swiveled a consternated stare between Neve and Seraphina. "Not that Grant isn't, like, a totally nice guy," she began carefully, finally pinning her worried gaze on Seraphina. "But Neve has a little bit of a point. It could cost you more than your reputation. Maybe you don't care about that, but I know you care about your career—"

"Part of which, in this business, is your reputation," Neve added, almost under her breath.

"It sounds like becoming Gallagher's apprentice could pay off in a big way, but will he go through with training you to step up as a partner one day if things go south between you two?"

"I guess we'll just have to be mature adults about our relationship. And anyway, working for Grant Gallagher isn't the be-all-end-all of my career, you guys. I have golden references from the university and partial credit for Sweetclover, thanks to you, Kay."

"Maybe," she conceded doubtfully, "but accolades fade fast, and you know it. Another six months from now, and Sweetclover is old hat. Someone will have taken the premise, expounded on it, and created the next hot-shot spa or club."

Seraphina wanted to get angry. If her life were a movie playing out on the Hallmark channel, she'd blow up and accuse her friends of trying to sabotage her new relationship, or cite jealousy, or even tell herself they lacked faith in her. But the truth was much less dramatic and slightly more depressing; they were worried for her and they were right to be. If it were Kay playing with fire by sleeping with someone as influential and well-known as Grant Gallagher, Seraphina would repeat all the same warnings and advice ad nauseum.

Subdued, Seraphina dropped her chin into her hand. "Can't I just bask in this good thing while it lasts? I believe Grant is a man of his word. And if he were to drop me because of a personal matter, well, he'd be less than a gentleman. I could hurt his reputation just as easily. Whatever happens, I'm the right person for that position, and he knows it, or he wouldn't have made the offer." She sighed. "And really, I need this. An apprenticeship with Grant Gallagher would make up for so much lost time."

Kay patted her knee with a crooked smile. "Maybe this is selfish of me, but I can't think of your efforts as a teaching assistant as time wasted. I needed you, Sera. You made a difference to me. I understand you feel you're out of the gate past the whistle, but I can't feel anything but utterly grateful you were around for me. You, my dear Seraphina, are one of the pillars of my excellence." She ended her spiel with a batting of her lashes, and a quick, fierce hug for Seraphina.

Kay and Neve didn't stick around much longer, sensing Seraphina's melancholy mood.

She spent the rest of the night and most of Saturday morning wondering why the one time in her life she'd find it entirely too easy to let go of her innate desire to control everything was also the one time losing control could be potentially disastrous to her career.

By Saturday afternoon, she was pacing her small apartment, finally moving past feeling sorry for herself. She was agitated and annoyed. She'd been fiercely independent her entire life. The only things she'd ever allowed to hold her back were her own self-doubts. She was, above all else, a calculated risk taker.

And Grant Gallagher was a huge risk. The possibility for ruin loomed, but so did other potential outcomes. Blurry, ill-defined outcomes. She didn't expect to fall in love or anything like that. But maybe they'd come to know a different kind of closeness.

Seraphina unearthed her cell phone from the pile of blankets on her bed. She tossed it from one hand to the other, mirroring her juggling thoughts. Okay, so they had some chemistry. At least, they had some hey-you-clean-up-real-good chemistry. But attraction could be a fickle thing. Grant had seen her razor-sharp at work and dressed to slay at dinner. The only real test left was the obvious; the unshaved legs, messy bun, morning breath, holey pajamas test. If they still had some zing between them on a lazy Sunday morning, when Seraphina considered herself at her most vulnerable, then this thing—whatever the hell it was—with Grant was worth what risk it carried. And if not, well, at least they'd fizzle out before things got too serious.

With steel resolve in her bones, she dialed Grant's number. "Hi," she said, when he answered. She heard the smile in his greeting, and her nerves kicked into a higher gear. She really didn't want to show Grant the most unattractive side of herself. But this was the only way. "I reconsidered your offer, and decided to counter with one of my own. We've seen what happens on a night out. But what about a morning in?"

* * * *

Grant hung up. He'd been asked out by women before. These were progressive times, and there wasn't anything strange about Seraphina calling and offering a date idea of her own. What had him scratching his head was the Go Nowhere policy. Seraphina didn't know it, but that kind of thing was straight up his alley.

By the time she showed up, he had cinnamon buns in the oven and fresh orange juice pressed for the next morning. As per the rules, he had on an old pair of blue plaid pants and was barefoot. He frowned and looked her up and down. "Jeans aren't fair game," he reminded her.

She ignored him, sniffing the air. "What is that? I feel like I just stepped into the spice aisle at the grocery store."

"You'll find out tomorrow morning. Tonight, it's take-out or delivery. Your pick."

She smiled tentatively, reached into a large canvas tote slung over her shoulder, and pulled out a handful of fabric. Pink plaid. "Delivery."

He guided her toward the guest bathroom to change, and took her bag into the bedroom and left it on his bed. He returned to find her in the hallway. The pink plaid turned out to be a pair of baggy shorts. She had swapped out the knit scoop-neck blouse for a light pink tank-top, sans bra. He swallowed. The top was so thin and old, he easily made out the outline of her nipples and the hard peaks. She had small, perky breasts, and the loose fabric draped over them enticingly.

There was something charged in the atmosphere, almost like they were playing a game they shouldn't be playing. And perhaps they were. A slow-building pressure, both similar and completely different from what had buzzed between them the other night, filled the room.

Grant excused himself to rescue the cinnamon buns. The trick was to pull them from the oven while just a hair underdone. The residual heat finished them off, and they cooled to airy perfection. He glanced over his shoulder. Seraphina had followed him and stopped just shy from entering the kitchen. She crossed her arms and leaned against the wall. "Do I not strike you as a baking man?"

"I was just considering taking notes. I burned cheese toast yesterday." She eyed the bowls in the sink. "You made them yourself?"

"Yeah." With a metal spatula, he carefully transferred the warm buns to a cooling rack and set the empty sheet pan aside. He'd rather have a pile of dirty dishes to wrangle Sunday evening than waste the time he had with Seraphina. A man had to have priorities, after all. "Kathleen, my, uh, mom, I mentioned her, right? She's disabled. Uses a walker. It was hard for her to get around, so she ended up with a lot of homemaking hobbies. Crafts, baking, that kind of thing. I liked to help."

"Oh." Seraphina paused and nibbled her lip. She came a few steps nearer, eyeballing the cinnamon buns while he drizzled pre-prepared cream cheese icing over the tops with a spoon. "It was just me and Dad when I was a kid, and he wasn't much of a cook. I grew up in the theater scene, eating a lot of whatever we could get our hands on."

"Here?" Little Rock was progressing culturally all the time, but twenty-five years ago, he couldn't imagine the theater scene was exactly swinging.

"Yep." Then Seraphina sprung. She snatched a cinnamon roll and backpedaled away. She squealed as he reached out and caught her by the waist.

Once he had her, his mind went blank. He simply stood there, her skin warming his hands through her thin clothes. "Just what do you think you're doing?"

She smiled wide and took a huge bite out of the roll.

He narrowed his eyes. Then he swiped it from her unsuspecting hand and shoved the rest into his mouth.

They stared at each other challengingly, mouths stuffed, then fell into fits of laughter. The first to recover, Grant shuffled to the fridge and pulled out the milk. He poured them each a tall glass and handed one to Seraphina. "I offer this to you freely," he said solemnly. "But leave my cinnamon rolls alone. Or we'll wake up tomorrow and starve."

She gulped milk and sighed, a smile still lingering on her lips. It lit up her entire face. Grant would've sworn in that single span of a few seconds, he'd never seen a more gorgeous woman. "Or we could order pizza to eat in the morning and have the cinnamon rolls now."

Her wide smile was luminescent, and Grant found himself grinning idiotically back at her. "Hm. They are best fresh," he conceded.

She grew suddenly serious. "And pizza is best cold."

He stroked his chin thoughtfully, but it was mostly an excuse to study her. Smiley and pajama-clad, she had an unidentifiable allure even the sexy, lacey red dress couldn't match. "You've been here all of twenty minutes, and we're already descending into anarchy."

She snorted, somehow a cute and dignified sound. "That's me. Harbinger of chaos and ruin."

He cocked an eyebrow at her. A joke for her was a poignant point of fact for him. Maybe not ruin, but she was definitely introducing an element of chaos into a very controlled environment. Likewise, he realized he was doing something similar to her life. "A little, yeah. But I'm not complaining. Not even a little."

She watched him keenly, as if searching for something behind his words. "Neither am I."

Well, if that was the score, Grant was in trouble. His grin persisted, despite the small stone of doubt that dropped in the center of his chest. He'd counted on Seraphina being the coolheaded one; the one to back out of this little arrangement before it got too serious, because he was hell and gone from being able to see their relationship with a rational mind. If they both dove in blindly, no one was going to save them. The aftermath would be what it was.

He lifted another cinnamon roll from the cooling tray. Warm to the touch, icing rolled lazily down the sides and over his fingers. He tore away a piece and held it out to Seraphina like an offering to seal the deal. "Anarchy it is. May we survive the night."

"Cheers to that." She took the bite of gooey bun straight from his fingers with her teeth. She laughed softly at his expression, her mouth full.

He stood there, staring dumbly, his hand still aloft, trying hard not to embarrass himself. The loose pajama pants wouldn't hide a thing.

An amused daredevil regarded him from behind Seraphina's piercing blue eyes. She held eye contact for a beat, then in exquisite slow motion licked the frosting from his finger, which was still suspended in the air between them, because she had turned his brain to mush.

Grant had a sudden vision of lifting her onto the counter, then realized there was no reason he couldn't make it a reality. Their gazes locked, he put the same finger in his mouth, sucking off the last of the sticky icing. He didn't waste another second, but wrapped his arms around her waist, got a hold of her ass, and lifted her to him. She squealed and flung her arms around his neck. In two strides, he had her on the counter.

Well, he'd known there'd be no hiding in these pants. He kept his hands wrapped tight around her waist and felt her back arch slightly as she drew in a breath. Her teasing expression became more solemn and her gaze watchful. Grant was the playmaker now.

Or so he believed. Every time he thought he had Seraphina figured, she proved him wrong. She reached down and ran her finger along the inside of the elastic band at his waist. His breath quickened when her light touch caressed his erection. She paused, grinned, then grabbed hold on either side of his pants and yanked. As the very thing he'd hoped to remain in some control over sprang free, completely of its own mind, Seraphina leaned back, slid her hips forward, and took possession of Grant's hand. She guided him up the wide-open leg of her tiny shorts. He was instantly rock hard when he realized what she was showing him. She had nothing on beneath the flimsy shorts. His curious fingers met soft, damp skin, and she made a small noise in her throat. At that point, the games were over. He grasped her hips and pulled her toward him as a hot, desperate desire ran like fire through his veins.

Seraphina wrapped her arms around his neck. She bit his ear, just hard enough to get his attention and draw a low growl from deep in his throat. "Anarchy is fun." She laughed softly, and Grant fell into oblivion.

Chapter 8

Grant woke up naked in his king-sized bed. That wasn't abnormal, but finding a soft, warm, and equally naked female next to him was definitely a delightful departure from his usual Sunday morning routine. He caught himself smiling at the red hair fanned out across the creamy white pillow at his side. Seraphina's face was buried in knots of sheets and blankets. Her bare leg draped across his, inducing vivid reminders of last night.

As much as he wanted coffee, he couldn't bring himself to extricate himself. Pinned down by her long, pale leg, he grinned and enjoyed the sensation until she began to murmur and stretch.

With care, Grant untangled himself from the bedding and padded into the kitchen, naked. He allowed himself a self-satisfied grin upon finding his plaid bottoms in a puddle on the kitchen floor where they'd been removed and forgotten. He slid them on. Coffee beans rattled pleasantly as he poured them into the grinder. He hoped the noise didn't wake Seraphina. He wanted to be the big hero who delivered coffee in bed.

Alas, it wasn't meant to be. The percolator had just begun steaming and hissing when Seraphina cautiously tip-toed around the corner. She might've made some effort to smooth down her hair, but there were a few tangles. Her bangs were skewed to one side. To Grant's pleasant surprise, she hadn't bothered with the modesty of wrapping a sheet around herself. She was gloriously nude, although made slight effort into covering herself with her arms. Even so, he could see the top of the triangle of thick strawberry blond curls where her thighs came together, and the swell of her breasts beneath her arms. His body responded immediately.

Meanwhile, Seraphina peered lazily around. "Have you seen my shorts and top?"

He laughed lightly. "Not since you removed them."

She looked at him then. "You mean since you removed them."

He shrugged one shoulder and took down two coffee mugs. "You asked so nicely. I couldn't say no."

He heard her little snort of laughter as she walked away toward the living room. Sated as he was, Grant still couldn't resist craning his neck as she walked past. Her hips had a leisurely swing to them, and the way her body moved brought back warm, fond memories of last night.

They'd been all over; the kitchen counter, the sofa, the rug in front of the large window, and the bedroom. Her clothes could be anywhere. He wasn't even sure in what order they'd been removed. They'd been there when he had her on the counter. Eventually, he'd flipped her over and pulled her shorts down. But, hard as they tried to get the angle just right, the counter was too tall. Then he recalled she'd been wearing them when he'd carried her to the sofa. Her top was long gone by then, but he'd pulled the shorts down with his teeth and proceeded to do other things with his mouth once they were out of his way.

"Look under the couch," he called.

"Found them!" Seraphina's triumphant cry came at the same time.

Grant poured their coffees. He picked up his phone from its charging cradle on the counter and dialed the closest pizza delivery place. After their rampant sexual activity—some fast and furious, some tortuously slow and tense—they'd returned to the kitchen in the small hours of the night and devoured every last cinnamon bun and the rest of the milk. Pizza ordered and coffee mugs in hand, Grant met Seraphina in the living room.

She was curled into the corner of the sofa, resting against an arm. She looked warm and relaxed, and Grant had a sudden desire to wrap himself around her and never leave his apartment again. Then he noticed the tablet in her lap. He sat and handed her a coffee. "Have you got your files there?"

She sat up straighter, her hands wrapping around the thick mug. "Thank you." She smiled demurely, almost shyly, as if last night hadn't happened at all. "Yes, I do have them, actually. I know you've gone over them, but I've tweaked a few things since."

"Let me see." He waited for her to pass over the tablet, which she did with mild reluctance. He set his mug on the end table and relaxed into the sofa.

He balanced the small device on his thigh, used his left hand to navigate, which freed his right hand to grasp and hold one of hers. From his peripheral, he noticed her look up sharply at him. He held still, wondering what she'd do. The thought of her pulling away made him unduly disappointed. He felt suddenly vulnerable and wished he hadn't initiated the small intimacy. But then Seraphina relaxed, and even readjusted so she could grip his hand back.

He fought off a stupid grin and made himself focus on Seraphina's plans. They were lightyears ahead of Roper's proposed blueprints.

The fireplace in the main parlor had been boarded up long ago, then reopened in the late seventies. Seraphina wanted to do more than clean up the structure. She wanted to enlarge the edifice and make it the focal point of the main reception area. Her plans called for a massive chimney, overlaid with a myriad of eggshell and ecru colored brickwork in the classic pattern to stretch from floor to ceiling. Side notations listed potential resources for the material, from other out-of-use sites, as well as local vendors. Apparently, there was a company in Jonesboro that collected and repurposed materials from historic buildings when they were dismantled or torn down. They'd likely have the bricks, which could be painted.

Grant nibbled his lip and squeezed Seraphina's hand. "Why aren't you bigger news? Look here." He tapped the screen where she'd marked for the re-installment of an old telephone booth. The original owners of this place were farmers, but the family had grown wealthy in later decades, and for a short run, the home had been used to house offices. She'd scanned a cropped photograph from the original building, circa 1940, when the phone booth had been installed, and another bullet list of notes were logged underneath. "That's genius. What's more, you want to make it operational. The Historical Society is going to love you. Do you really think you've got a bead on where the original booth ended up?"

Seraphina snuggled closer. Her breath moved the hairs on his arm as she leaned into him for a closer look at the small screen. "I'm about eighty-percent certain. It took a couple days of digging through some archives at Town Hall, but I found the records from the estate sale in the fifties, which was the first time the building switched ownership. It had been owned by the same family for generations up until that point. The Robichards even managed to hang onto the property through the Depression. I may have traced the sale of the telephone booth to the buyer, but from there it's a lot of conjecture. Still, even if I can't find the exact one, I can get a refurbished replica. God bless the internet."

"Amen," he murmured, scanning her notes with renewed appreciation. "So again, why are you bothering with the likes of me? Seraphina, you're a remarkable talent. You should be focusing on your own business. You'd give Neve Harper a run for her money. And myself." He grinned sideways at her. "I've been looking for an excuse to expand outside of Arkansas."

Her lips had turned down. "I have half the experience you and Neve have, that's why. I don't have a solid reputation to fall back on. Sweetclover is the first real thing I have in my portfolio. You know that, Grant. It was all I had to recommend myself for the position at your firm, besides the years I put in at the university."

He shook his head. "Why the late start?"

She glanced away from him. Maybe he'd hit on something uncomfortable. A seed of curiosity planted itself firmly in his gut. "Come on, I'll swap a story of mine for one of yours," he bargained. "I think we've been as intimate as two people can get. What's the harm?" He grinned at the blush that crept up her neck to infuse her cheeks.

"Maybe," she conceded. "But this is different." She met his gaze squarely. "There are different kinds of intimate."

He twirled his finger in a circle between them. "So this is just a sex thing. I was wondering when were finally going to dredge up a label."

"That's not what I—I didn't say that." He hadn't thought it possible, but her pale skin flushed an even deeper rose.

Grant found it annoyingly attractive. His reaction threw him. He didn't expect to be so affected by Seraphina's reticence. "You're right. I'm sorry. It's probably for the best if we keep a few barriers up."

"No." She shook her head. "I'm just insecure. As usual. It's not like my history is some special secret. It's just…well, it's embarrassing. And I don't tell many people. Although, it's fair to say not many people ask."

"We're not exactly the type to invite personal questions, are we?"

She blinked, her gaze morphing into something like surprise, as though he'd said something that warranted meditation. "No. We aren't." She gazed at him for a span of five seconds before breaking away.

"Do you want me to go first? Hi, my name is Grant Gallagher, and I'm emotionally handicapped."

Seraphina grinned sheepishly. "If you wouldn't mind breaking the ice."

"All right." He made himself relax, forced an easiness into his bones he didn't feel. Even so, he held Seraphina's hand tighter as the words began to flow, stuttering at first, then gaining strength as he continued. "I was basically dumped on Kathleen's doorstep when I was eight. I don't know a lot about my dad, other than he's a giant prick, and nothing at all about my biological mother. Of course, you know this much already."

"That's a spectacularly shitty start."

"Indeed." He pressed his lips together and nodded. "But there you have it. The great and terrifying Grant Gallagher is one vague father figure away from being an orphan. I'd probably be a lot angrier about the abandonment if it weren't for the fact that Kathleen is pretty much the most amazing human being on earth. She was fifty when I came to stay with her. A club foot and mute from a stroke in her forties, thanks to some underlying heart condition doctors didn't catch until it was almost too late. The two of us, we were a pair."

Seraphina had snuggled close enough to his side to rest her head against his shoulder. "Your dad left you with an old disabled woman? It doesn't sound like she was in any position to take on a child."

Their clasped hands had shifted to his lap. Grant hadn't even noticed when he'd put aside the tablet. His free hand stroked the line of her knuckles. "Like I said. A giant prick." He laughed quietly, amazed at how easily the story spilled from him. It seemed like he'd been waiting a lifetime for just the right person to tell, and here she finally was. She didn't have an alternate view to offer. She wasn't a savior, come to drag him from his pit of self-containment. On the contrary, Seraphina inhabited a pit of her very own, thus making her perhaps the only person in the wide world who understood his alienation. How they managed to bridge the gap between their two islands was a mystery for the ages, but maybe they'd find a way.

"I see her every day," he continued. "I don't even know if she likes having me around, but I can't not see her. I feel like I owe her everything. She's in her late seventies now, still putting around with her walker. Keeps a little pad and pen in her pocket and writes me notes as I drone on about work. I never know what else to talk about. I mentioned you, though. That seemed to make her happy."

Seraphina was still as a deer caught in the lights of an oncoming car. She cleared her throat delicately. "Am I newsworthy?"

"Yeah, I think so. Looking back on our first meeting, you could see why you might stand out. I don't regularly get into heated arguments with designers I hired sight unseen. In fact, it's been a good long while since a designer has spoken against me, thanks to my 'terrifying' reputation. I was vexed, to be honest, but Kathleen was tickled. She actually suggested the apprenticeship."

"She did? But why?"

Grant bit his lip, glad Seraphina hadn't glanced up to scrutinize his face. He had no idea what he might give away. "I may have suggested she'd like you. You're a lot like me. She figured if she'd like you, then I must like you, too. She does that sometimes. Ferrets out the meat and potatoes while I'm still trying to make sense of the garnish."

"So," Seraphina drew out the word thoughtfully. "You like me because I argued with you?"

"I like your stones." He shrugged and laughed. It was the truest thing he could've said. She had a grade-A body, a mind like a steel trap, and talent she didn't seem to realize, but what had crawled under his skin and settled to stay was her temerity. "I don't look for doe-eyed obedience in the people who work for me. I hire for talent. Behind real talent, there's always a fire. Because we're artists. I've had to step away from that side of designing, because now, my art is a business. I'm ruthless when need be. I never suspected the necessity would turn me into whatever people think I am."

"You're nothing like I expected," she said quietly. She pulled away from his shoulder and sat up, only to twist and lie down with her head on his lap. "When Neve Harper thinks you're scary, I have to take her at her word. It's usually dead on target. I kind of can't wait to tell her she's wrong about you."

He shifted uncomfortably. "Well, I think simply being forward and looking people in the eye while you negotiate can earn you a few whispers in this industry. I don't smile much. That seems to strike an unfriendly figure." He knew he made people uneasy. He even accepted that he used the preconceived notion to his advantage. He wasn't sure how he felt about Seraphina giving away his secret. "Is it worth seeing her fall to give away my only advantage over Neve? She's fierce competition. She hasn't beat me out yet, but she damn near took the Baylor and Tack remodel right out from under me. Damn near. Besides, she can't possibly be as bad as people say."

"Having met Neve, I swear upon my very soul, she is every inch what people say she is. Abrasive, crude, opinionated to a fault, and usually spot-on. She gets it right almost every time. It's tiresome. At the same time, she's a compelling person. And a strange friend to have. You want to kill her, but you also want her to like you."

"Well, now I know."

"She considers you a worthy rival, if that's any balm."

He scoffed. "Until she gets to know me, at any rate."

"And you have plans to get to know Neve Harper, do you?"

"Most definitely. If she's a friend of yours, it's merely a matter of time."

* * * *

Seraphina wasn't sure how she felt about that. Defiantly, like a dragon hoarding gold, she wanted to keep parts of herself hidden away from Grant—his potential scrutiny and inevitable judgment scared her to pieces. That's how friendship, or any close relationship, worked. At first, people kept an open mind. But pretty soon, like Kay and Neve, they were tossing out admonishments and opinions like confetti at a birthday party.

Grant brushed her bangs back from her forehead. "You look pretty cute in my lap like that. So, tit for tat. Your name is Seraphina, and you're…"

She gusted out a heavy sigh, a grin pulling at her lips. Grant didn't look so bad from this angle, either. "Hi, I'm Seraphina, and I too am an emotional handicap." She licked her lips and tried to decide the best place to start. She couldn't recall she'd ever told the tale in full before. It wasn't the kind of thing a young girl would be compelled to dish to her friends. "As I mentioned before, I was a theater rat. My dad and my mom separated sometime after I was born, but before my cognizant memory was functioning, apparently, because I have practically no memories of her. I have Dad's story of how things went down." For a second, she wished her story was as simply straightforward as her dad leaving her on some kindly old woman's doorstep. It was almost hateful to think, even to herself, but maybe her life would've been better that way. Grant continued to stroke her forehead, like she were a puppy in his lap, listening attentively.

She felt silly but stayed put. "You'd think the whole theater gig might've given it away sooner, but I guess not. Sometimes, we see what we want to see. And my mom saw a perfectly straight man who wanted to marry her and have a kid. Except, my father is not straight. Back then, though, things were different for men like him. If you wanted a family, you had to go about it pretty much the way society expected you to. When I was very young, my dad…" She paused and cleared her throat. "He had a, uh…well, an affair. With…you know. A man. My mom found out."

Grant's face screwed up into a grimace, but his lovely blue eyes held an ocean of pity. Whether for her deceived mother, or for the confused child Seraphina had been, she couldn't guess.

"My dad says that my mom was floored. He sort of suspected she knew, but her reaction to his affair made it crystal clear she'd had no idea. I guess they tried to work things out at first. Dad had this huge weight lifted, and he was happier. He was sorry for the affair. He didn't want a divorce. He just wanted Rebecca—that's Mom—to accept him. You know, he loved her. And me. And he wanted his family and figured we'd all just get over it. Move on. My mom went looking for answers, though. She sought help, at first from counselors, then eventually the local church. She got super involved. Started reading their pamphlets on the devils of homosexuality, buying into the fiery sermons. For her, religion became a lifeboat, rescuing her from a storm of hurt and confusion."

That part had always struck Seraphina as fair. She could understand Rebecca's search for answers, for anything to make sense of something crazy and strange; something so few others could relate to. It wasn't exactly unheard of, but if Little Rock still had a small-town mentality now, how much more so over twenty-five years ago. Even now, small Southern cities clung to their prejudices and xenophobia.

But her mother's actions were less easy to justify. "She left. She packed her things and left us both. Dad says one of the last things she said to him was that he'd corrupted me the moment I was born. As a gay man's daughter, I was ruined before I ever drew my first breath."

Grant inhaled deeply and whistled. "Shit. I hate to say it, but good riddance. I mean, unless you think you'd have been better off raised by an ignorant bigot." He paused a beat. "Sorry."

"Don't apologize. You're right. The abandonment stings, but I've never once wished she'd have taken me with her. My dad is many things, not all of them great. But he's honest. The only person he seems to judge unfairly is me."

Seraphina decided she'd had enough of Grant's pets. She knew she was imagining it, but they felt more a thing of pity with every stroke. She sat up and put a few inches of space between them. "All that talking, and I haven't even got to the stuff that matters yet."

Grant's thick forefinger traced a path across the back of her hand. She remembered those clever, clever fingers. Unwillingly, her gaze traveled to his mouth. His lips were pressed together. His gaze was downcast. He didn't appear to be enjoying her life story any more than she was.

"He's hard on me, that's all." She tried to inject a small measure of levity into the explanation. She was bringing them both down with her weird, pathetic tale. "You ever just miss the mark with someone? One misunderstanding after another. If I distance myself, then I must be ashamed. He sees my mother's shadow looming behind me. If I call to tell him news, good news in particular, then I'm a braggart, better than him. Again, shades of Rebecca Fawkes coming out. He keeps expecting to see my mother and ends up missing me entirely."

"Hm. You should've gone first. My story would've lightened the mood."

Seraphina cracked a smile that took mere seconds to become full-blown laughter. "You're right. I'm far too serious for my own good."

"Nah." Grant shook his head, a slight grin tugging at his lip. "I don't believe that. For people like you and me, there's no such thing as 'too serious.' We adapted to our environment."

"That's not better. You think our pasts define us?"

"Not at all. We evolved as a means to move forward. We're a product of our experiences, but I don't see us sitting here blaming our bad luck and shitty decisions on our parents. Seems to me we're two successful, well-adjusted adults."

"Hm." Seraphina grew quiet. She let Grant's words tumble inside her head. "You ever consider listening to people on couches full time? I hear there's good money in it."

He laughed softly. "No, I think not. I have to be invested before I can care. I'm Grant Gallagher, remember? Callous. Terrifying. Cold." Their gazes met and held. "But I sense an impending thaw. Makes me nervous."

Seraphina kept her expression studiously somber, but her heart hitched in her chest in a wild, sudden surge of something like hope. "You're telling me."

Grant cleared his throat, and they both seemed to find something interesting on opposite sides of the room. When she felt comfortable in her own skin again, and less like Grant could see down to the fiber of her soul, she smiled disarmingly. "So, how about a tour of Tanbee House? I've seen the specs, but I wouldn't mind the chance to poke around." It was the sort of thing she liked to do alone before a big project began.

Grant gave her a measuring look. "A short visit is actually on my itinerary. It's one thing to scan blueprints and layouts, take in measurements and notations. But you don't get a solid sense of what a home or office has the potential to become until you see the bones for yourself."

Seraphina smiled and didn't care if she looked crazy. "It was cute at first, but the list of things we have in common is starting to creep me out."

Chapter 9

The balmy night air felt different tonight—alive with subdued but playful excitement, like a kitten wriggling its bottom, poising to pounce. Seraphina was wise to the phenomenon now, though, and recognized the feeling as her reaction to Grant's quiet, prowling presence beside her as they strode down the dark streets with their hands linked.

They'd meant to visit Tanbee House earlier, ideally while the sun still lit the sky, but other things had distracted them: pizza, sex, and a movie. It was of dire importance that Seraphina watch Die Hard. She'd never seen the film, much to Grant's consternation. She still hadn't seen the film despite his efforts. They had both succumbed to naps ten minutes after the opening credits.

Now it was late, the stars were out, and they were strolling through Little Rock's historical Governor's Mansion district, passing under pale street lamps and past looming plantation and carriage homes. "Maybe we should've waited. We both have to work in the morning. My boss isn't the understanding type. He'll be upset if I'm late."

"Yeah, I heard that guy is a real prick." Grant's amusement curled his lips into a soft smile. "All the same, I'd like to show you the place before tomorrow, when we have the first team meeting. We need to confirm the demolition schedule, begin processing orders for our supply contacts." He paused, as if suddenly recalling Seraphina wasn't new to the business. "Just another day at the office, I suppose."

Seraphina sighed as they rounded the corner, where a four-story Georgian home stood. Several windows were shuttered, and the elm tree in the front yard was half dead. "Kay lives in one of these monsters. She's been renovating the last three years. I love my job, but when it comes to personal space, I'm a turn-key kind of gal."

Grant squeezed her hand so lightly she hardly felt the pressure. "Not into fixer-uppers?"

As always, there was more to the conversation between them than the face value of the words. It was like they spoke in a code they'd learned in preparation for meeting each other. The night was almost eerily quiet as they moved farther from the constant downtown bustle. Seraphina's shoes scuffed lightly on the spotted sidewalk. "I don't have an exact image in mind of my perfect dream house. I'm not looking for a place to create an imagined perfection. I think, rather, that I can find comfort and peace in something as it is."

Almost imperceptivity, his grip tightened. Layers and layers.

Finally, on the block behind the Governor's Mansion, Grant pulled her to a stop in front of a blockade. Hulking concrete barriers were placed across the span of the street, and an eight-foot-tall chain link fence made a wall around the operation already in action. The house and the street in front of it were cordoned off completely, and would remain so until the major work was complete. By the time Seraphina started laying new flooring and painting, she hoped the road would be clear.

Grant pulled a key ring from his pocket and let them inside the fence after quickly unlocking a padlock. They approached a sage green carriage house, glaringly illuminated by an orange street light placed near the door. They were on a side street that didn't cut through to the next block, but turned abruptly north. The sidewalks were cracked and neglected. Seraphina frowned. "The city is financing more than the building renovation, I hope."

Grant's face was a study in concentration as he counted out keys on an old ring, finally holding up a small silver one and squinting against the light. "Another company is in charge of the external beautification."

"Well, I'd at least shoot them an e-mail. These orange lights are murder."

The steps up to the embellished wooden door rose up right off the sidewalk, two crumbling cement blocks that must've been added onto the structure during the seventies renovation, likely replacing a wooden staircase. Seraphina reached into her purse for the pad and pen she kept there and made a hasty note under the poor lighting. She'd already pulled dozens of photographs of Tanbee House for her files, but she scribbled a reminder to check if the original staircase was worth replicating. It would ultimately depend on style and material.

Grant struggled with the ill-fitting metal on the ancient lock. "This week," he grunted, "I'll get the second set of keys to you."

He'd answered her unspoken question. As project leader, she'd appreciate the ability to come and go at any hour. The property was hemmed in by a leaning privacy fence, but it didn't appear to circle much area beyond the structure itself. However, out back there was an empty field, which would eventually become a cultivated garden spanning the distance between Tanbee House and the Governor's Mansion, to make for easy passage from one building to the other. A landscaping company from Texarkana had scored the job, much to Seraphina's disappointment. She would've liked Free Leaf Concepts to have picked up the contract. It might've meant a few weeks working with Kay, who was a delight to collaborate with.

Seraphina bit her lip. Except when she made very fine points about not sleeping with one's boss. All too fine, Seraphina mused, casting an appreciative glance over Grant's superbly male form, clad in loose Levi's and a soft flannel shirt as he finally worked open the stubborn lock and pushed open the old wooden door.

It scraped loudly against the floor. Seraphina pulled a face at the dirt under her shoes, and the soft grating feel of debris being crushed into the floor. "I should've expected it to be this dirty."

The darkness inside the house was absolute, until Grant flicked on a flashlight he'd had tucked into his back pocket. The light swept an arc across the room, illuminating patchwork flooring, stained, distorted walls, and the massive busted up fireplace Seraphina desperately wanted to save.

She didn't need to see the old house to know it was wrecked. Most of the place would need to be torn down to the foundation and built back up, and not only for aesthetic purposes, but also to appease the code gods. Electrical and plumbing would have to be rerouted. The how wasn't Seraphina's concern, as Grant had so kindly pointed out to her in their first meeting, but the where was entirely in her hands. A small thrill went through her.

Grant had approached the fireplace. He brushed ancient dust and dirt from the mantel, which protruded a solid foot out from the brick chimney. He whistled. "You're sure about keeping it?"

Upon seeing it, she couldn't be more certain. She joined Grant, unable to stop a smile from playing across her lips. "It's a monster, isn't it? It should be preserved. So much of Tanbee House has to be redone, remade, and re-shaped. I can't think of anything more lovely—or important—than displaying a link to its humble beginnings. We wouldn't be proper Southerners, wallowing in our history, if we tore it down."

"The Historical Society should've asked you to write the proposal."

She winked. "Who says they didn't?"

The flashlight beam splashed over the brick and busted wood in a vivid whiteness only an LED bulb could manufacture. Seraphina easily made out Grant's expression in the glow of the light's wide aura. Grant stilled as he looked at her. For a long moment, she waited, lost in her own thoughts of where his might have wandered. She had a feeling they held back as much as they dared to share.

He answered her unspoken question with a soft kiss. His lips brushed lightly across hers, but his breathing had grown labored, his manner weighted like something heavy had come over him. Seraphina didn't ask questions. Instead, she returned the tentative kiss, matching his mood. He deepened the contact between them, sliding his tongue expertly into her mouth, inviting her to come out and play.

A distant crash broke them apart. A muffled thud followed. Seraphina was close enough to inhale Grant's lemony scent in her startled gasp. Her hand raced to his chest in some feeble, instinctual gesture of protection, both offering and seeking.

Grant clasped her wrists and held still, his head cocked, listening. Seraphina held her breath, clutching him and straining to recall which way the noise had come from. Inside, parts of the walls had given way, exposing black sockets and littering the floor with age-old abandoned stacks of crumbled wall material, eaten and torn away from neglect, infestation, and abuse.

They were in the main room, labeled a parlor in the blueprints from the seventies. The kitchens were a narrow room off to the right. A doorway to the immediate left of where they stood in the parlor led to a library, and in the back of the library, a small bedroom.

"Someone's here." Grant's whisper was almost alarming in the aftermath of their stillness.

"I heard something after the crash. Either the canning shed or the back bedroom." The whisper from her throat fell like a shout on her ears, and she winced.

Grant didn't seem to notice, but nodded his agreement. "The bedroom," he murmured.

There were no connecting doors. If they were wrong, they'd lose their man as he made his escape from the canning shed. Grant was staring at her, and she realized he was waiting for her approval. Or at least an agreement. She nodded, and he took her by the hand. As silently as possible, crouched like cat burglars, they moved to the left of the fireplace, toward the open door leading into the library.

Library was a generous term. Seraphina didn't think the few scattered, looming bookshelves quite qualified the space for such a lofty credit. Lamps affixed in between them looked to be original thin and brittle glass. The room was long, running over half the length of the house, flanking the main parlor to the north much as the kitchens did to the south. Grant held the flashlight down and angled behind him, but there was nothing for it; the room was awash in the bright white LED light.

The bedroom, at least according to the specs Seraphina had studied, was among the smallest rooms, affixed to the back end of the library like an afterthought, and barely beating out the attached canning shed in square footage.

If someone was inside, there was nowhere for them to run.

They'd almost reached the closed door when the sharp sound of glass shattering made them freeze in their tracks.

Then Grant was gone from Seraphina's side. He rushed at the door like a left tackle after an indecisive quarterback. The beam of the flashlight danced wildly across the room. He didn't slow down, but met the old wooden door with his shoulder, knocking it clean off the hinges. It bounced up and fell back, clattering against the doorway before getting wedged at an angle in the frame, preventing it from falling to the floor.

Seraphina froze for the space of a breath, waiting for what came next; a cry, a shout, or the thick sound of Grant tackling someone. When no noise came, she went forward to investigate.

Grant stood by the only window in the small bedroom. The pane had been busted out. Only jagged shards remained. Seraphina approached, scouring for any evidence left behind of the intruder. Maybe a piece of cloth snagged on the broken glass or a bloody smear from a cut so the police could gather DNA. She placed a hand on Grant's bicep.

He was still, utterly quiet, and his face was drawn as he stared at the busted out window.

She rubbed the tensed muscle of his arm to get his attention. "I didn't bring my phone. Let me see yours. I'll call the police."

Grant looked at her then, but shook his head. "Just kids. They won't come back. Now they know someone might be here at any hour."

His voice was stern, and while the words didn't make him seem particularly troubled, his expression said otherwise. Seraphina blinked up at him, perplexed. "Right. Sure. Some kids vandalize your work site, damage property, and we ignore it?" She glanced around the room, awash in the light of Grant's flashlight. The walls were intact in some places, crumbling in others, and flat out missing certain sections. Apparently, they hadn't updated the insulation back in the seventies, because in those bare spots, only the ribs showed, along with a few old mildewed bird nests and thick cobwebs. "We should look around. Try to find out what they were doing in here."

"No. I told you. Just kids." Grant grunted, then left the room, shouldering past the door he'd removed from the hinges.

Seraphina stared after the retreating light with her mouth agape. Not because Grant had left her there, or because he wouldn't even have a look around after the building had been broken into, but because Grant hadn't spoken to her in that tone since their first meeting.

Standing there, with the room growing darker by the second, Seraphina realized the steepness of her trajectory with Grant. Somehow, they'd gone from zero to ninety in a matter of days. For the first time, she made herself look down and cast a critical eye on where she stood—on a ledge. The view was dizzying, and the fall would be devastating. Not only for her career, but for her heart. She also realized, with stunning dismay, that she didn't really know the man at all. It had taken only a few words for him to remind her of that. It was like coming down from a strange high. By the time Grant called her name, a slight question in his voice that she hadn't been trailing behind him all this time, Seraphina felt decidedly more sober than she had in days.

Grant was making his way back toward her as she stumbled across the library. She ran into a table she hadn't realized was there, and almost tripped over an overturned chair.

"Those might be worth saving," Grant mumbled, cocking his chin toward the table and chair as they met in the middle of the library. "Even if they're from the seventies update, they're old. Like the fireplace." The words held a hint of suggestion, maybe even an air of apology. It wasn't much as far as olive branches went. Maybe he hadn't meant to leave her in the dark, but he had, and he'd been a dick, too. Bringing up her pet project wouldn't fix what had gone askance between them.

And it definitely wouldn't undo Seraphina's epiphany about their relationship. She sighed in relief as the light flooded her path and didn't answer. Right now, she'd be content to use the furniture as fire wood. She just wanted out of here. And away from Grant.

He began to move toward the exit again, this time slower, deliberately checking over his shoulder every few steps to make sure Seraphina was behind him. They made the walk back toward downtown in stony silence. Grant fidgeted. He seemed to realize he'd made some kind of mistake, but was struggling with how to breach the gulf. Seraphina was content to let the chasm grow and grow. She didn't break the heavy silence, and when they came upon busier streets, she hailed a cab for herself. She told Grant she'd see him in the morning.

He stared at her. She had one foot in the cab when he finally managed a coherent sentence. "Um, so, I was thinking. Kathleen mentioned she'd like to meet you. Are you free tomorrow?"

Seraphina ducked into the cab, gave her address to the driver, and then looked at Grant one last time. "I don't think I am."

* * * *

A tap at her office door jarred Seraphina into the present. All while getting ready for work that morning, she'd been going over the weekend in her head, trying to figure out at what point things had turned completely upside down. She'd forgotten the delicate gold necklace she liked to wear with today's ensemble, and she felt out of sorts. Part of her had been waiting for Grant to appear, even though she seldom saw him outside of his office. He hadn't summoned her, either. The man had a job to do, she reminded herself sternly. A company to run. And besides, she didn't know what she had to say to him, anyway.

The man who'd knocked was a handsome stranger; a more than welcome distraction from her repetitive, useless thoughts. "Hello," she said, offering an inviting smile to the man's apologetic one.

"Hey, there. I'm Marc Curry. General contractor. I'm running the Tanbee House dismantling, as it were."

"Oh. Of course. Nice to meet you. Please, come in."

Marc swaggered inside—really no other way to describe that lingering stroll in those faded deep blue denim jeans. His lazy smile was charming, and his brown eyes were lit with interest. There was a shyness in his manner she found utterly likeable. Shame she hadn't met this guy first. Maybe she'd have never lost her mind over Grant Gallagher. Too late now. For all his good looks and charm, Marc Curry lacked Grant's sheer presence. His eyes were nice, but they didn't zero in on her very soul.

Still, Seraphina caught herself returning Marc's smile. "What can I do for you?"

He swept a thick forefinger into the front pocket of his jeans and pulled out a small key ring. "Just met with Mr. Gallagher. He asked me to bring you these. One for the padlock that's on the gate surrounding the site. The smaller, older one opens Tanbee House." He held out the keys to her.

Seraphina took them with a frown. She bit her lip. "Did he mention the window?"

Marc's eyebrows went up. They were fine and straight, light brown like his hair. He was better looking than Grant. More open. "The broken one? Yeah, no worries. We were going to replace it anyway."

He didn't mention how the window had been broken, and Seraphina didn't want to push. She might have some sway, sleeping with the boss, but she wouldn't make a liar out of him by giving the general contractor a different story about the window. "Thanks, Marc."

"Yeah." He grinned. "Maybe I'll see you around the site, huh?"

She eyed the keys in her hand. "Maybe you will."

For several minutes after Marc left, she stared at the keys, wondering if she had the guts. If she hadn't embarked on a completely inappropriate relationship with Grant, would she even question her next move? Would Neve or Kay hesitate? Not in following their instincts, no. If Seraphina needed convincing, she'd found the means.

She stood up, then came to a dead halt as Brendan Berkley stepped nonchalantly into her office. "Brendan. What a pleasure."

He smirked at her dry greeting. "That's kind of you. But don't fake it on my behalf, please. And my apologies for tracking you down before you've even had time to plow through your first cup of coffee."

She let her brittle, forced smile drop. Her hands clenched at her sides. "What do you want?"

He took a step closer. His hair was brushed back in the trendy, current style, shaved close on the sides. The thick black frames of his glasses hid his eyes well, and made him difficult to read. He wore a checkered button-up tucked into impossibly tight black jeans. Not exactly office attire, but Grant wasn't a stickler about such things. "Look, Seraphina, I'm here asking you for a fresh start. A clean slate. This morning, Roper told me I've been assigned to shadow Ophelia to get a wider feel for the company before I begin looming over Annie's shoulder. Apparently, I need some pretty steep inside knowledge to best facilitate smooth operations as Mr. Gallagher's assistant. Since Ophelia has been assigned to you, it appears we'll be working together for the next several months."

Her mouth fell open. She quickly closed it, refusing to let Brendan see that he had one up on her. Information was power. "Should prove interesting."

Brendan sighed and ran a hand through his hair. "Please. Grant took a huge risk hiring me. I have more to prove than any other person working for him, and no one else in this city has been willing to give me so much as a chance. Hell, he was the only one who even interviewed me after what the LRPD put me through. I know you're friends with Oliver and Kay. I know how determined Oliver is that I'm hiding something. But if it were true, don't you think I'd have skipped town? Or sued Oliver for harassment? I could get his badge taken away. But I don't want that. I just want to move on with my life and my career."

Seraphina considered. Brendan Berkley was almost certainly involved in the drug ring Oliver had taken down inside Free Leaf Concepts, but the evidence simply wasn't concrete. She loved Kay and believed in Oliver, but for the first time, a small sliver of doubt shimmied up her spine.

But then she recalled how Brendan had somehow known there was an undercover agent at Free Leaf. He'd mistakenly believed it was Kay, and tried to convince her he was also working undercover to entice her to share privileged information. There were coincidences, and then there were clues, and it didn't do to confuse the two.

Seraphina scooped up her tablet and walked around her desk. She and Grant were overdue for a talk. She brushed past Brendan without glancing at him. "We'll see." For now, it was the best she could offer.

* * * *

Annie's outraged squawk was the only warning Grant got before Seraphina charged into his outer office. She was a study in passion. He recognized the flush in her cheeks, the wildness in her eyes, and the way she took in each breath like fuel fanning the flames. Her pinched lips were new, though. As was the ire glinting behind her blazing blue irises. A few angry strides ate up the space between them. She wore a forest green pencil skirt that tapered to just above her knees, and it accentuated the swing of her hips. Grant cleared his throat and sat up straight.

"I will not work with Brendan Berkley." She said that and nothing more. She crossed her arms over her cream-colored silk blouse and stared.

Grant tapped his pen on his desk and did his best not to let his anxiety show. How would Ophelia like this handled, he wondered wryly. He had no choice but to be a degree of honest. Enough to convince Seraphina to move forward. "I'm not asking," he said simply, keeping his voice light. "You've been assigned a job. So has he. I expect you both to accomplish those tasks to the best of your abilities, and with the professionalism our clients expect from Gallagher Interiors."

Seraphina didn't appear chastised in the least. Instead, she grew suspicious, her eyes narrowing. "This isn't right. First, you deliberately choose Roper's designs—"

"That was an impartial decision."

"My ass. I'm not stupid enough to believe for one second you preferred his work to mine. If you're going to tout professional behavior, I'd start with being less obvious about your shows of favoritism."

His anger came slow, but it came with force. Her impertinence made his chest feel heavy, like hardening cement. He stood up. "You are an employee here. And the first to stand over me in my own office and dictate terms to me. This is unacceptable. You're dismissed."

"No." Her jaw hardened. "I'm not leaving without an explanation."

"Our relationship outside of this building has skewed your perception. You work for me on my terms, Seraphina. Or you do not work for me. There were more qualified applicants for your job."

"Threaten me all you like. But unless you're prepared to call in security, I'm not moving. You owe me answers." To further make her case, she sat down in one of the chairs facing Grant's desk.

He stood over her, blood pounding in his temples. He warred against himself. If it weren't for Ophelia, he'd fire Seraphina on the spot, their hot weekend together be damned. Business was business, and this wasn't how he conducted his. But in this, he was essentially powerless. There were consequences to having important friends, and it had never been more evident than now. He exhaled slowly, forcing himself to calm down. Eventually, his heart rate slowed, and he returned to his chair. Seraphina wouldn't be cowed, which equally annoyed and impressed him.

Mostly annoyed. "I owe you?" He ran the words over his tongue, disgusted with the way they tasted. "So, those were favors you did me. I see. Well, it's unfortunate we can't keep our short-lived affair a secret. It won't sit well with the designers who lost Tanbee House to you."

Her brilliant red eyebrows gathered in confusion. "What?"

"You think it will go unnoticed, how you strode into this office as if it's your right to do so? Or that you'll face no disciplinary action? You think Annie is so loyal as to be above juicy breakroom gossip? If the people who work for me haven't already figured out we were sleeping together, they'll certainly piece it together after this." He didn't miss the way her eyes widened at his use of the past tense. She had to see it. There was no way they could continue after this. By forcing his hand, she was making a statement. Favoritism, indeed. "Try not to take it too personal if you get dirty looks from a few of the office women. Lucia has been trying to seduce me the better part of a decade."

For the first time, some uncertainty crept into Seraphina's voice. "That's not what I meant. You don't owe me...for that. I just meant..."

"It wasn't favoritism." He cut her off swiftly, irritated to find his feelings were more than a little hurt. There was nothing else she could have been referring to. He had no idea she'd expected him to pay her back at all, let alone on company time. He was mildly floored to find she saw him as indebted to her. "Desperation. Roper self-sabotaged the project, deliberately to keep me from giving him Tanbee House. But with his files deleted, it would've been too obvious, even for me, to keep him on. He wants more creative enterprises, but I need him on the important city projects."

Seraphina snorted, a delicate sound despite her anger, an anger that came off her like waves of heat. "You think a couple of fun renovations will keep him from leaving the company?" Her eyes widened as his head snapped up. Her hand flew to her mouth, even though it was too late to stop the words, now they were out and floating between them.

"Roper is leaving? He said this to you?"

Seraphina merely blinked. Eventually, she lowered her hand, and her throat bobbed as she swallowed. "I'm sorry. He asked me not to say anything. He wanted to tell you himself, when the time was right."

Grant stood up again. He drew his hand into a fist, but stopped short of slamming it onto his desk. He'd never lost control in front of an employee, and he wouldn't start now. His fearsome reputation didn't need eye witness accounts. He spoke through gritted teeth, and locked his gaze onto a spot beyond Seraphina's head, because he couldn't bring himself to look her in the eyes. "This is a gross breach of trust between us. Your commitment is not to Roper. As my apprentice, it's to this company. And to me." He inhaled deeply. "You would leave us shorthanded and in peril of defaulting on contracts signed years in advance to keep Roper's confidence. You both owe me time to prepare for the departure of someone as instrumental as Roper. And you have both failed me." Finally, he looked at Seraphina, but only so she could see for herself that he meant every single one of the next words he uttered. "Get out. If you force me to involve security, I will have them drag you from the building."

Chapter 10

"I'm sorry. I really am, but Grant's right." Miserable didn't quite cover how Seraphina felt. Her hands shook as she brought the chai tea to her lips. It was sweet of Roper to offer to buy her a mid-morning drink after she'd ratted him out, but he didn't strike her as anything more than mildly upset.

He sipped iced coffee through a straw and gazed at his phone in that heavy-lidded way people had. Only a slight shrug indicated he'd even heard her. "I would've had to come clean eventually. He is right. I didn't want to leave him in a bind. But now he's so pissed I was going to bail, he hardly looked at me when he called me up to his office. I doubt he tries to convince me to stay on now."

"Really? I get he's mad, but it'll fade."

Roper finally looked up from his phone. His gaze on Seraphina, he took another long sip from his drink. "Not Grant. Grant doesn't let anything 'fade.' That's what makes him such a bull to deal with. He doesn't backtrack or change his mind. And once he says 'this is how it is,' then that's exactly how it is. Guy's a shark. Move forward or die." Roper shook his head in an appreciative way and returned his attention to his phone.

The words dismayed Seraphina. She leaned back in her chair, glad for the relative privacy Roper's distraction afforded her. Roper had forgiven her easily, and even apologized for asking her to keep such a secret in the first place. He hadn't completely succeeded in hiding his disappointment at being summoned by an upset Grant, and it almost made Seraphina feel worse somehow. Better had he ranted and raved. By being so nice, she only felt further indebted.

You owe me.

Her face burned hot at the memory of the carelessly flung words. How idiotic. And untrue. Grant Gallagher didn't owe her a thing, and she had no idea what on earth had possessed her to make such a claim. Because she'd opened herself up to him, given him a piece of herself? But then, he'd done likewise. In every sense, with the exception of their respective job descriptions, they were on equal footing. He'd been incredulous and livid, and Seraphina couldn't pretend he should have felt any other way. She hung her head and gripped her tea container. The cup was growing cool in her hands. She had to apologize to Grant, and she had a feeling mere words wouldn't suffice. Some sort of compromise—no, sacrifice—would need to be made.

She sighed and rose from the small table, offering Roper a slight grin when he looked up, eyebrows hitched in question. She glanced at her watch. "I should get back."

Roper let her go, again reminding her there were no hard feelings between them.

Back at the office, Seraphina hunted down Brendan Berkley. She found him in the second place she searched, the breakroom.

He sat picking at a loaded baked potato in a black Styrofoam container and speaking animatedly to Lucia, of all people. "Yeah, yeah," he was saying. "Swift Appraisal and Pawn. Guy who runs it does the best deals in town. You should try there. You'll get a fair price if you're sure the ring is solid silver."

Lucia mumbled something back and Brendan laughed. Seraphina cleared her throat. Lucia glanced her way, stared for just long enough to convince Seraphina everyone and their grandma knew she'd slept with the boss, then made a quick excuse to leave. Brendan gave her a quick wave and turned to Seraphina with an open, curious expression, his spork poised over his potato as if he didn't intend to take another bite until she announced her intentions.

She tried to conceal her defensiveness. She deliberately uncrossed her arms as Brendan blinked owlishly from behind his thick square frames. "I've behaved less than professionally," she admitted coolly, forcing her pride to the back of her throat. "I'm not certain I trust you, Brendan, nor can I say I much look forward to spending months in your company. However, I will endeavor to leave my personal feelings at home each day, and arrive here each morning focused on the task at hand, prepared to work beside whoever shares that goal. I won't put my personal allegiance ahead of my professional one, which is to Gallagher Interiors."

Brendan's grin came slowly. "That's all I ask."

Seraphina nodded shortly and left him to his lunch. Then, she crashed Annie's waiting area once again. Only this time, she did her best to appear embarrassed and chastised. She pleaded pathetically for a word with Grant.

Annie's frown was deep, and it formed thick wrinkles on either side of her chin. "He's out."

Seraphina accepted this without complaint. She left quietly, and stepped into the hallway. Once away from Annie's disapproving stare, she withdrew her phone from her pocket. She hadn't wanted to text, but she also didn't want to leave a vague message with Grant's overprotective secretary.

I apologized to Brendan, and owe you one as well. I will work with whomever you see fit to assign to Tanbee House, without complaint. She paused, bit her lip, and considered. Long messages were the bane of everyone's text inbox. But if Grant declined to speak with her again, she needed to say everything while she could. He couldn't block her; not so long as she still worked for him, anyway, but she still preferred to stop short of harassing the man. Would like to see you. To explain.

There. She'd get her chance or she wouldn't. How she could explain, she had no idea. She still couldn't fathom what had compelled her to make the claim Grant was somehow in her debt, and she hadn't time to sufficiently dig through her myriad of strangled, stunted emotions to figure it out. Perhaps she would, by the time Grant deigned to reply.

To her amazement, he did so immediately. Filed a report this morning about the intruder at Tanbee House. Nothing else. Nothing about their heated exchange, and nothing about Brendan.

She found Ophelia in her office, sorting through stacks of pages. Some were sketches, and some were color palettes.

Ophelia glanced up and smiled wide, then launched into a report. "Cedar can be sourced locally, and recommended if you intend to stain the wood used to construct the new walls. I also found suppliers for black walnut and teak. Marc Curry estimates three weeks for them to have Tanbee House ready for plumbing and wiring, as well as foundation concerns addressed. He suggests you meet with him before they begin rebuilding the necessary walls and infrastructure. He's concerned you'll end up with a patchwork interior if you keep the original white oak in some spots, as outlined in your plans. But he also says he'll know more after he completes his initial inspection today. I told him I'd have you get in touch."

Impressed with Ophelia's efficiency, Seraphina took the proffered pages, detailing suppliers and their contact information for each source of wood. Teak was the gold standard, and the price reflected it. The right type of cedar, too, could put a hole in their budget. The black walnut seemed to check all the right boxes: durable, widely available, and not too expensive. She handed it back. "Excellent work, Ophelia. I spoke briefly with Marc earlier today, but I'll make time for an in-depth meeting this week. I'm leaning toward the black walnut, but he may have other ideas."

Ophelia was quiet for a moment. Seraphina had the sense she was working up to something. A short indrawn breath was followed by a pause. She made another quick inhale before finally speaking. "Seraphina, I hope you'll reconsider working with Brendan."

Seraphina's snort was distinctly unladylike. "Spoken like I have a choice if I want to head the Tanbee House renovation. For what it's worth, I've apologized to him." She studied Ophelia's expression, but gleaned nothing from her dark, steady gaze. "Why? Do you know him personally?"

"No." A faint smile ghosted over her painted lips. "But I trust Grant implicitly. And if he wants Brendan to shadow me as I assist you on the Tanbee House renovation, I've got to assume he thinks it's the best way to introduce Brendan to the company's infrastructure."

Maybe. It was possible she'd taken Brendan's appointment personally, when in fact Grant had actual reasons. She thought of the keys burning like a chunk of hot coal in her jacket pocket. She'd love to know those reasons, if they did exist. Brendan hadn't been anything more than a lackey, albeit a highly-placed lackey, at Free Leaf Concepts. Coffee fetcher and file shuffler. What value did he bring to Gallagher Interiors?

"I'd better go," she told Ophelia. "You've done well. If you wouldn't mind moving on to other source materials. I don't want to shop at Lowe's for finishing products. Metal work, hinges, and doors. Find me custom shops, or at least a few that offer unique wares, local if at all possible."

On her way out the front of Gallagher Interiors, Seraphina dialed Kay.

Kay answered immediately, sounding slightly out of breath. It could mean any number of things, as Kay didn't save her spastic energy for any one task. She could be jogging, pacing around the large drafting table inside her office, or simply thinking too hard. "Sera, my loveliest friend."

Seraphina smiled. Kay simply had that kind of power. "Hey. Listen, this is important. Brendan Berkley has been assigned to assist me on the Governor's Mansion project. I tried to get him taken off, but Grant isn't budging. But I wanted to let you know, I'll be watching the guy like a hawk. Last night, someone was inside Tanbee House. If it weren't for Brendan's involvement, I wouldn't see anything strange about a squatter making use of the abandoned site, but something about Grant's reaction seemed off."

"Whoa, hold on." Kay's mild distraction dissipated, and worry settled into her voice. "What do you suspect?"

"Er...well, nothing. Not yet. It's just strange. Grant's insistence that Brendan sit in on the project. A glorified secretary, I'm having trouble seeing how this prepares him to be Grant's personal desk jockey. Then there's the fact Grant hired the guy in the first place."

"And the break-in?"

Hell. Was she going crazy? She smoothed her hair and wound through the midtown streets, through crowds of shopping mothers, harried businessmen all wearing shades of the same tie, and the usual aimless pedestrians— mostly college students with a few free hours, eyeballing the buskers and food cart peddlers. "Someone was inside Tanbee House last night. They broke a window to get out. Grant says he reported the incident, but last night he wouldn't even investigate. Almost like..." She couldn't bring herself to accuse him of hiding something. "Never mind. Maybe he was trying to protect me in case the intruder was still around."

Kay's silence stretched long. Only small considering hmms in her throat let Seraphina know she hadn't dropped the call. "I have to say, it's a stroke of luck if you're sure about becoming a spy for Oliver. The department won't let him back on the case, at least not as long as Brendan remains a person of interest. But if you could get some hardcore evidence, or even simply pass along information, you might happen upon just the thing we need."

"What good is evidence if I can't prove anything?"

"Start carrying a camera," Kay suggested in an obvious tone.

"You mean like the one built into my cell phone?"

"No, don't use that." Kay's voice turned serious. "Oliver says stuff gets booted from court all the time because it's hard to prove a photograph wasn't altered. There are a million apps you can get these days to play with pictures. Get a real camera, and because most civilian e-mail isn't encrypted, I'd save them onto an SD card, rather than e-mail them as attachments. It'd be nearly impossible for, say, Brendan's future lawyer to claim pictures were altered if they were never digitally stored or transferred."

Seraphina felt her eyebrows climb. "Wow, Kay. You've really picked up a few things. But it'd look weird, wouldn't it?"

"No one will think twice about you snapping pictures here and there if you say you're using them for a design board. Or to create a before and after portfolio to present to the city when the renovations are complete. If they push, tell them your camera phone sucks. Most do."

"Kay, has anyone ever told you you're a goddamn genius?"

"Once or twice, but not nearly often enough. Although, you guys are slowly coming around to fully appreciating me in all of my wondrous glory."

Seraphina rolled her eyes. "Forgive us our humanity."

"I'll consider it. Oh, and there's Amos with my new rhododendron samples. Got to go. Thanks for offering to do this, Sera. If stuff gets weird or uncomfortable, or you feel your loyalties are becoming divided, Oliver and I will understand if you want to step back."

They ended the call, and Seraphina shuffled to the bus stop, then left the line abruptly. The walk to Tanbee House would do her good, and give her some time to marshal her thoughts. She didn't want to be left scrambling for explanations when she surprised Marc Curry. She hadn't taken two steps when her phone buzzed, and Grant's name sprung to life on the screen.

* * * *

Grant's heart turned to ash and fell away as soon as he entered Kathleen's room. He'd forgotten he'd sent along instructions late Sunday for the staff to put out an extra place setting at lunch, on the assumption Seraphina would be joining him.

Kathleen was dressed for company in one of her finest church outfits, a calf-length pink and purple floral dress she adored and saved for the most special of occasions. Her face lit up when she saw him, and her eyes darted past him, smiling nervously as she bobbed her head to see around him and catch a glimpse of a guest who wasn't there. The smile faltered when she realized Grant stood alone in the doorway. She seemed a deflated child, giddy with anticipation, only to discover she'd been let down.

Grant stood frozen, immensely shamed that he'd forgotten to call ahead and cancel, and feeling like the biggest asshole on the planet. When had he last brought someone to meet his mom? Or given her a reason to take down her white-streaked gray hair from its bun and ask one of the nurses make a braid for her that ended in a small lavender bow draped across one stooping shoulder. And maybe he was crazy, but Kathleen's pale flesh showed evidence of a slight application of rouge, a habit she hadn't bothered with in two years or more. He remembered being a boy, watching her use a tube of peach-colored lipstick to draw dots onto her cheeks, then smoothing it for ages, blending, blending, and blending.

She was utterly charming and lovely, and he couldn't stand to disappoint her, or to have had her don her most cherished dress for nothing. He smiled, hoping his anxiety didn't show in the lines of his face, and waved a careless hand, the other fishing his cell phone from his pocket.

"She's coming," he assured her, in the blithest manner he could muster. "I'll just call and make sure she's not stuck in traffic."

Kathleen met his smile with one of relief, and nodded, almost shooing him back out the door to make the call.

Grant paced in the hallway. Seraphina finally picked up, a hesitant question in her greeting. "Hi."

"Seraphina. I'd forgotten I'd called ahead to Heritage Acres. Kathleen is—"

"Expecting me to have that lunch," she finished softly.

He might've imagined the tinge of disappointment, but he thought not. Her unspoken favor grated against his pride, but he'd swallow it whole for Kathleen's sake.

"I understand. I just left the office, actually. I can be there in ten."

He couldn't respond. He was glad when she hung up, unintentionally saving him from an awkward, bumbling reply. He stared at his phone for a beat, his estimation of Seraphina rising against his displeasure at her behavior that morning, and then cresting it like a wave breaking onto the beach.

As simply as that, he forgave her. He couldn't help it. She owed him nothing, and still, she hadn't wavered or hesitated, even though he was fairly certain she'd been on route to another errand. A petty person would've used this as an opportunity for a small measure of revenge. She could've hurt him, and chose not to. Not for the sake of brownie points, or because she was dying to meet an elderly mute. Just because she was decent, and so did the decent thing.

She arrived in less time than promised. Grant had joined Kathleen at the table, assuring his happily anticipating mother that their guest was on her way. She gripped her walker—she steadfastly refused to use the wheelchair with company—and rose at the same time Seraphina's head poked through the doorway and she knocked tentatively, then stepped inside. Seraphina wore an uncertain smile, but her eyes were kind as she greeted Kathleen. Kathleen smiled wide, her head bobbing in lieu of a spoken greeting.

Grant expected the hour to pass in agonizingly slow awkwardness, but again, Seraphina surprised him, confidently and adeptly taking charge of the conversation. She didn't talk about herself, which was Grant's way of communicating with Kathleen. Instead, she asked his mom a million questions. What did she like most about Heritage Acres? Did she really enjoy playing bridge? Did she have a best friend or a favorite nurse? To his surprise, Kathleen's smile widened each time she picked up her pad and pen to reply. Seraphina reacted to each note as if they were words said aloud, creating a cohesion and flow as natural as any spoken exchange. Halfway through the meal, Grant began to feel like a second centerpiece.

There because it was expected and a nice addition, but without offering much tangible substance.

Every time Kathleen set her mug of tea or fork aside to respond to one of Seraphina's queries, Grant realized how little he himself offered Kathleen. All this time, he'd thought he'd been doing her a favor. But now it seemed uncomfortably clear he'd stifled the poor old woman, robbing her of an opportunity to express herself. He seldom asked questions, assuming she'd rather not be reminded that she couldn't easily reply. But reply she did, happily and near constant, beaming at Seraphina's interest and curiosity.

His introspection drifted apart like breaking clouds as he came to realize they were talking about him. His gaze swung from one to the other. Seraphina covered her mouth, and mischief danced in her pale blue eyes as they alighted on him. Kathleen's wide grin threatened to split her face in half, and she had her pad tucked toward her chest, hiding the last thing she'd written from view.

He narrowed his gaze. "What?"

Without so much as a speck of guilt, Kathleen slowly turned the paper around. There were no words, but a stick figure wearing a skirt.

Grant covered his eyes and groaned. "Oh, no. You told her the story." While he'd been daydreaming, Kathleen had been diligently writing out one of the most trying moments of his young adult life, in bits and pieces as her small writing pad allowed. The story, he called it. The one he wished would've died a quick death. Even so, he couldn't help an answering grin, because no matter how embarrassing the tale behind the drawing was, he could see the humor all too easily.

"It was for drama club. Did she explain that, at least?" He offered his pained expression to Seraphina. "The club was basically an all-girl club. And me. Even the drama teacher was a woman, and it was her grand idea to gender swap the whole play, have all the girls be men, and the one guy dress as the only lady. A character, mind you, fond of short skirts and sequin festooned blouses. As a comedy, casting me as a bedazzled female only heightened the farce." He shrugged. At least Kathleen had only given up an unflattering stick figure. Somewhere, actual photographic evidence existed. "I fought and argued, but in the end, it was too perfect. I didn't mind until the play ended. I was last in the train of girls, bowing and waving as I followed them off the stage. Some jock kid snuck up onto the stage on the other side, creeping behind me as the audience giggled. The giggling became one collective gasp when he yanked down the pink flimsy skirt."

Seraphina's eyes widened, mirth so evident he still couldn't wipe the grin from his own face. He felt the flush start from his neck and brush up his face like a spreading wildfire. Even now, all these years later.

He sighed. "You know, the little costume was designed for...well, the little undie things that were supposed to go beneath the skirt, they were obviously made for a girl. Too small for me by half, and I'd worn a loose, flowy pair of boxer shorts that day that came to mid-thigh and would've been visible beneath my costume. I didn't have time to run back to the drama classroom and dig through wardrobe for something suitable before my time on stage, so I improvised."

Seraphina dropped her hand, and her smile went from ardently amused to shocked. "You didn't..."

Kathleen chuckled silently, her hand tapping the table in time to her breathy laugh. She nodded vigorously, and Grant decided it was worth the mortification to see such glee in her wrinkled face. Her eyes were bright, and her skin flushed. The rouge was almost redundant.

"I did. I'd gone commando. And thus, showed everything I've got to the entire assembly at Cary Johnson High. I actually think it would've been worse if I'd managed to stuff myself into those small pink underwear, personally."

For a solid minute—he counted each passing second as they crawled by—Seraphina laughed. And laughed. She laughed until tears gathered at the corners of her eyes, and she brushed them away with a delicate swipe of her pinky. Kathleen glowed with pride at having entertained their guest, completely unabashed as she met Grant's gaze across the table. Despite the heat still lingering on his face, he had no regrets. He'd gladly let Kathleen dredge up and rehash every last one of his worst childhood escapades to see her light up like she did now.

Seraphina gamely offered an embarrassing story of her own, about a boy in junior high who'd displayed his ardent love for her the only way a young boy knows how—by torturing her with a Whoopee cushion for an entire semester. He managed to slip it beneath her at pep rallies, in the cafeteria, as she gathered with other students in a classroom, and once just as she sat down adjacent from him in a starkly silent library. She'd confronted him, finally, with a sucker punch to his jaw, and he left her alone after that. Only years later did he confess to the crush.

She rolled her eyes at Kathleen. "Men," she said, wearily. "They claim we want them to read our minds. But at least we don't act in direct opposition of what we feel. It never once crossed my mind to show I liked a boy by pulling his hair or throwing rocks at him. Or, God forbid, keeping up nine weeks of systematic public humiliation."

To this, Kathleen pulled a face and nodded in agreement, then batted away imaginary gnats as if to say to hell with them all.

Grant's hour with Kathleen passed more quickly than it ever had, and he surprised himself by feeling reluctant to put an end to the gathering and head back to the office. In the hallway, after saying their good-byes, he shrewdly assessed Seraphina. "Her birthday is next week," he offered. "I don't take her out very often, but I thought she might like a few hours away from this place. Maybe a meal not taken in a cafeteria or next to her bed."

Seraphina's smile was something less than what she'd given to Kathleen. Still, there was some strain between them. "I'd love to be there, if you're inviting me."

He nodded. "I think Kathleen would like to have you there." He paused, cleared his throat. "I haven't seen her that relaxed, happy even, in a long time."

Seraphina was pensively silent. "She's sweet. I wouldn't mind getting to know her better."

Grant held back a smile, because Seraphina didn't offer one. He didn't know if she'd see it as him misunderstanding the undercurrents between them, or pretending they weren't there. "She's certainly worth getting to know."

"Well, thanks for having me, but I have to go. I was on my way to…" Her blue eyes were hooded and refused to meet his as she dipped her chin in a small gesture of farewell. "Somewhere else," she finished, in a forced light tone. "I'll see you back at the office this afternoon."

Grant watched her go. He didn't know why his gut suddenly felt heavy with apprehension, but he was pretty sure it had something to do with Seraphina's secretive errand. Instead of following her, he dug his cell phone from his pocket and dialed Ophelia. She'd know the next move.

Chapter 11

Marc Curry didn't seem all that surprised when Seraphina let herself into the chain link enclosure that surrounded Tanbee House. He strode toward her in long, purposeful strides with an easy smile on his face and a yellow tool belt swinging in time with his hips. She swallowed. Some men wore their sexuality like an accessory, and some, like Marc, managed to do it and remain completely unaware of the fact.

He grinned good-naturedly, briefly nodding an affirmative to some question posed to him by a passing fellow workman, and waved, "Didn't expect to see you again so soon. We just started busting up the place this morning. Not to toot my own horn or anything, but you might be surprised at how much we've accomplished in a handful of hours."

She peered at the old house, then pulled a yellow notepad from her satchel. "I want to take notes, see for myself what's been claimed reusable or a complete loss."

Marc's face grew serious as he turned his attention the house. "To be honest, I'm in favor of gutting every inch of the place. We're finding decent bones. Structure just needs to be brought up to code and reinforced where it's load-bearing. But walls, flooring, even the ceilings"—his voice ended on a disparaging note—"pretty much anything you'd have to look at every day, I'd toss."

She nodded when he turned to meet her gaze again. "I'll likely agree with you." She'd only seen the place in pitch darkness, but she'd gotten a pretty good feel for the degree of dilapidation they were dealing with.

Another crew member, laboring over a sawhorse in thick coveralls and a thin red plaid shirt, hollered for Marc.

"I don't need an escort," she assured him. "You can get back to your guys. I've got on close-toed shoes, and I'll grab a hard hat before I go in."

He grinned swiftly, taking her measure so quickly she hardly noticed the sweep of his eyes, down and back up. The appreciation in the curve of his mouth was less subtle, but she could tell it was respect for her sensibility, not for how well she stacked up in her neat office clothes. "I guess I'll leave you to it, then. Should be a stack of hats near the door. Watch your footing, especially in the south wing. It's cordoned off, but no one will stop you if you want to look around. Just be careful. The floor was so bad, we tore it up first thing and made walkways from planks set across foundation beams."

The south wing; these rooms were the old kitchens, where they'd ordered plumbing installed during the seventies. Here, she hoped to create two large restrooms, to serve both the staff and the public, since the plumbing was already there. It would only need to be updated. "Thanks. I'll be most diligent." She rolled her eyes at herself as she walked away. Sometimes, things inside her head didn't sound stupid until they passed her teeth.

She snatched up a hardhat and plopped it on her head before ducking inside. With sunlight filtering into the windows and open doors, chasing shadows from the corners, Seraphina noticed a degree of disrepair she hadn't last night. She'd known the place was a mess, ill-used for too many years. But she hadn't been able to see how the remains of the walls were eaten and rotted in so many places, the questionable slope and discoloration of the ceiling inside the main parlor that spoke of an ancient roof leak, or the poor state of the cheap materials they'd used back in the renovations during the seventies.

It almost wasn't worth saving; a traitorous thought for any born and bred Southerner. Oh, how they revered their history. Seraphina clucked her tongue. She'd come to investigate the bedroom, where the window had been busted out, but she wouldn't turn down an opportunity for an in-depth survey.

The parlor where she stood held the giant fireplace, a sorrier thing than it had appeared in the wash of a flashlight. The room was a nice size, though, wider than both the kitchens and the library, perhaps longer, too, and large enough to house a comfortable reception area, waiting lounge, and maybe a set of low-walled cubicles.

Off to the right, two large mirrored arches led into the old kitchens. She could see the patchwork catwalks the crew had erected to get around, and had no desire to test her balancing skills. Time enough to have a look when new flooring was laid down.

It still didn't make sense. Cupper Cottage, the property originally slated for the project, had larger rooms and more square footage overall, despite the misnomer, plus a second floor, and also sat closer to the Governor's Mansion. Why the sudden switch to Tanbee House, a less suitable location, and how, she couldn't quite understand. The city could takes months, years even, to greenlight renovations on historical sites. Yet the switch from Cupper Cottage to Tanbee House had been almost instantaneous. A mystery for another time.

She made her way back through the parlor, and entered the library. The room almost appeared vandalized, even though what little she could see last night appeared in those same places and positions today. She didn't spend much time here. All said, the walls in this one room seemed to her almost salvageable, but it would take closer scrutiny to decide for sure. She intended the old library to serve as the private office of whatever city official would reign here, as well as their personal staff.

She paused at the door at the end of the room, recalling the silhouette of Grant's tall, broad-shouldered form as he'd stood there and barked at her. She glanced down at the yellow lined paper she still gripped and pressed her lips together. So much for taking notes. A sigh escaped her when she finally entered the small room. There were built-in wooden shelves in surprisingly good condition lining the far wall that she hadn't noticed last night. The window was off to her left.

Or rather, a hole was, boarded over with a single large piece of plywood. The shattered window and its frame had been removed, probably first thing this morning. She sighed. Any clues left behind were long gone.

She glanced around. In between the bookshelves, the walls were spotted with holes, large ones that showed the wooden slats behind them, leaving four inches of open space. She studied the holes, noticing a peculiar sameness—almost a pattern. It was as if someone had taken a mallet to the wall, punching out foot-wide holes.

Seraphina shoved her little pad of paper into her bag and approached one. She grimaced and stuck her arm inside, searching the space between the walls. Her fingers brushed a crossbeam—a tidy little shelf for anyone wishing to hide something here. Methodically, she began to search every hole in the wall. She had no idea what she was looking for, but someone had broken into this room, specifically.

Her fingers brushed against something, waking her from a mechanical stupor.

"Looking for lost treasure?"

Seraphina's heart leaped into her throat. She yanked her hand from the wall, knocking loose debris to the floor. She cursed herself for her reaction. She hated to appear guilty. She didn't turn around to look at Marc until she had her face under control. She fixed her features into polite surprise. "You startled me." She offered a breathy laugh. "I was inspecting the primary wall, expecting a hairy spider to crawl up my hand any second." "Could happen. The cobwebs suggest spiders have lived well here in the past." He took a few steps inside and peered around the room, his gaze scanning the ceiling and tattered secondary wall. "What's this room going to be for? When it's remodeled?"

Seraphina straightened and brushed the dust from her hands. "The new library. I want to keep as many of the original bookshelves as possible. If you wouldn't mind making a note to set them aside. I'll have a central table, a place for private councils or staff meetings." She pointed to the wall separating the old library from the room behind Marc. "Tear this down and rebuild it three feet over. Details are in my plans."

"I've gone through them, but I won't study them with a fine-toothed comb until we have good bones." Marc frowned, turned his head, and ran a hand down the wall beside him. "Thin," he said agreeably. "Boards feel loose. Maybe some rot in places." Then he nodded. "Well, I just came to check on you, make sure you hadn't fallen into the floor somewhere."

"Thanks." She didn't smile, in case he took it as an invitation to hang around. "I'm fine. I think I'm going to spend another minute in here. I want a closer look at some of these shelves. If we can't reuse them, I'll want duplicates made, perhaps, for use in the reception area."

Marc bobbed his head. "You got it."

Finally, he left, and Seraphina blew out a long exhale and closed her eyes. The man moved like a ghost. She hadn't heard a single floorboard creak under his boots. But then, he'd inspected the floors and probably knew to avoid the weak spots.

She waited several heartbeats to make sure she was alone, then returned to the hole she'd been searching. Her fingers wriggled until they finally found purchase on a small, smooth item. She struggled up on her tiptoes, and at last managed to grip it between her first two fingers. Ever so carefully, she withdrew the tiny package.

Her eyes went wide at what she retrieved and let settle in her palm. No bigger than a fifty-cent piece and round as a golf ball, the clear plastic closed around a loose white substance. Seraphina's heart thudded in her chest. She suddenly knew with deadly certainty Brendan Berkley's purpose in being assigned to Tanbee House.

But the question that plagued her wasn't why he'd stash drugs in an old historical building, or how he'd managed to get himself in the professional position to retrieve the drugs.

But rather, how deep was Grant Gallagher's involvement. He'd hired Brendan. Assigned Brendan to a position that allowed him access to this specific property. Her stomach churned sourly at what it all appeared to add up to.

She felt around inside the hole. This time, she pushed a long-forgotten piece of lumber against the wall and used it to make herself tall enough to reach farther. Her hand touched upon a whole pile of the soft, round packages. They felt like rubber balloons filled with flour. Malleable and heavy for their size. She stepped back and tried to think, pacing a tight circle around the room as she did. "Damn. Kay was right. I need a good camera."

She growled, frustrated with herself. She needed evidence. Real evidence. She'd take one of these to Kay and Oliver, so the PD could confirm the substance. But she couldn't prove where she'd found the stash without some kind of evidence, and Kay had been pretty clear that her cell phone wouldn't cut it.

She smoothed her hair, physically calming herself as well as mentally. She'd come back at night, with camera equipment, and she'd tear away the wall until she could get a decent shot of the stash. Then, somehow, she'd make sure Brendan Berkley got caught well and good this time.

* * * *

"Marc called. She's there." Grant gave Ophelia the news with a wry twist to his lip. He rubbed his hands together in an effort to ward off his anxiety. They played a long, questionable game. There were so many elements that could go wrong, so many things left to chance, with nothing but the calculated hope that they might go as predicted. A large part of his frustration lie in being nothing but a game piece himself. He wasn't the play caller or the mastermind, just another token to be arranged as deemed fit by the powers that be.

He didn't mind. Or he hadn't, anyway. But in the end, he didn't know if he'd have the right words to explain it all to Seraphina. Or if she'd believe he hadn't hired her for this purpose, but for her own merits.

Ophelia had her head bent over Seraphina's notes. It was almost as if she'd picked up on his thread of thoughts. "You know, she's pretty incredible."

As if he hadn't figured that out. "Yeah. She is. You know what I think? I think I don't appreciate the pointless subterfuge. We know what we're after, we know who's responsible. Why are we putting Seraphina smack in the middle of everything?"

Ophelia looked up at him with a soft groan. "Grant, please. Time and time again, we've gone over this." She set the notes aside and approached his desk. She crossed her arms and leaned one hip against the small antiquity.

Here, in the hidden inner office, Grant let his inherent chaotic style run amok. He didn't have to concern himself with neatness or appearances. They'd called it strange when he'd had two offices created, but he had to maintain a particular image. He glanced at the stacks of random papers and files, the large scrolls of blueprints stacked in corners, and plants Kathleen misguidedly gifted him every so often gone bone dry and wilted in their pots. This was definitely not the face he could afford to put on his brand for employees and clients. And yet, he couldn't work up an ounce of creativity in the clinically well-ordered outer office.

He knew rumors swirled about his supposed lack of vision and talent. Those who met with him in his office saw the starkness as an extension of Grant's personality. They called him a figurehead and a crook, stealing the ideas of his designers and stamping his name across them for the sake of profit. As ever, he didn't care what people thought or said about him, because the designers he supposedly robbed of their ingenuity had seen his inner sanctum and had an instant kinship with the madness creativity usually wrought. And as long as those who worked for him trusted him, well, the rest could think what they like.

Ophelia made a strange departure for him. She gave off an aura of authority that, in some cases, trumped his own. He didn't like her position, even if he understood it. "Seraphina is important because she's our link to Oliver Pierce. He can't investigate Brendan Berkley hands on. Not unless we want Brendan to go through on that harassment claim and destroy every ounce of evidence Oliver has gathered against him so far. However, if Seraphina supplies evidence without Brendan's knowledge, legally obtained as a private citizen, Oliver can use it. Publicly, he's been distanced from the investigation. On the inside, he's the figurehead, while Donald Cappricci handles the reins from Jonesboro. If the fact we've had to separate them by the width of the state of Arkansas doesn't tell you something, I'd think a little harder on it. Now, we've got to be more diligent than ever. Brendan isn't the catch. He is the means. Seraphina, our Trojan horse."

Grant leaned forward on his elbows and steepled his fingers, gazing at Ophelia over the ridge of his fingertips. "Has contact been confirmed?"

Her smile answered before she gave voice to her satisfaction. "She's in. And it has to be Seraphina. Because Brendan expects her to mistrust him. He'll expect her to give him sidelong glances. Her suspicion is driven by her loyalty to her friends, and he won't find anything odd in that. He certainly won't expect her to investigate him on Oliver's behalf. If it were you, he might begin to question why you hired him. He might begin to question how easily you took him on despite his reputation. You have to appear to have his back, to believe in his innocence. In the very least, believe in his right to a second chance, and that Tanbee House is his opportunity to prove himself. You have to make certain he believes that's why you agreed to his petition for that specific project."

"Meanwhile, we're simply facilitating?"

Ophelia gave him a flat stare. "Yes. We rigged the city planning council to switch to Tanbee House at the last moment, securing it before the drugs could be removed. We put Seraphina in position, knowing full well she'd immediately inform Kay Bing and Oliver Pierce of Brendan's new job with you. We know his organization has been moving drugs through the abandoned property. We just need to give Seraphina time to find them. We also know Brendan will be watching her closely, and her movements should put pressure on his. The broken window ruse worked. She went to Tanbee House to investigate on her own."

He sat back with a frustrated huff. "And I get to be the bad guy. She'll suspect I'm involved. It's my company. And I did what you asked. Gave her a reason to go back to Tanbee House to investigate. I still don't understand why the lead investigator doesn't seize the drugs we know are there."

"We don't want the drugs. We want the people making them. And Brendan Berkley is going to be the rat that leads us back to the warren." She frowned, showing some regret for Grant's plight—the merest hint of sympathy. "If our success comes at the cost of your relationship with Seraphina, so be it, Grant. You signed up for this."

He nodded. "And can't regret the decision."

Besides, when the governor himself came knocking, even someone as powerful as Grant Gallagher didn't say no. Seraphina had already been hired, so it was all too easy to put their plan into motion; a complicated game designed to bring down one more leg of the massive drug ring afflicting the entire state with modified magic mushrooms that were killing people.

Since Oliver had brought down the operation inside Free Leaf Concepts, occurrences of overdoses and hospital reports had dwindled. But they weren't stopping entirely. According to the street reports, the drugs were still available, but premiums had skyrocketed. Victims nowadays were of wealthy stock, in one case the son of a senator. That turned out to be the turning point that led both law enforcement and city officials to devise a deeper offense. It almost seemed absurd that so much of it hinged on one woman.

"Tell me one more time why it doesn't make sense just to tell her what we're doing."

With more patience than he expected, Ophelia crossed her arms. "Grant, think. Seraphina is not an actress. She's a designer. The first time—and I do mean the first time, because Brendan is no fool, and he will be vigilant—that she looked at him with any measure of satisfaction rather than the distrust he expects from her, it's over. One wrong look, one miscalculated step, and she'd give the whole thing away. Do you think she could hide her gratification that Brendan hasn't been forgotten by the LRPD, after all? So long as things go their natural course, with subtle guidance from us, the better our chances are of bringing this guy down once and for all." Ophelia pushed away suddenly, checking her watch. "Speaking of, your three o'clock is nigh. I'll be in here if you need me. Quiet as a mouse."

"Recording device going?"

She almost looked offended. "I'll worry about my job. You worry about yours. Get in there and convince Brendan he'd better think long and hard about how and when he plans to get access to Tanbee House. Scare him off temporarily. Long enough to give Seraphina some time to come across the stash. She's smart and determined, and she's not going to quit poking around until she finds out why someone would break into an abandoned house. You asked Marc to increase security?"

Grant rose from his untidy desk and straightened his tie. "It's done." In the absolute order of his outer office, he sat behind the desk and waited until Annie announced the arrival of Brendan.

He decided Brendan was a careful fellow. His hair was combed just so, his khaki dress shirt attractive against black slacks and a tie but two shades off. Complement and contrast, in precise and circumspect quantity. Very designed. Very purposeful. His thick black framed glasses suited his long face and small eyes. Even his body language, as he fluidly entered the room and both sat himself and greeted Grant with a quick smile, spoke of a particular calculation.

Grant didn't like him. He covered his aversion with a polite nod of his head. He couldn't make himself offer the man a smile if the whole investigation hinged on it. "Brendan." A short, cursory greeting.

Brendan grinned. "Mr. Gallagher. A pleasure." He rubbed his hands together and surveyed the office. "I admit, I'm curious as to why I'm here."

Grant settled back and watched Brendan with careful attention. He enjoyed how he squirmed while trying to hide the fact that he was uncomfortable under Grant's steady gaze. When Grant was satisfied Brendan was no longer at ease, he spoke. "I wanted to check in. I understand your unfortunate involvement in the investigations into Free Leaf Concepts left something of a sour note on your reputation. As we saw with Ms. Fawkes last week."

He made intentional mention of their being seen together in public. He wouldn't allow Brendan to think for one second he could hold his relationship with Seraphina as some sort of bargaining chip. There was one issue settled.

"I hope my employees are treating you fairly. And I hope you'll find some satisfaction in working with Seraphina. I'm sure she only requires some time to warm up to you." He left off with something of a question in his tone.

Brendan responded as he'd hoped. "I'm sure. I mean, we had very little contact at Free Leaf. She was buried in the Sweetclover project, which she did a remarkable job on. And I had other duties. We rarely crossed paths. I understand she's personal friends with the investigator who led the undercover operation, and it's reasonable that should color her judgment. She just needs to get to know me better."

Something in the slick edge of his smile chilled Grant. He had a sudden premonition he could guess how Brendan considered he might win Seraphina over. He'd find it all the easier to attempt if he discovered she and Grant had called an end to their affair. He wanted to sigh out loud. One more thing Seraphina could question when all of this came to light. Would she believe Grant wanted to rekindle things between them, or decide he'd simply done it to thwart Brendan? If he could just tell her everything now.

Brendan was already talking again, probably a reaction to Grant's stony silence. "And I'm motivated. To do a good job for you. For her. To earn my reputation back in whatever manner I'm able. I'm grateful for the opportunity." A slight smile stretched his lips. If he imagined it covered the hunger in his gaze, he was wrong. "I'm already impressed with how efficiently this place runs. I mean, I've never seen the city council and the historical society work so smoothly together. The swiftness in which you got them to approve Tanbee House in the place of Cupper Cottage is nothing short of a miracle."

For the first time, Grant let his smile stretch wide. "Yes. I'm rather proud of that." Proud of how we cornered you so easily, you weasel. Brendan's application had hit Grant's desk two days after the proposal to switch properties cleared. To no one's surprise. A good old bait and switch, and now they had Brendan right where they wanted him. "I wanted Tanbee House all along," he said, letting his self-satisfied smirk run over his mouth, marveling in how Brendan was utterly ignorant as to the reason for it. "The layout is better suited to our needs. Once they approved Cupper Cottage,

I decided it was worth convincing them one property wasn't so different from another. If you never swing, you always miss."

Brendan nodded. "I can't thank you enough for allowing me to join the Tanbee House team. It's a real honor. I—"

"Not an honor." Grant cut him off swiftly, coldly. He let the grin fade from his face. "An opportunity, as you said, and nothing more than that. A scale large enough for you to make a mark and prove I made the right decision. I like to think my judge of character is one of my strongest abilities. I would take it as a personal affront if you were to prove me wrong."

He watched Brendan's Adam's apple bob with great satisfaction.

"That's all Brendan. I hear Seraphina already has Ophelia hunting down resources for materials. I'd suggest making sure I don't get left out of the loop, were I you."

Brendan scuttled from Grant's office more quickly than he'd entered, and less certain. Some of the cockiness and surefootedness had abandoned him. In the end, Grant's role in all this may remain a secret, and there'd be some public fallout for his bad judgment in hiring Brendan Berkley. In the very least, he could get a few good swipes in while he held some degree of power. He decided he didn't dislike the man, after all. He despised him.

Chapter 12

Kay's concern shone through her indistinct hazel eyes like beacons. She and Oliver shared a glance all but dripping in some unspoken communication, before Kay turned back to Seraphina. "You've got to be careful. If he suspects you're actively investigating him, Brendan won't hesitate to conclude you're doing favors for Oliver. Maybe pretend to give the guy a break or something?"

Seraphina couldn't control her expression. Her lip curled in distaste, and her eyebrows rose. "Really? You want me to pretend to his face he's not the most dishonest, crooked loser I've ever met?"

"The reality is we never proved a thing against him," Kay pointed out hesitantly.

"The court might require proof. I don't," Seraphina averred. "It's all too weird, and you won't convince me otherwise. The break-in, the drugs, Brendan's sudden involvement. Hell, even the way the city council switched properties. That's unheard of. It can take months to wade through all the bullshit and red tape to be able to renovate a historic property. And Grant, well, he's successful because he's intelligent, one would suppose. But where is the sense in taking a chance on someone like Brendan Berkley?"

Oliver grimaced, ran a hand through light brown hair about due for a trim, and swung his doubtful gaze between Seraphina and Kay. "There is such thing as coincidence, and it has screwed over guys in my position over and over again, all throughout history."

Kay cocked her head. Seraphina opened her mouth to speak.

Oliver held up a hand to ward off their impending protests, which had to be written all over their faces. He had a natural ability to assume control that way, through simple gestures and an overall kindly attitude. He gave direction like merely a wise suggestion. Plus, he was utterly adorable. Not

Seraphina's type—she liked a sharp, honed edge and a hint of darkness that Oliver lacked. He and Kay made a singularly perfect couple.

"I don't believe that, either," Oliver offered. "Brendan's connection stinks. But unless we—no, strike that—unless you, Seraphina, can directly tie him to the drugs hidden inside Tanbee House, we have nothing. I'm blind. I can't set up a sting. If he were to get wind of me investigating his workplace, he wouldn't hesitate to lodge a complaint that could cripple the entire investigation. Those involved at Free Leaf Concepts haven't even gone to trial yet, and I could botch the proceedings for the DA before they ever set foot in front of a jury."

Seraphina drooped within herself, but outwardly kept her shoulders squared. She didn't believe for a second she could do this on her own. But she also couldn't bring herself to tell Oliver and Kay it was useless to hang their hopes on her. She hoped the helplessness she felt didn't come through in her voice. "I'm not a private investigator. I'm a designer. What can I do?"

Oliver grinned as he held up the plastic sandwich bag. It held the small balloon of white stuff she'd brought him. "Already, you've done a lot. We'll have this tested as soon as possible. And before you go, remind me to get a quick sample of your prints. Pretty sure I've got the stuff around here somewhere." He glanced around, as if the kit would spring up nearby.

Kay rolled her eyes, smiled, and patted his knee. "I know where it is. Scatterbrain."

"Busy brain." He tapped his temple and gave her a wide-eyed stare of admonishment.

Kay shrugged and glanced at Seraphina. "He does work some crazy hours. There's more than one angle to the investigation. He thinks Brendan Berkley is the lynchpin, but there are still plenty of other avenues to explore."

Oliver turned to Seraphina again. He scratched his chin thoughtfully. "Just make sure you keep your head down. If Brendan has his hands in this, we want to catch him moving the product, which he'll have to do before Curry brings down that wall, right? Keep Kay in the loop on your timeline, casually. But should Brendan get wind you're watching him, he might abandon the drugs. And even with them in possession, it'll only add up to more circumstantial evidence against Brendan. If there's anything I'm sick of, it's evidence that can't tie this guy down."

Seraphina pressed her lips together and tried to stop caring for five minutes. Just a small reprieve. She'd been more than happy to accept Kay's dinner invitation in exchange for the evidence she collected. She had a queasy feeling, hauling around a bag of white powder in her purse, and was more than relieved to hand it over. "Are your people still having trouble recreating the super shrooms?"

Kay rolled her eyes. "And have they come up with a worse nickname yet? Call them mad caps. Or death fungus. Anything but super shrooms." She hooked a thumb at Oliver and gave Seraphina a wry stare. "These guys got no imagination."

Oliver rolled his eyes right back, but a smile tugged at the corner of his mouth. "Yeah, because giving stuff catchy names makes it easier to hunt down. To answer your question, Sera, yes. Still struggling. They've created the mushrooms as we assumed they were made, using the African dream plant, but an element is missing. Apparently, the batch we took in the bust was unfinished product, and what we collected from the salad Kay was dosed with is also different."

Unease rippled through Seraphina, and she noted the shiver that shook Kay's shoulders. Her face mirrored her thoughts. Someone had slipped the shrooms into a salad, which Kay had eaten. Luckily, she didn't finish it, or she might've died. Even the small dose she'd taken had brought on intense hallucinations and put Kay on bed rest for days.

"We have no idea how they complete the process, but now we know for certain there's another step to creating their specific drug." Oliver shrugged, and the weariness of searching for answers that fought to elude him was clear in his bearing. "Could be another plant they spliced. Another street drug incorporated into the process. Could be what they had growing at Free Leaf's greenhouse compound was a trial run for a different formula. We'll figure it out. But in the meantime, that stuff is still out there. Not spreading as rapidly, but we get local reports every couple of weeks, so they're still producing."

After that, the three of them fell into a congenial silence, each focused on their inner thoughts. The day had been a trial, and Seraphina didn't appear to be the only one going through a rough stretch. If she'd had doubts about helping Oliver, he'd effectively squelched them.

At least relaxing in Kay's harmoniously gorgeous kitchen took some of the sting from her day, much like a hot soak after a tough workout. Probably a designer thing. Seraphina was uniquely in tune with the quality of the elements, the labor, and the vision it had taken for Kay to have pulled together the remarkable room. It was a flattering display of stainless steel, soft whites, and the whole spectrum of blue hues and tints, evident in everything from a display of glazed dishes to the mosaic backsplash that glinted in the light of the pale blue pendants that dropped down from the high ceiling. The food was takeout, but that was almost the second reason they gathered here. They'd really come for the atmosphere. It was a happy place.

"How's the rest of the reno coming along?"

Kay brightened immediately, as she always did when someone brought up her pet project. "Amazingly fast, with my extra set of hands." She grinned and winked playfully at Oliver. "The foyer, as you saw, is complete. We found paneling that matches the original hardwood floors near exact, and wallpaper stunningly close to the original. We started in the library last week, but we're having some disagreement over the hideous fireplace."

"It's marble." Oliver's tone suggested that was his argument in whole.

Kay shook her head. "See? He thinks the material is worth salvaging, but it's wrecked and can't be repaired."

"I think the dents and dings are part of the charm."

Seraphina surprised herself with a snort of soft laughter. "I'm not even sure I could argue with that logic."

A short while later, she said good-bye to her friends and took a city bus to a pharmacy near midtown. She picked out two disposable cameras and decided she'd go shopping for something with more consequence later on. Something with bells and whistles to make the best of every photo op. But for now, for tonight, the cardboard wrapped cameras would suffice. Definitely no altering the evidence that came out of these things.

Tanbee House was deserted with the crew long gone. Seraphina's nerves jangled as she spotted an unmarked patrol car drawing close, coming to a halt between her and the fence surrounding the site. The door opened and the officer stepped out. He smiled in that way they had. Something they must teach at the academy. It was meant to put her at ease, but only succeeded in making her feel like he knew more about her plans than she did. She swallowed and introduced herself.

Still with that smile, he greeted her in return. "You have identification on you, ma'am?"

"Yes, of course." She dug her license out of her bag and handed it over. He didn't seem particularly concerned or watchful. But he also didn't seem inclined to let her anywhere near Tanbee House. "I'm Seraphina Fawkes. I'm in charge of the renovations here."

He nodded, eyeballed her driver's license. "Hm. Well, we've got Marc Curry listed as the guy in charge. And without him here, or his consent expressed to us in person, we're to keep the property secure." An apologetic smile. "Sorry, ma'am."

She cleared her throat. She was disappointed, but there was time. As long as she got photographic evidence before Marc's team stumbled onto the drugs—which she believed Brendan would prevent at all costs—then she had some time. She promised the officer she'd get her name on that list and headed back the way she came. At least if she couldn't get through, then neither could Brendan.

* * * *

The tap at Seraphina's office door startled her. She snapped her head up from the blueprints spread out around her, and she stared open-mouthed at the man in the doorway. "Dad?"

Daniel Fawkes's deep green eyes were the color of pine needles. He had an absence about him; a kind of distraction that made her feel like half his mind was elsewhere. He wore the suit of a restless, underappreciated, temperamental artist. He was effortlessly fashionable; his hair carelessly mussed, but attractively so. Just like he'd always taught her—hide the effort, make it look easy, and never let them see you sweat.

"May I?" He indicated a chair with a distinct note of impatience, as if he expected her to command a sovereign's respect here in her inner sanctum.

She smiled in an effort to ease away some of the tension he carried into the room, which proved difficult as always. Her dad didn't call often, at least not for idle chat, and she could remember only a handful of times in a span of years he'd stopped by her workplace to see her. Never had his visits preceded good news or happy times. A few times to borrow money, and then swear to never borrow money again, because she was so judgmental about the loan. Not once had she ever said a wayward thing, but that was Daniel.

"Don't be silly. Come on in. I'm just eyeballing a few things. I'm kind of in research mode while I wait for the contractor to get me good bones to work with." His gaze had gone vacant, so she stopped talking about herself and carefully set aside her work. "It's good to see you."

He looked well. Healthy. His olive skin was dark, so he'd been getting sun lately. "Yeah, well, that's just it, I'm hitting the road. I was going to call, but that seemed cheap. And I knew I couldn't count on you stopping by anytime soon." He took the proffered chair, dropping into it languidly.

"Wow. You're really leaving town." She didn't frame her surprise as a question he might take some offense to. Like she doubted him, or his determination, or his ability. "That's... I'm happy for you."

Doubt clouded his expression. "That right? Well, good. I thought you might have some objection."

"No, no. Of course not. Why would I?"

Her dad glanced aside. His Greek bones were more evident than ever in his profile; the long, patrician nose and the high, cutting cheekbones. He took a moment to adjust the old duster jacket he wore. It was strictly a style choice, because the weather certainly didn't call for one. But he made it look good. Beneath he wore a thin white cotton T-shirt with a V-neck. Eventually, he sighed and the look he gave her was heavy with sympathy. "Because this is it. I can't imagine why I'd come back. I've been roofing, you know." He paused a moment to let her absorb that. No wonder his skin had grown so dark, if he'd spent the summer laying shingles.

"Dad, you could've told me. I know a hundred general contractors who—"

"Told you what, sweet pea?" Despite the endearment, there was a hard edge. "That I haven't done any real work in the last half decade? That I was a stay-at-home stepdad for a couple years, for some kid who never liked me all that much, anyway? No more than my own ever did. Look, I didn't need your pity, Sera, and I didn't need your help. I still don't. I find myself suddenly free and single, and I've got an audition lined up at the biggest theater in Phoenix, so don't you worry about me, dear. I'm here because I'm worried about you."

Seraphina knew her mouth was hanging open and worked to close it. Her dad had spent the last few years being a stepdad, and had never said a word about this other family, this other life? "Why… Why wouldn't you tell me something like this?"

"So I wouldn't have to listen to this. Right here. If I needed a job so bad I couldn't get one on my own, maybe I would've come to you, maybe—"

"Dad, no." There was a bubble of silence as they both took in her interruption. Suddenly, she didn't care if he was disappointed, or if every single one of the words that came of her mouth next were the wrong ones. "You had a family, all these years? Another child?"

"Not blood," he explained, exasperated. "Ron's boy. A thirteen-year-old smart-mouthed kid."

"Do you think that could possibly matter to me? I thought—God, I'm so stupid sometimes. I thought we were both alone. Both abandoned. That one thing was the connection I've always clung to between us, despite however else you and I may differ. At least I wasn't left completely alone. At least I wasn't the only one who understood the hurt in being tossed aside for being defective. I have led a lonely life. All this time, I could've had a family to spend holidays with? I could've had a stepbrother or stepsister? For years, you tell me? Why on earth would you keep something like that from me? And why would you keep me from it?" As quickly as her anger and resentment had billowed up like black storm clouds, they dissipated and scattered. Daniel looked defeated. Beaten and depressed. She corralled herself, breathed calmly. "Please. Help me understand."

"Because of this right here." There was no apology in his steady gaze. He was stone. "Because it didn't last. We both know it never does. And instead of both of us having broken hearts, this time it's just the one. Just mine."

A tear hovered on her bottom lashes. Emotions were roiling up from the depths to strangle her. It was almost like she'd been abandoned again, tossed aside while her father enjoyed a family life without her. At the same time, she saw the pain in his gaze. "But you wouldn't be alone. We'd still have each other."

"Only that would make this next part harder, wouldn't it? Sera, I'm telling you now, I ain't coming back. That relationship was the only thing holding me back. It's over, and I'm out of time to keep waiting around for things to get better and stay that way." He waved his hands around the room, his gaze bouncing around her meager personal belongings. It landed on the photograph of him perched next to her printer, earning her a small, wry grin. "You got all this. You have not ever needed me. I daresay you never wanted me that bad."

"I did," she shot back. "I did. It's just that nothing I've ever been or done is good enough for you. I'm not Rebecca. But she's who you see when you look at me."

Daniel shrugged. He shook his head sadly. "Seraphina, I love you the best way I know how. Sometimes, I don't think your mom needed a reason to take off. Maybe I was pushing her toward it long before she found me out. And yeah, you look just like her. More than that, you talk like her, you move like her, and speak the way she did. Maybe it's not fair that we never got any closer. But I needed the distance."

"Just like you need it now." Seraphina swallowed, her throat thick. So strange, so unthinkable. Her father had been in one relationship all this time, years, and never once offered to introduce his boyfriend to his daughter. Swiftly and ruthlessly, the facts and their inherent truth clicked into place.

She peered at him, for the first time taking some satisfaction in knowing her appearance and bearing made him uncomfortable; made him remember a pain he'd turned around and inflicted on his own daughter. "Just like you've needed it my whole life. You've always been so quick to accuse me of being ashamed of you. But did Ron even know about me? Did your stepson?" Daniel's silence answered her. "You never told them I existed. Because the truth, Dad, is that you're ashamed of me. I'm not even a real person to you. I'm just this big, fat, walking, talking reminder of your own bad luck. Every time I succeeded at something, you saw Mom succeeding without you. Every time I did well for myself, you saw something good come from her and couldn't stand it. God forbid Rebecca Fawkes come back and see her daughter was more her blood than yours." She smiled without any trace of humor. "That's right. I'm Rebecca's daughter. More than I was ever yours, and now I'm finally up to speed. You could've let me in on the secret years ago and saved us both so much heartache. I've wasted a lot of time trying to be enough for you."

He wasn't sorry. Just tired, evidenced by the thin line of his mouth and the circles beneath his eyes. Tired and anxious to leave, his toe tapping and his fingers drumming. But not sorry. Daniel glanced up at her, his thoughts unspoken but clear as crystal. Are you done yet?

"I'm done." She gave a little shrug and looked away. An emptiness like creeping fog stole through her. She was numb as her father rose from the chair and left her office. The door clicked quietly shut behind him. Hours passed before it opened again.

* * * *

Grant frowned at his watch. He stared at Seraphina's office door, paced a tight circle, trying to appear nonchalant in case there were any other stragglers, then approached again only to falter and lose his courage.

Apologies weren't that hard. Rare as albino peacocks, but not impossible. She'd stayed late tonight, working through the day inside her office, for which he was personally grateful. He wanted to come to her on her turf, not summon her into his office again. He wanted to speak to her as Grant to Seraphina, not Mr. Gallagher to lead project designer. Ideally, that didn't happen at the office. But to convince her to meet him somewhere else, he'd have to give her a good reason. An apology for being a dick had to be a decent starting place. The surety and easy confidence that were his trademark abandoned him. He forced his way through it, feigning what didn't come naturally, and finally rapped his knuckles across the door twice in quick succession.

Several beats of silence passed. Then Seraphina's muffled voice invited him inside.

Grant took a second to compose his features and square his shoulders. He didn't want her to see his nervousness. He needn't have bothered. He opened the door, took one look at her face, and shut it quickly behind him. "What's wrong? What happened?"

Seraphina's blue eyes were almost vacant as she stared at a spot on the wall. She seemed to shake herself, then gradually meet his gaze. She

smiled wanly. "Sorry. I had a visitor earlier. Some family news." Her low,
bitter laugh caught Grant off guard. "If you can really call it that."

He sat down and leaned toward her, palms resting on his knees. "Tell me."
He winced at the command in his tone, but Seraphina didn't seem to notice.

She shrugged. "My dad came by. He's moving to Phoenix. Which is
great. I'm glad he's chasing his dream or whatever. They say it's never
too late." Suddenly, her eyes grew round and wet. She blinked fiercely,
battling against some building emotion that stiffened her shoulders. Her
hands fisted on her desk. "She must be a burden to you, no matter how
dutifully you bear it. Maybe because you feel you owe her something, but
I hope you appreciate how lucky you are. I could've used someone like
Kathleen in my life." Her pinched lips formed a grim smile. "Still could."

Grant didn't ask any more questions. He knew loneliness when he
saw it, and the echoing of abandonment made hollow wells of her eyes.
Another tendril of understanding twined between them. He stood and
pulled Seraphina to her feet, gently gripping her elbow. First, he hugged
her, burying her inside the protective circle of his arms. Then he helped
her gather her things and prepare to leave.

"I do know how lucky I am. I've always known," he responded softly,
once they were ensconced inside a cab, directed to Seraphina's studio
apartment in midtown. The weather had been indecisive all day, alternately
scorching hot and overcast. Finally, a few of the scattered clouds broke. Light
rain fell onto sun baked streets, causing mist to rise from the pavement.

Seraphina didn't move her gaze from the window, but she nodded.
"It's stupid to feel so abandoned when he was never there for me, anyway.
We hardly spoke."

Pain added a strangled twist to her words, and Grant guessed there was
more to the story. But he didn't push. They rode the rest of the way in silence.

Seraphina led him inside. He couldn't help a smile as he studied her
cozy apartment. They were tight quarters, but she made the best of them
with stylish touches and clever furniture placement. What the apartment
lacked in natural light, Seraphina made up for with candles. Clusters of
them on every surface, in big clear vases filled with glass beads. Some
were wedged inside wrought iron holders on the wall. From the small table
where she'd dropped her keys, she picked up a book of matches and began
lighting several as she moved farther into the living area.

A vast variety of potted plants gave it the feel of a courtyard off the
French Quarter in New Orleans. Flowers in every color, some in bloom,
some in tightly curled buds, and some brown and drooping. Leaves, small
bushes, and a vine trailing over the window frame and up the side of a

decorative wooden ladder resting against the wall, the rungs providing shelfs for even more plants, all embellished the small space with warmth and life.

She caught him ogling. "Kay," she explained, her smile tight but genuine. "Since she started working for Free Leaf Concepts, I've become the recipient of a tiny horde of greenery. I had a few of my own to start with, some flowers that aren't too difficult to keep alive, and I guess she assumed I must have a green thumb. Or maybe she feels bad that I don't have a yard. I make an absurd effort to keep them all alive. But I manage, because I feel like I'd disappoint her otherwise, and Kay just keeps bringing them. Vicious, like most cycles."

"Well, it's nice." And it was. Humble. Cozy. Seraphina didn't live on the budget he did, but for all that, he couldn't think of anywhere else he'd rather spend time. Small flames made dancing shadows on the walls. It brought to mind images of long-stemmed glasses of rich dark wine, and the soft orange glow of candlelight on bare skin.

Seraphina had gone into the kitchen, which butted against the far wall, divided from the living space by a small island. She flipped on a dull light over the sink and began hunting through cabinets. "I usually heat up a can of whatever looks yummy on the label."

He snorted softly and came up behind her, setting his hand atop hers. "I heard all about the burned cheese toast. Instead, why don't you give me permission to rummage in your pantry?"

Her eyebrows rose dramatically. She peered up at him, and they were almost nose to nose. "I don't think there's going to be any rummaging in my pantry tonight, mister."

Grant pressed his lips together. "I stepped right into that one." It was nice to see her smile return, however briefly. "But in all seriousness, I'll cook. And in return, you let me stay the night." She'd taken a step back from him. He quickly held up a finger. "Nothing to do with your pantry. Not your metaphorical one, anyway. Just let me stay."

Such indecision. She bit her lip and backed away until she bumped into the island. Her arms crossed her body as if she was fighting off a chill. She watched him like the answers to all of life's questions were scrawled across his skin. Finally, she spoke, a low murmur he hardly caught. "Today, my dad reminded me of something important. Things don't last. Nothing ever does."

His lip curled into an involuntary grimace. "I think nothing has lasted for him because he's a tool. You wouldn't have to go any farther than Heritage Acres to find an old woman who'd disagree with him wholeheartedly.

Forgive my saying so, but only one of those two opinions is worthy of the high regard they've both been given."

Grant didn't move until Seraphina exhaled a deep breath and relaxed her shoulders. "Okay. You can stay."

Chapter 13

Roper paused in the doorway of Seraphina's office and coolly appraised her. "I peeked at your updated plans. They look good. The black walnut. Cost effective and pretty."

She smiled wanly. "Just like me."

He chuckled softly and came inside but didn't sit. Nor did his strange expression change.

Seraphina pulled her hands away from her laptop and settled them in her lap. She cocked her head to the side. "I don't know how to invite you to get to the point without sounding rude. So, would you like a coffee or something? Maybe you'd like to discuss the weather while you warm up to your topic?"

A smile broke through, but the thoughtful look in Roper's eye didn't quite disappear. He shrugged and took a seat. He rubbed his hands together and leaned forward. His expressive eyes were wide and earnest. "I don't think you're rude. I think you're efficient, among many other things. I know it might seem weird that I care at all, given that I'm counting down my days here at Gallagher Interiors. But it's professional integrity that drives me to ask why you're spending so much time at Tanbee House."

The question caught her off guard. Seraphina licked her lips and settled back into her chair. She wrestled with the answer. She couldn't tell the truth, but she had to have a believable lie. She'd spent a few hours the last several days sniffing around Tanbee House. She'd yet to achieve the privacy necessary to further investigate the drug cache in the wall, and Marc had adamantly refused to pass her name along to the nighttime security team, because the risk of getting injured on site in the dark was too high.

Before she could decide where to straddle the line, Roper sat back with a sigh. "Sorry. I know, it's not my business. I just heard a couple of

Marc's guys complain. They say you're underfoot. Marc doesn't mind, because you're not out there trying to usurp his power and boss his crew around. But it hasn't gone unnoticed that you're delegating a lion's share of your job to Ophelia. As far as I can tell, you're using the free time to hang around Tanbee House at a time when you aren't needed there. Until Marc's crew put down a subfloor, wire, and plumb, there isn't much for you to do." Roper paused and rubbed his cheek. "I guess I'm just curious. If I were running this thing, I'd be a little more hands on, but on this end."

Seraphina cleared her throat and decided some measure of honesty was necessary. Her reputation was still too young and fragile to withstand rumors of laziness. She stood carefully and came around her desk to lean against it. She lowered her voice a degree or two. "You are correct. Under normal circumstances, I wouldn't spend any time at Tanbee House during this phase. Or not much, anyway. I trust Marc and his team to do the job, and yes, I find myself in the way most of the time. In fact, there are times it's deliberate. To slow the process. See, I think I found something. Or rather, I think there's something to be found."

Roper's mouth opened and closed again. His gaze scanned the ceiling before meeting hers again. Shrewd, his expression, and she didn't blame him for his skepticism. "Can you give me a little more detail than that? Like, what are we talking here? Gold hidden in the walls?"

Her pulse skittered. Then she realized in a shell like Tanbee House, the walls were the only place something could really be hidden. For a moment, she'd thought his wild guess was less than a guess. "No. Not to say what I suspect doesn't have value. I don't intend to take it for myself, if that concerns you. More like I need to prove or disprove its existence." She couldn't be more misleading and simultaneously truthful than that.

"Huh." Roper stroked his chin. "Where'd you get this from? Did you stumble across something in the historical society's archives?"

"Uh...um, no. Well, sort of." Her mind leaped and ran, grasping for purchase. If she couldn't convince Roper of her intentions, he may decide to do some digging of his own. "Evidence suggests a house was used for stowing away goods. I can't prove the location is Tanbee House, but some of the pieces fit. It's all supposition at this point. I'm merely investigating." The lie made her skin prickle with unease. It would be easy enough to prove her a liar.

But Roper seemed to relax. He nodded. "Oh. Okay. That's pretty neat, huh? What does Grant think?"

Seraphina stood up straight and checked her watch. She didn't have anywhere to be, but she hoped Roper would feel her impatience and be prodded into wrapping up his little interrogation. "I haven't spoken to him. Not yet. Without proof, there's not much to say. Although, it's hard to imagine he hasn't had some of the same concerns as you. And he seems like the kind of man who knows what's going on." She prayed that would be enough to keep Roper from mentioning a word of this conversation to Grant. She wanted to wring her hands and mumble prayers, but maintained her calm in front of Roper. If she had to explain herself to Grant, she'd ask for a likely cover story from Oliver. If anyone had something up his sleeve, it was a man whose undercover work demanded he have an answer for everything.

Whether he realized it or not, Roper reacted to her nonverbal cues. He stood and brushed invisible lint from his slacks. "I'm not questioning your ethic or anything, Seraphina. Or your integrity. Or, for that matter, your intelligence," he added with a quirk of his lip. "I expect you'll go to Grant if you find anything cool." His smile widened. "I hope your hunt goes well. Sorry if I came off a little…"

Seraphina responded to his trailing sentence with a disarming smile. "No harm, no foul. I appreciate your being forthright in your concern, and giving me an opportunity to explain myself. And you're probably right. I've pawned off enough of my job on Ophelia and Brendan. I hope to wrap up my little detective scheme soon and dive in, both hands on the wheel and eyes on the road."

He waved her off with an almost embarrassed smile. "Forget I even said anything. Really. I didn't mean to accuse you of not working hard enough."

"I understand," she assured him. And she did. She might've initiated the same discussion had she been in his shoes. Roper might be ready to walk away from Gallagher Interiors, but he obviously still cared about the company. As if he weren't already too likeable, that endeared him to her. She walked around her desk and tapped a key on her laptop to wake it up. "I'll let you know what I find," she offered. "Should I find anything at all."

"Yeah, cool. I hope you do. For fun's sake, if nothing else." He waved, walked through the doorway, and had hardly taken a step beyond. "Oh, hey. Didn't see you there, Brendan. Did you need to speak to Seraphina?"

Seraphina's small hairs stood on end as Brendan slowly stepped into view. Their gazes locked, and she fought to keep her surprise and anxiety veiled. His eyes were difficult to read behind the thick frames resting on his nose. Had he heard everything? Nothing? There was no telling by studying him. She couldn't give away her nervousness, so she covered it with irritation. "Do you always linger outside doors before you enter them?"

Brendan didn't skip a beat. "I wasn't waiting. Just passing through at the same time Roper walked out." A careless grin blossomed on his face, and he clapped Roper on the shoulder. "Sorry, bud, just bad timing. I'd be more careful before merging into traffic if I were you."

As she slowly lowered herself into her chair, Seraphina had to wonder if the playful jest held a hint of true threat. Or perhaps a word of caution meant for her own ears.

Roper took the joke good naturedly. Because he was Roper, and how else did the man take anything. "I'll look both ways next time." Roper took off to the left, and Brendan continued on his path, taking him past Seraphina's open door. He glanced up and his smile fell away before he disappeared again.

So much for no harm, no foul. If Brendan had picked up even half of her conversation with Roper, there was potential for both.

* * * *

The next week and a half were among the longest in Seraphina's professional career, if not her life. There were a few stretches of college, finals week for example, that came close, but those lacked the depth of anxiety she felt as opportunities and chances kept slipping her by. Time and time again, something thwarted her efforts to capture the drug stash on film. She was kept late in a meeting, or Ophelia caught wind of her plans for a late visit to Tanbee House and joined her. Sometimes, she even had actual job duties to attend to.

She'd distanced herself from Grant as much as possible. A difficult thing to achieve, after the night he'd spent at her apartment. That night, something formed between them; a closeness she both craved and mistrusted. It was entirely too possible she was projecting her daddy issues onto Grant. One man walked out of her life without a backward glance, while another seemed all too eager to step into the vacancy left behind. Until she could sort out her feelings for Grant, keeping him at arm's length seemed the wisest course.

The camera purchase had been more of an ordeal than she'd expected. Not the actual buying part. Oh, no. The weight of the sleek new Nikon in her hand made her hum with satisfaction. It was a gratuitous piece of equipment. Unfortunately, it didn't allow for stealth. She'd bought a bigger purse and kept the Nikon swathed in a silk scarf.

She'd managed to keep Brendan out of her hair by attaching him firmly to Ophelia's hip as they worked together to order preliminary supplies and scout local sources for as much as possible. She'd even sent them out of town, off on a bargain-hunting trip to find a flea market Neve had raved about way out in the mountains. Brendan's ignorance was key. Seraphina had no hardcore evidence the stash was his, but if it was, he might decide something were off if he caught Seraphina lugging around a Nikon to and from the work site. If he thought for a second she had any kind of evidence, he may bolt. Or abandon his stash. Which, according to Oliver, would defeat the purpose entirely.

Marc Curry was another matter. Seraphina could hardly mask the vivid flash and tell-tale click of the camera. With him, she had no choice but to trust he'd find her sudden interest in photography not particularly notable. When she explained her desire to make a before and after portfolio for the city, documenting Tanbee House's rebirth into the current century, Marc had frowned and glanced around the shell of the house. "You're sure they want a reminder?"

The man had made a particular nuisance of himself, wanting to move on to the bedroom as soon as they'd cleared the old kitchens. She'd had a ready excuse, if a bit feeble. She asked for more time, since she was still quibbling with herself as to whether moving the wall was truly necessary. It was, but she'd hang onto that excuse as long as Marc let her get away with it.

Marc hadn't been overly understanding of her fickle artistic process. He'd parked his hands low on his hips. "I've still got to tear down these useless secondary walls, brace the foundation, check for trouble spots like mildew and pests, and install insulation and drywall. You've got loads of time to figure out the pretty stuff."

She recalled the way he'd said pretty stuff with a hint of disdain and a small dismissive wave of his hand, which had sullied her impression of him probably more than he realized.

And here he was, yet again, trying to make her life difficult. This was her last chance, and he wouldn't make it easy. She was beginning to wonder if he wasn't intentionally impeding her. If Brendan could get hired, surely he could get someone else inside the company, as well.

Sera checked her watch. Kathleen's birthday dinner was a short hour away. The small gift wrapped neatly and tucked away in her purse weighed on her. It would either be a huge blunder or a blinding success. She'd decided maintaining distance between herself and Grant didn't necessarily mean keeping Kathleen at arm's length. Kind, wise, funny, and sweet, Kathleen embodied the female presence Seraphina had always craved in her life. The last thing she wanted was to be late for the party.

So she couldn't afford to screw up her carefully laid plans to gain access to the bedroom before Marc began dismantling the following day. It was now or never. "Of course. We shouldn't forget our humble beginnings. And ideally, I'd like to get the sun coming down, casting that eerie glow into the old bedroom. I've got keys, and I promise to lock everything down before I leave. I'll leave before it's dark out. I won't be long at all, in fact." She injected a note of dismissal and a shot of command into her tone. Marc didn't outrank her. Nor she him. But she wasn't going to budge on this, and he couldn't make her.

For a moment he watched her, as if gauging her determination. Finally, he shook his head, gave her a final doubtful glance, and then nodded. "If you say so. You're the creative brain, after all." With a short farewell, he and his crew began shuffling toward the exit.

She moved slowly as they filed out, letting the click of the camera punctuate the thudding of work boots on wood. While a few men remained to complete small tasks of their own before clocking out for the day, Seraphina began cataloging in earnest.

She fully intended to go through with the before-and-after venture. A Then and Now collection she could present to the city as a sort of appreciative token for their being so accepting of the plans for Tanbee House. Besides, she ought to do something useful, besides pretend to be an amateur sleuth.

Even as she rolled her eyes at herself, a thrill ran up her spine. There was something exciting about this undercover operation stuff. Despite the warmth of the day still clinging to the inside of the house, it could've been the dead of night for how anxious she was. She glanced around in between snaps and flashes of the camera, probing darkening corners and empty doorways for shadows that shouldn't be there. Maybe she was being silly, getting inside her own head, but the break-in hadn't been a joke. She didn't want to stick around any longer than she had to, heightened security or not.

Twilight came slowly, clear daylight shifting into a cheesy orange-ness. The beauty of it defied her inept description. Carefully, she photographed her way toward the bedroom. Once inside, she didn't waste any more time, but rushed to the hole where she'd found the small baggie and stuck her hand inside.

Relief spiked as her fingers brushed across the rubbery outside membrane of the small round packages. They were still there. She stuck the long camera lens down into the hole, as close she could manage without blocking the flashbulb, and snapped several pictures. She checked the small screen for quality—useless evidence if the image she captured wasn't clear. She smiled at the clear photo. They were golden. With that knowledge came a swift desire to get the hell out and away before it was too late. Too late for what?

She had no idea. All the same, some nameless fear tickled her senses and tapped restless fingers across her spine. Her head swiveled, checking her surroundings once, and then again. She forced herself to stay, clawing past her sudden anxiety, to take another dozen or so artistically arranged photographs of the bedroom. It would be questionable if there were none in the finished portfolio.

With that done, in careful, measured strides, she left Tanbee House, locking up everything nice and tight. She stood at the gate for a beat, catching a glimpse of the patrol car as it rounded the corner. What would happen when Marc Curry's crew dismantled the wall and discovered the drugs? Would they be retrieved by then? Would the authorities get involved? They might have to shut down production.

Seraphina didn't know the answer to any of those questions. Nor did she have any idea if she'd done the right thing. Technically, by telling Oliver, she'd reported finding the drugs to the authorities. But even she wasn't naïve enough to believe spying for him was considered the "proper" channels. Her mind ran through a litany of potential laws she was breaking.

Eventually, she flung the worries away and strode toward the busiest street in the area, where a cab could be easily hailed. She'd answer for her crimes, if it came to that. Of course, another part of her was shaking its head at her lack of faith. Oliver and Kay would never abandon her to fend for herself. She should know better than that.

* * * *

Grant didn't realize the depth of the tension coiled inside him until Seraphina slipped into the restaurant. A sigh escaped him, one he hoped Kathleen hadn't heard, and he waved, greeting her with a warm smile. Kathleen perked up when she noticed, and began bobbing her head to catch sight of their final party guest.

The three of them were seated equal spaces apart at a small round table that allowed an intimacy for close conversation. Grant had been careful to avoid making anyone feel like a third wheel. Himself included.

He smiled wryly at Kathleen's beaming face, her cheeks bunched into perfect round apples from the force of her smile. Her face was flushed a rosy pink with delight. Today, she wore a dress he'd given her as an early birthday gift, since she'd already donned her very best the day she met Seraphina. He couldn't have her attend her own party wearing anything second best. She adored the sweater top, white with fat yellow roses, and the thick yellow cotton skirt that went with it. He might've lost touch with how to talk to Kathleen—really talk to her, the way that Seraphina did so naturally—but he had his mother's taste in clothing down to a fine science.

As a greeting, Kathleen reached over and held one of Seraphina's hands for a beat. The smile shared between them sent something warm and somehow foreign sliding around in Grant's chest. He squirmed, unable to pinpoint what had made him suddenly uneasy. No, not uneasy. Nor easy, exactly. Something undefinable. For now, he put it from his mind as just another tick on the list of new and strange things Seraphina made him feel.

"Ladies, plan on a light breakfast. Because dinner is going to be a doozy. You're not going to be hungry again for a good, long while." He winked at Kathleen, knowing she'd get a kick out of such funny words coming from his mouth. When the waitress came around, he allowed his mom to write out her drink order, because it made her feel better to do so. He didn't begrudge her what independence she could manage.

But when it came to the food, he stepped in, ordering family style. He chose three appetizers, always carefully keeping Kathleen in mind. Stewed brussel sprouts and prosciutto sounded atrocious, but he noted Kathleen's small approving nod as he added it to his request. Twice-baked sweet potatoes with honey butter, and after conferring with Seraphina, a fruit and cheese platter. After that, he added entrees and sides on a whim. Rosemary pot roast and roasted root vegetables, a favorite of Kathleen's. Shrimp scampi, barbeque shredded brisket, fresh tomato and pesto gnocchi, and lemon pepper and dill salmon. He added a bowl of fresh pickled vegetables, a basket of soft potato rolls, creamy grits with smoked cheddar, and collard greens and ham. His last request before the waitress scampered off was a stack of small plates, for passing and sharing, and the dessert menu.

"It's a lot," he confessed to Kathleen's consternation. Seraphina's expression mirrored Kathleen's thoughts, eyebrows high on her forehead. "It's a party," he reminded them. "Besides, I'm sure you wouldn't mind taking any leftovers home with you for tomorrow. Not that the meals at Heritage Acres are anything to sniff at, of course."

Seraphina smiled when Kathleen shrugged and nodded affably. She scrawled a note. Thank you, Grant.

"You misspelled 'you're welcome.'" The quip won him another smile. He'd never seen her smile so much. She always had a happy, lighthearted disposition. She always appreciated his small jokes, and effortlessly lightened the moods on days when he came to her with a heavy heart or burdened mind. But today, Kathleen shone like the sun, sweeping her beaming smile over the whole world. She scribbled again. It's all one and the same.

He shrugged at that. As if somehow taking her out to dinner for her birthday made up for the years she'd taken care of him. That it seemed so effortless to earn her gratefulness almost made him ashamed. Why didn't he do things like this more often? He couldn't recall when he'd stopped being her burden, and she'd become his.

Seraphina didn't help matters, the way she genuinely embraced Kathleen and enjoyed her company. Then he recalled that Kathleen was something of a novelty to her; a wise older woman, with a ready smile and a good heart. Any envy he harbored at how quickly the two of them became friendly dissipated then and there.

Their round of iced teas was delivered, with thick wedges of lemon clinging to the lips of their glasses. Seraphina took a sip through the straw, her pale, round blue eyes open wide and sweeping from Grant to Kathleen. "Okay. I was going to wait but I just can't."

She leaned to one side, her face disappearing as she ducked and rummaged through her purse. She came up with a small rectangular item, slightly bigger than her palm, and wrapped in garish paper. "I'm nervous. I won't be able to relax until I give you your gift."

She handed the package to Kathleen, who took it with a shy smile, slightly shaking her head. She set the present down to pick up her pen, but Seraphina stopped her. "No, please. I know you're going to say something incredibly sweet, and it'll just make me feel awful if I got this wrong."

Grant had an idea of what the gift might be. The shape and apparent heft was telling. He was both chagrined and shocked at himself for not thinking of it first. Years ago, in fact. "Go ahead, Mom," he urged.

It was strange to watch his self-assured mother fumble with the paper self-consciously. He wondered when the last time she'd been given a gift by someone who wasn't him. Kathleen's eyebrows gathered in puzzlement as she withdrew the big, black cell phone, the size of a small tablet, from the wrapping.

Seraphina flushed red. "I hope you like it. This one is special, because I modified it. See?" She showed Kathleen a brilliant yellow button on the side. "That's an on and off button," she explained. "Just one press. And once you turn it on, there's a screen with a single icon."

Kathleen grinned as the screen lit up at the press of the button, seemingly delighted the device had responded to her command. The grin stretched her mouth wider, and she held up the screen to show Grant. One icon. A fat yellow notepad and blue pen.

"Just a tap with your finger." Seraphina's careful guidance was patient. "A new screen comes up. See? A list of names. Right now, there's just two. Me and Grant."

His mom held the phone up to show him again, her confusion gone now. A few taps of her finger, and she'd come to the list. And there was his name, just above Seraphina's.

Seraphina finally smiled, relieved by Kathleen's easy handling of the device. It was a bit large for her hands, but no larger than the pad of paper she carried with her. And for the sake of Kathleen's eyesight, it would need to be a bit large. Seraphina pointed to Grant's name. "Then you tap whichever name you like to open up a conversation. I checked with Heritage Acres, they've got Wi-Fi. So, no matter where you are, or what time it is, you can talk to Grant." She shrugged humbly. "Or me. Any time at all."

Kathleen's eyebrows gathered again, but this time in concentration. She set the device down and leaned over it, typing with her fingers as if the flat digital keyboard were a typewriter, although slowly as her hands adjusted to the size. Food arrived, and still she typed, slowly and carefully, as Grant and Seraphina arranged the dishes and small plates around the table.

Grant handed Kathleen a plate with a pile of brussel sprouts and mashed up sweet potatoes at the same time she tapped the 'send' button and sat back, pleased with herself.

Seraphina had just picked up her fork when her phone jingled. She pulled it from an inside pocket of the soft brown blazer she wore. Her eyes scanned the screen, and then she was laughing girlishly, her head tossed back, and her free hand reaching for Kathleen's. "Well." And that was all she said, after a judicious throat clearing.

Grant looked from one woman to the other. "Well?"

With a surreptitious glance at Kathleen, Seraphina showed him the message.

My friend Bettie has one of these and she lets me type her messages sometimes. She likes to send pictures of little red rockets to Mr. Bill.

He felt his face flush and ducked his head to hide the burning blush. Well, indeed. He had no idea Kathleen knew what an emoji was, let alone that she had some little old lady friend up to date on the, uh, peculiarities of sexting. The devious twinkle in Kathleen's eyes as she delicately scooped a bite of sweet potato informed him she was not ignorant as to what the red rocket implied.

He rubbed his face and blinked at Seraphina as she giggled into her napkin. Her face was red, too, but for an entirely different reason than his own. Such a pair they made.

And there it was. That moment. The moment. A moment he'd recall for the rest of his life.

He loved her. He looked around himself, at Kathleen, happily tapping away on her new device, gleeful in her ability to communicate on a brand new level, a level denied her for years. At any time, she could reach out. He looked to Seraphina, who maybe didn't realize how open she became in Kathleen's presence. Her edges softened, her careful poise relaxed. Grant swung his gaze from one to the other and saw a family forming, bonds reaching and stretching, effortlessly breaking through erected barriers. Suddenly, he couldn't think of anything he wanted more than to make Seraphina apart of his family. It was a small circle, damaged by old hurts, one that only someone who knew something of that sort of pain could fill. They could heal together. They could heal each other.

He gazed at Seraphina wonderingly, acknowledging the uneasiness he'd felt earlier; a response, he realized, to his heart tumbling over in his chest.

She caught his stare and cocked her head. "What?"

"I think we should do this more often, that's all."

Kathleen took a break from her tapping to glance up and nod. Seraphina's phone jingled again. She read, then smiled up at Kathleen. "You're welcome, of course. I'm so glad you like it. Right now, there's only the messaging app, but there are games and other programs you can add. I can stop by anytime and fix it up however you like. Bigger letters or a different background picture."

Kathleen tapped out another message, a faint smile on her face as she did so.

Seraphina's phone pinged. "Hm. Well, I'm glad Bettie will have you to message when she has insomnia. You should know, I don't sleep well, myself. If you ever find yourself staring at the ceiling in the wee hours of the night, you might try me."

Kathleen nodded gratefully to that, but Grant doubted she'd do it. "You could text me, too. Any time, ever." Him, now, she might feel no qualms about disturbing in the middle of the night.

The rest of the meal went by in an easy companionship Grant couldn't recall feeling in a good, long while. Maybe not since his college days, when he'd had a group of friends he saw regularly. He didn't have many friends these days, and if he had, there was little spare time for him to indulge in their company. He went nuts and ordered every slice of cake on the dessert menu, which the three of them passed around and around, debating whether the chocolate tart was better than the cheesecake. He wallowed in the high color on Kathleen's cheeks and her girlish bashfulness when a circle of wait staff arrived to sing "Happy Birthday," their voices carrying across the entire dining room.

He was almost shocked to realize they'd spent nearly two hours at dinner. He decided it had been, all said, one of the best days in a very long time. It wasn't every day, after all, that a man realized he was hopelessly in love, or found himself surrounded by happy women. One who loved him, and one who could learn to. His heart ached for the possibilities today represented, a future where days like today were commonplace instead of blips on the straight line of his existence.

A shuttle from Heritage Acres arrived to take Kathleen home. She hugged him hard around the neck, and Seraphina, too, mouthing her thanks more than once. She wedged her new cell phone down in the purse where she held her old pen and pad.

He and Seraphina stood on the corner a short while later, uselessly hailing cab after cab as they whizzed by without seeming to notice.

"Walk?" she suggested after one more failed attempt.

Grant nodded. A cab would be quicker, but they weren't so far from Seraphina's apartment. From there, he'd try again for a cab. He sighed. "I can't believe I never thought to do that for her."

Seraphina shrugged. "It was a gamble. I had no idea she had any kind of experience. Most of her generation don't have any use or desire for technology." She laughed softly. "I'm going to carry that message about the red rockets with me until I die."

He rubbed his forehead. "Oh, God. Don't remind me, please. I'm working hard to expunge that part of the meal from my memory banks."

That only made her laugh harder. "I just, you know, I was thinking of her the other day. And I wanted to let her know it." She paused and sniffed. "I thought how nice if I could send her a quick note. Or call her. Sometimes, it's nice to hear you're on someone's mind. And it came to me that a text isn't so different from her written messages, if she could figure out the program."

Grant nodded and they walked along in silence. The streets had abandoned their usual hurry and bustle as the sun disappeared behind the towers of downtown. At night, the city seemed a different place. He was reminded of their first dinner date gone awry, and smiled.

"Listen, Seraphina. I want to…" He paused. He had no idea how to tell her he wanted to help her investigate Brendan without giving away Ophelia's whole operation. He realized he had no way to explain that he knew what was going on, and wanted to come down on her side. "Um, well, I want to bring up the, uh…it just seems like maybe there's something going on." He regretted that his words made the laughter fall away from her face completely, and morphed her expression into a guarded one. He fumbled for the way in, like feeling his way through a dark, unfamiliar room. "It's just...you've been distant. And focused, but more than just overseeing Marc's deconstruction of the site. He says you're there often, even though you needn't be. I wanted to tell you that whatever it is, I'm here. And I don't know if it's the kind of thing you require help with..." He swallowed, hoping he wasn't going too far. "But I'm willing. To help, that is. With anything."

At some point, they'd quit walking. Seraphina turned away from him, worrying her lip. He watched her as a light breeze blew the ends of her hair around her shoulders. A tortuously long moment passed. When she met his eyes finally, hope sparked. But then her gaze narrowed, and she glanced away with a heavy sigh. "No, thanks. I won't insult your intelligence by pretending something hasn't snagged my attention. But it's nothing you should worry about." Her smile was a ghost of the usual thing, not reaching her eyes.

He nodded his acceptance. His heart fell to realize she didn't trust him, and his frustration mounted. Not with Seraphina.

Ophelia was to blame. And he resolved to confront her.

He had his first opportunity late the next morning. A quick text had Ophelia waiting in his inner office by the time he arrived. He greeted her with a nod and shook off his coat. "We need to discuss the plan."

"Oh?" Ophelia's eyebrows rose challengingly, and her mouth was a firm line. She disapproved already and she hadn't heard anything yet.

Grant didn't care. He took his chair and leaned back, straightening and choking up his tie. "Seraphina doesn't trust me."

"She doesn't need to."

He bit back the reply that wanted to launch from his tongue. Ophelia wouldn't care about the personal nature of his concern. If he was going to force her to concede, he'd have to do it on terms she'd understand. "Does it not undermine what we're trying to accomplish if Seraphina decides I'm working with Brendan, or that I know what's going on and am doing nothing to address criminal activity happening right in front of my eyes?"

Ophelia shook her head and started for the door. "Grant, I understand your concern. But Seraphina's suspicions about you are not what I'm worried about, and they're not what could undo this whole thing. In fact, it's as good as we could hope for that she's distanced herself from you while she's looking into the activities at Tanbee House. It means that Brendan doesn't suspect your involvement, and that is paramount. Because you're the tip of the iceberg, Mr. Gallagher. Seraphina's suspicion, he expects. If she starts digging around, asking questions…well, that's no surprise. She's not Oliver. She's not a threat to Brendan, as far as he's concerned. He's a career criminal. I'm sure he intends to run clever little circles around her. Her sniffing around is a joke. But you're another matter. If you're always at her side, he'll conclude you've decided she's right about him. That's best-case. Worst? He begins to suspect he's been set up."

She didn't wait for his response, and he was almost glad. Because at the moment, he didn't have one. At least not one Ophelia would appreciate. He'd get nowhere through her. But there were other parties to whom he could make his case.

And would. He rose again, donning his coat once more. He waved to Annie as he stalked past her. "Hold my calls. Cancel my meetings."

He grinned at the string of polite curses that followed him out the door.

Chapter 14

Grant stood on the front porch, marveling at the size of the huge old Victorian and wondering why on earth two people needed such a massive home. What did Kay Bing and Oliver Pierce do with all the extra space? Unless they were planning on opening a bed and breakfast or having a passel of kids, then maybe they'd require such a sizable home. He couldn't decide if it was rude to ask or not.

Oliver answered the door. Light green eyes held him in a steady gaze. "Hello." There was a hint of question in the greeting.

Grant cocked his head at that, amused. "Come now, Mr. Pierce. You know who I am. You might even guess why I'm here."

All pretense of confusion fled. Oliver grinned and sighed heavily. "Guess you better come on in. Wouldn't do for someone to see you here."

"Someone named Brendan Berkley," Grant dared as soon as they were inside the foyer, safely behind the closed door.

Oliver regarded him as his amusement faded. "Or any one of the people he works with, who may or may not have been recognized by our tech team as they rode slowly past my house, or trailed me on public streets. I'm watched all the time. By my people, and a few of his."

His boyish impression hid the tension well, but upon closer inspection, Grant noted the lines of strain around Oliver's eyes. "Then I owe you an apology. But I took precautions."

Oliver shrugged and walked away. "The department's put out word I left town, so I'm not technically here, anyway. We haven't seen any movement in the last week around the house. And we have contingencies in place. Be prepared to hire Free Leaf Concepts for your interior green needs, should word get out you stopped by."

"Understood." He followed Oliver through a well-lit foyer, paneled in rich oak. "Original hardwood?"

Oliver glanced back with a grin. "Kay would be utterly delighted to hear you ask. Yes. She refurbished it herself."

"I wouldn't live up to my reputation if I didn't notice floors like these. They're incredible. I could tell they were old, but the condition is almost startling."

They entered a gorgeous high-end kitchen in shades of pure white and soft blues. Oliver's grin widened as Grant stood in the doorway and whistled. "Yeah, Kay did this, too. Design and most of the dirty work."

Grant sat where Oliver motioned toward a chair at a high granite bar. A moment later, a glass of lemonade slid toward him. "Thanks."

"Eh." Oliver shrugged. "It's the kind of kitchen that compels one to be a gracious host." He didn't join Grant at the bar, but poured himself a lemonade, took a long sip, then settled against the counter. "What's this about, Grant?"

The question was affable enough, but Oliver couldn't entirely hide his anxiety. Grant made him nervous. "Seraphina." A direct answer for a direct question. Oliver only hitched his eyebrows slightly, so Grant continued. "I understand the position I'm in and the part I play. I understood that when I agreed to do this. But as you know, there are always unforeseen circumstances and concerns that crop up in any big venture, especially one relying so heavily on everyone doing what they're supposed to do. For example, if Brendan hadn't applied at Gallagher Interiors following our takeover of his stash house. Or if Seraphina had turned down the Tanbee House job."

"I hear she nearly lost it. To a guy named Roper."

Annoyed, Grant met Oliver's stare with a hard one of his own. "I still have a business to run. Seraphina would've been assigned Tanbee House, regardless. At the time, I wanted to ensure I had Roper's services under contract for the job. Circumstances intervened, and here we are."

Oliver only sighed wearily in response.

"Look, I'm more than happy to be a part of the team that takes down Brendan Berkley and the jerks he's working with. But I did not agree to do so at a personal loss."

"Personal loss? What do you have to lose here, Grant? Your company is working on the most extensive sting orchestrated in decades by law enforcement in this area, an operation the entire city from the governor to the city planning commission has some small part in. You stand to gain a great deal."

He repeated himself. "Seraphina."

The other man shook his head. "You can't appear to be helping her."

Grant should've guessed. "Ophelia's been in touch."

"My captain and I are running this thing from the opposite sides of the state, all for the sake of keeping Brendan in the dark. If he gets wind of any weird vibes, or becomes suspicious, Seraphina is the only thing we have to hang his misgivings on. She's critical. Brendan knew going in that she was employed with you, and she's a risk he'll have accounted for."

"Meanwhile, she can't decide if I'm involved or not," Grant shot at him. "She doesn't trust me. I'm only asking for the ability to let her know she can. She's not a stupid woman, and she knows Brendan is up to something. But I hired him, and I put him on the team to give him access to Tanbee House. My general contractor is pretty sure she's found Brendan's stash—" He stopped as Oliver nodded confirmation.

"She's in," Oliver said. "Seraphina got us a sample and photographic evidence last night. We know Curry will discover the drugs today if he stays on schedule, which means Brendan will have moved them by now. We kept him out of Tanbee House just long enough to give Seraphina time to do what we needed her to do, which is be my link to the investigation, without tipping off Brendan."

"Just arrest the bastard already."

"That's not the plan, Grant. I have only indirect contact with the team running this, so I couldn't make that call if I wanted to. That's why every step has been so meticulously planned, and must be carried out with the same precision. There are too many moving parts to throw a wrench now. Besides, we don't want to bust him moving the stash. We want to see where he takes it next. But in the meantime, we're garnering what we need to make an arrest and a charge that'll stick when the time comes. He's not slipping past me again."

"Well, if the drugs are gone, Seraphina will guess Brendan figured out how to access them. And even more good reason to question my involvement. I've made it all a little too easy for Brendan. Maybe even Brendan will see that."

Oliver shook his head. "You've played your part well, Grant. And I'm sorry, man, but I have to ask you to keep playing it. For a while, we worried you getting cozy with Seraphina would make Brendan nervous, but because you stood up for him so well the night he ran into you, we've seen no deviations from what we expected of his movements."

"How do you know all this, if you're so far removed from your own investigation?"

"Carrier pigeons." He laughed at the look on Grant's face. "Not quite, but close. I can get information, but I can't give new directives. I can't do anything but sit here and hide and hope we're right that Brendan would feel more secure going after the drugs if he thought I were out of town. So far, no pigeon has arrived to tell me anything. But then, maybe you'll hear before I do."

Grant narrowed his eyes, confused. Then his phone rang, and Oliver smiled wide. Grant glanced at Marc Curry's name before answering briskly. "Marc. What do you need?"

"Boss. We found something pretty strange behind one of the walls."

His gaze slammed into Oliver's. "Yeah? What?"

"You should come see this for yourself." The man's voice lowered. "She just got here."

"I think I'll do that. Thanks for letting me know." He ended the call and gave Oliver an appraising look. "They found something. But Marc's reaction doesn't suggest drugs, but something less incriminating."

Oliver didn't ask any questions but rose and took their nearly full glasses and set them by the sink. "I suppose I should keep my eyes peeled for a pigeon today."

At the door, before walking out, Grant faced Oliver. "You're telling me you didn't go outside the rulebook during your investigation into Free Leaf Concepts? Because some might question how Kay got involved."

Oliver pressed his lips together and conceded. "I perhaps unwisely involved a civilian with whom I may or may not had developed feelings for in my investigation, 'tis true."

Grant nodded knowingly. "Then you understand."

In an instant, he knew Oliver did. But the pity in his gaze didn't outweigh the determination. "The main difference is that Free Leaf was my investigation. I had the power to make the call. Unfortunately, the deal you signed on for doesn't give you that kind of leeway. This isn't your boardroom and you're not calling the shots. Besides, Seraphina is pretty dead set on bringing Brendan down. If you were the one who ruined it, I'm not sure she'd agree the ends justify the means."

Grant rubbed his jaw thoughtfully. "Maybe not. I'm not sure why she takes this so personally. Like Brendan is doing all this to spite her."

Oliver shrugged, but his smile widened. "It is personal. For me and for Kay. And that makes it personal for Seraphina. Because that's the kind of person she is. I mean, yeah, she's kind of imperious and scary. Threatening, one might say, in the right light. You should've seen her playing mama bear when she thought I was using Kay. But…well, there you go. Mama bear. Brendan messed with Kay. Now, he's gonna have to deal with Seraphina." Grant sighed and ran a hand through his hair. "I don't like that she feels like some sort of lone crusader. Like she can't trust me. And I'm not allowed to do anything about it. But if it's the way, then it's the way. Suppose you're right, and she'll thank me more for the deception than if I screw up the operation and Brendan slips like smoke through your fingers again. I commend you. If it were me, I feel like a bird in a cage. You should be out there running him down. Must take quite a bit of willpower to hold yourself back."

"You don't believe it's my idea to sequester myself like this, do you? I'm taking one for the team, Grant." Oliver clapped him on the shoulder, the friendly gesture at odds with the bitter edge of the words. "I know you are, too. And so is Seraphina. If you think it sucks that she'll suspect you of being a criminal for a little while, imagine how pissed she's going to be when I admit I was behind this whole charade. Between her and Kay, there's a good chance the next time we meet will be at my funeral."

* * * *

Seraphina caught the tail end of Marc's call, swiftly putting together who he spoke to. A few specific murmured words sent intuition roiling through her.

There were times when she believed women's intuition a simple misnomer that curious, nosey women liked to claim. If you seek, so shall ye find. But she couldn't discount the few times in her life when her bones seemed to know something before her mind came around to noticing it, and a truth unveiled itself through no effort on her part. In this case, Marc's tone and timing drew clues together like a hook caught on a string, dragging the ends together until they made the neatest of bows.

Seraphina turned away from the hubbub in the bedroom, where a thick crowd of crewmen gathered around the wall they'd torn down. They were arguing about whether or not they had damaged the rare find with their swinging sledgehammer. The man with the hammer disagreed. She stepped close to Marc, close enough to threaten his personal space. "You've been watching me for him."

Marc's eyes grew hooded, and he kept his gaze on his phone. "I've been keeping an eye on my worksite. It's my job."

Seraphina felt the muscles in her jaw work. "You've been reporting to Grant. Specifically about me. Don't deny it. I'm going to call you both out the moment he arrives, and he won't appreciate your cowardice. Why does he have you watching me?"

The truth was plain in the lines of Marc's frown.

Her intuition had struck true. "What cause could I give Grant to spy on me?"

She hadn't expected Marc to answer, but he surprised her with one. Well, as much of an answer as he could give, at any rate, accompanied by the shrug of one shoulder. "I don't know. He asked to keep an eye on you, that's all. Not to interfere or ask questions, but to let him know when you were here and what you were working on. So there, that's what I've done. Now, you want to know why, you ask Mr. Gallagher, because I don't know, and I wasn't dumb enough to ask. Mr. Gallagher isn't the kind of man you question. Not if you're just one of the hard hat boys, anyway."

Seraphina rubbed her eyes, disbelief warring with indignation. "Do you even know what was found back there in the wall?"

Marc's cheeks wrinkled as his mouth spread into a sort of considering grimace. "Not a damn clue. But it looked heavy, old, and valuable. I have them pulling away as much of the wall as they can so we can get a better look." He gestured at the camera hanging around her neck. "You might want to get a few pictures while the thing's still where we found it."

Brendan. He'd found a way inside and removed the drugs.

Her jaw clenched, she left Marc standing apart from the group and entered the bedroom. For just a moment, she drew the parallel between elbowing her way into the crush of men inside the room, and her forceful determination and unwavering conviction that Brendan was involved in this and she was going to prove it. She blinked back frustration. It wasn't her job to prove Brendan's guilt. She was a designer, not a detective.

The man who'd been swinging the sledgehammer fervently denied he'd touched the damn thing, and declared loudly to the room at large that he wouldn't be held responsible for a chip in something over two hundred years old.

Seraphina frowned at that. Gradually, the men began to clear out as she elbowed more and more of them aside for a clear picture. Enough of the wall had been torn away now for her to get several good shots of what appeared to be the base of an antique brass candle holder.

Behind her, Marc called for his men to file out. As the room cleared and quieted around her, Seraphina began pulling pieces of splintered wall away from the supporting beams. Marc joined her. Without a word, he gingerly grabbed the base of the candelabra and began to gently work it out and away from the wall. After a few moments, he pulled the base free, and the rest followed. He held the candleholder upright for their mutual inspection.

Seraphina took several photos. "That's different," she murmured. The candelabra was cunningly wrought brass shaped into a pair of cherubs joined at the hip and their feet gathered to create the base. Their arms rose up separately, creating two hollows for candles.

She noticed how the surface shined, odd given the apparent age, then wanted to smack herself. Of course the candelabra was shiny. Not dim from being stuck inside a wall since the seventies, because it had only been there since the drugs were removed. If the item were part of the official investigation of Brendan Berkley, a discerning detective would note the irregularity. Unfortunately, Seraphina was all they had. She wondered, not for the first time, how in the hell such important things had come to depend on her inept handling.

Marc shrugged. "I don't know much about candlesticks. I'm more than happy to let this be your problem."

She realized with a pang just how big of a problem it was. She also recalled Brendan's eavesdropping. Seraphina heaved a sigh and pulled her cell phone free of her jacket pocket as Marc left the room. She dialed Oliver.

"Hey."

"Hey, yourself. So, we knew our guy was on a tight schedule." She peered after Marc's retreating form through the open doorway as he walked the length of the library. Confident she wouldn't be overheard, she didn't dissemble. "Brendan had to get the drugs out before today. He did more than take them. He made a trade." She described the ornate candleholder in detail for the confused detective.

"That's not passing strange."

"Some kind of ploy, maybe?" She bit her lip. She had other suspicions.

Oliver's voice sounded tired. "Or a damn head game. His way of letting you know he's playing, too, and already a step ahead of you."

The slow smile curving her lips surprised her. "So he may think."

"Exactly. We can swing this two ways. You can feign shock at the discovery..."

"Or irritation?" she suggested. "Brendan should expect this to confuse and exasperate me. I was hoping the crew would find his drugs, after all. Tell me, were you able to catch the guy who did the swap? I can't fathom Brendan would risk his own neck."

"You fathom correctly. I received a message that the lackey Brendan dispatched was picked up a few hours later. He no longer had the drugs on him, so they suspect a dead-drop nearby. So far, the guy won't turn on Brendan. He claims he wanted to poke around Tanbee House for materials to swipe." He loosed a frustrated groan. "As per usual, we're left with a token piece of circumstantial evidence."

Seraphina hefted the candelabra. "Maybe not." The loose ends of an idea tickled her brain, but was too vague. She'd need time to think. "The candleholder isn't so rare as to be one of a kind, but it's unique enough we might trace its sale. What should I do with this thing? It's evidence, right?"

"Yeah, but not yet. Not until the team moves on Brendan. I'm going to reach out and see if we have enough for a search warrant yet. Your drug sample and photographs might be enough to sway a judge. They don't mind circumstantial evidence when it comes to search warrants. But they're real sticklers at trial." He paused, and when he spoke again, the words were weighted with something like despair. "Securing the warrant is a double-edged boon. If nothing comes from the search, we'll have given away our game to Brendan. Ultimately, it's the captain's call. In the meantime, hang onto our evidence until we can rightfully call it evidence. Snap a few photos for me, too. Don't seem too interested in the candle thingy, or give Brendan the impression we think we might be able to use it against him. He wouldn't have used anything that could come back to bite him, so I have some pretty serious doubts the candlestick will be any use to us. But I'd be a shit detective if I didn't exhaust every avenue."

She had no idea how Oliver could stand his chosen profession. She couldn't imagine spending day in and day out trying to worm her mind through the crooked thoughts of crooked men. "You got it. I'll swing by the drugstore and print what I've got on my storage card and bring photos by tonight. Kay gave me the whole speech on insecure e-mails."

"That's my girl. But not tonight. This close on the heels of the discovery, we shouldn't risk you being caught here. For all I know, Brendan's hip to the fact that I didn't actually leave town. Chill for a few days, give Brendan time to relax, and me time to find out our next move. In fact, you should communicate through Kay after this. If I can, I'll send a runner for the photographs."

"I probably should've called her to begin with." The scrape of heavy boots falling heavy on wooden planks sounded behind her. "Gotta go."

She didn't wait for a reply, but punched the button to end the call. Soon, crewmen were trickling back into the bedroom, sledgehammer guy taking possession of his tool once again. She backed out of the room, clasping the dirty candelabra to her breast like a child.

Still, a half-formed thought niggled at her. She put it away, and focused instead on how best to confront Grant. So far, her apprenticeship was off to a rocky start. But she couldn't in good conscience continue working with Grant if her suspicions were true. She was more inclined to believe he was in cahoots with Brendan with each passing tick of the clock. The possibility would be disastrous for her, professionally or personally. It would be just her luck to find herself falling in love with a criminal.

* * * *

"How do we keep ending up back here?" Grant rubbed his cheeks, not hiding his despair. It was late. Barefoot and wearing only black sweatpants, he felt somehow vulnerable and at a disadvantage. Meanwhile, Seraphina stood at his door in a fine temper. Her steel-gray pea coat and towering heels were like battle armor. He'd waved her inside with a dispassionate shake of his head.

No one told him how trying this would be. Nor advised him on how to avoid Seraphina's confrontations. She did more than suspect him now; she very nearly accused him outright of involving himself in Brendan Berkley's more nefarious activities.

"For what other reason would you set a watchdog on me?" With the ease of someone in comfortable territory, Seraphina stalked into the living room and tugged off her coat, laying it across the back of the couch. He wondered idly if she realized how freely she moved in his space. "I don't believe it's anything to do with my job. This spying is personal, somehow."

"Look, be pissed off if you want, but consider my position. You mentioned trust. Well, you could've trusted me with the truth when I asked for it, Seraphina. I trust you to do your job. But sneaking around a construction site and getting in the way of my crew...that's not behavior a man like me lets go uninvestigated. Today, Roper told me you thought you might find something inside Tanbee House. Him, you trust. Me, you lied to."

He knew the answer. It struck him as fatalistic to ask. But ask he must, lest she decide he already knew the answer. He had to play his part for Seraphina as well as he'd done for Brendan.

Her response was to glower. "I didn't lie. I asked you to trust me, and I insinuated to Roper that you had an idea of what I was about and were letting me do my thing. Apparently, I didn't convince him, nor was I right about you."

"If you see it that way, then yeah, I guess you were wrong. But if you were in my shoes, you'd have done the same thing. And I didn't ask Marc to spy on you. I only asked him to alert me when you were on site, and to mention anything that seemed weird or off. Like the camera you started hauling around."

He should stop there. Part of him wanted to press her until she caved and offered him the opportunity to earn her trust. Some other rebellious part wanted to push until he saw for himself how deeply her distrust went. And yet another far smaller part of him knew he was risking the investigation to push her so blatantly into opening up. Taking one for the team. The reminder didn't settle the sourness in his gut or assuage his guilt or self-pity.

"I have my reasons," she said through gritted teeth. "The candelabra is an antique. It's worth something, perhaps. I should look into it." She started to say something more, then paused as if rethinking the decision. "Actually, the candle thing is probably junk. I'd like to hang onto it, though."

But of course. She'd like to keep Oliver's evidence safe. Oliver had probably asked her to. And Grant could admit nothing. He waved her off as if none of this mattered at all. "Whatever you like. You're the woman in charge."

Seraphina's blue eyes pierced him like small knives as she studied him. He regarded her openly. Although he was hiding something, he didn't feel guilty or furtive. The difference lay in that he was looking for any excuse to put it all out in the open. She was the one intent on keeping secrets. If she spilled and confessed everything, he'd match her and put her concerns to rest, laying the blame for his silence firmly at Oliver's feet. But after both Oliver and Ophelia warned him, he couldn't be the one to break the silence between himself and Seraphina. He'd respond to her outreached hand, because he'd owe her compensation for the trust she'd have to put in him, but he couldn't—wouldn't—break character for the sake of his own vanity.

And that's all it was, he realized. Seraphina thought he was a bad guy, and it rubbed him raw, even if her misconception was a wrong he would eventually have the opportunity to right.

He smiled halfheartedly at her continued scrutiny. She seemed lost in her own thoughts. If her expression was any indication, they weren't good ones. "Have you eaten? I made red beans and rice. I used turkey sausage instead of kielbasa, but it's decent."

Like pulling the stopper from a tub, the tension leaked from Seraphina. Her gaze fell away, and she sighed almost piteously to herself. "Food sounds nice."

Later, they sat together on the sofa. Seraphina had kicked off her heels, and their feet tangled together. They watched old reruns of Buffy and stayed up late, hardly speaking. Despite the contention between them, a pull still existed. Grant just hoped it would still be there when all was said and done, and the secrets between them were laid bare.

Chapter 15

Seraphina faced the dark of the pre-dawn hours to reach her apartment. She'd learned the hard way Grant did not accept their after-hours activities to excuse tardiness.

Under the steamy water raining from the showerhead, something inside her rattled around uneasily. Last night, she'd gone to accuse Grant of spying on her, a thing he readily admitted to. He'd explained himself, and had only seemed wearied by her offense. And yet, she'd ended the night with him. In his bed and in his arms. The scent of his freshly laundered sheets still clung to her skin. She was split in two, and neither half of herself could condone what the other did.

She couldn't fathom a man as insightful as Grant Gallagher could be ignorant as to what was going on under his very nose. Indeed, having set Marc to spying on her spoke of a man who paid attention and saw between the lines. Yet, he seemed to have an inexplicable blind spot when it came to Brendan.

She couldn't reconcile the two sides of Grant, and in turn, she was becoming split in two. When she was acting on Oliver's behalf, Grant was the enemy. But at the end of the work day, she sought him out as she had no other in her life. She yearned for him, for his company, his companionable silence, his feather soft touch, and his warm gazes. How could she deny him her trust while freely handing him everything else of value she possessed?

She couldn't wrap her mind around her inner divide. Eventually, the investigation would end. If Grant ended up on the bad end of events, she didn't know how she'd ever recover. Maybe she'd keep loving him anyway, just as she kept going to him despite her misgivings. She'd be one of those women who stayed faithful to an incarcerated lover. She'd write him long, endearing letters, and they'd enjoy conjugal visits once a month.

She snickered to herself, impressed she could amuse herself despite her issues. Even so, the imagery was enough to make her think long and hard about her feelings for Grant as hot water sluiced over her, and steam rose to fog the mirrors. She drew uncomfortable parallels between her need for approval from both Grant and her dad. Did she really care about Grant, or was she trying to earn the respect from yet another man who doled it out sparingly?

Her father's abandonment plagued her still. Sometimes, she caught herself checking her phone without knowing why. Or glancing at the calendar to count the days since her last talk with her father, an old habit to keep herself from ignoring him for too long. She squeezed her eyes shut and knotted her fists. Her dad may have left town, but some remnant of him would always be with her, shaking its head in annoyed disappointment.

It wasn't fair or rational to ascribe the attitude to Grant. But no matter how tightly she held to the knowledge, no matter how Grant differed from her father, what remained was how they affected Seraphina. And in that regard, she was the same needy, desperate girl she'd always been, seeking approval even if it came with damaging side effects. She didn't trust Grant, yet she was falling for him. So typical of her. She toweled off and made a complicated decision. She couldn't compromise herself anymore.

An hour later, she found herself standing in front of him in his office.

Today, he had a small smile for her. It was full of fondness and warmth, and a corner of her heart railed at her for what she was about to do. "Good morning," he said amiably, with a short glance at his watch. "I wasn't expecting you. I have a meeting, but I can spare a minute."

Seraphina inhaled deeply and steeled herself. "I don't want to see you anymore."

The open happiness on his face was swept away by a look of confusion that slowly melded into hurt. He didn't even bother fabricating a façade for her sake. He didn't feign carelessness or indifference as she'd expected, but stood and made a swift demand. "Why?"

Why, indeed. She'd wrestled with the answer all morning. Even now, she couldn't be sure if she wasn't merely making excuses out of fear. She had so few close ties. As much as she'd wanted a tight bond with her father, maybe she'd been the one to hold back, after all. It'd take a professional therapist, probably, to sort out her issues, but the clearest thing her mind fastened onto was the vulnerability of her increasing intimacy with Grant.

"Because," she began softly. She paused, licked her lips, and gathered the threads of what she needed to say. "Because I think some part of me is only drawn to you by a need to be validated. I need your approval to feel valued. That need is at odds with my better judgment. Everything in me cries out warnings against this." She vaguely waved her hands between them, exasperated with herself. She could barely think straight, let alone put her mystifying emotions into clean, precise words. "My head says what's between us is bad news, my heart wants to charge blindly ahead. I can't help but question why I'm so torn, why a part of me holds back. And none of the answers make me feel better. If anything, they convince me to reassert my reasoning, and do the wise thing."

Her answer didn't appear to do much for him. He cocked his head to the side, his brows gathered in puzzlement. Then he stood and walked slowly around his desk, pondering as he moved with his usual powerful grace. "You can do better than that. I mean, if you don't like me, that's understandable. I'm not to everyone's taste. If I'm an asshole, well, that's not a bad reason. But needing my approval? That's just silly. No, this comes back to the whole trust thing." He shook his head; his lips were a thin line and his gaze piercing. "I don't know how to convince you I can be trusted. No, that's not true. I could convince you. But there would be costs. And as much as I believe you're worth it, it's simply not my call to make."

She suspected he knew more than he let on about her activities then. "Okay, fine. It's confusing and contradictory to everything else I feel about you. And it casts a parlor on all of my other emotions. I don't trust the thing inside me that draws me to you. And I'll remind you, you've had a man keeping tabs on me, and that's no sign of trust. So all the other stuff can't mean a whole lot. Not if it's missing a crucial piece of the foundation relationships are built on. Even if you can look past that lacking critical ingredient, I can't."

"And I suppose it's too much to ask for you to have faith?" He didn't wait for her reply, perhaps guessing how she'd respond. "Distrust was never my motive behind keeping up with your activity at Tanbee House. Curiosity. Concern. But never distrust."

"Even so, I can't shake the belief that I'm drawn to you for all the wrong reasons."

"Seraphina, there's nothing wrong with wanting validation. It's not a sign of weakness. Rather, it's a very common desire of those who question their abilities or their choices. You think I never doubted myself? Never sought Kathleen's approval for the decisions I was making about my life? Or confirmation from my peers? Even some I didn't admire. Because I placed value in their respect. It's nothing but a compliment to me that you care for my opinion. It means I'm important to you. And it's not so strange you had the same desire for your father to likewise approve of your life. Those aren't parallels anyone should be surprised to find themselves drawing." He came closer and took one of her hands into his. His brilliant blue eyes followed the line of his thumb as he traced it along her skin. "I'm an expert in compartmentalizing. I have to be to run this company with a cool head. When I say I value you as a professional, it is exactly what I mean. I respect you as a designer and as a woman." His gaze came up and met hers with an intensity that stilled her. His voice grew deeper. "If you care so much for my esteem, then don't leave me. I would disapprove most ardently. Because I must admit to a particular bias in your case. For the record, you meet every standard I have, and then some. I value you. I respect you. I care about you. I..."

In the tension-riddled wake of his slight pause, Seraphina's pulse galloped, and time seemed to slow. Her breath held, her muscles froze, and her skin prickled. Foreign sensations assaulted her in that brief space of seconds.

Grant's gaze dropped again, as if he didn't have the nerve to look her in the eyes. A piece of her heart went out to him, because she recognized self-doubt as surely as she felt the hum of truth and earnestness in his words. Still, they were no less of a shock to hear, spoken on a whisper, flavored by his soft laugh.

"I love you. My head and my heart are in complete harmony over the matter, so it's an unpleasant revelation to hear you say yours are in discord."

When she didn't respond, he let go of her hand and stepped away, turning his back to her. His hands slid into his pockets. "Well. You feel how you feel, I suppose. If you'll excuse me, I have a meeting to prepare for. But should your mind ever catch up to your heart, I'm here. Right here."

* * * *

Grant heard the whisper of Sera's shoes on the floor fall away as she left his office. Tension and misery thrummed through him. In a sudden burst of insight, he realized he hated Brendan Berkley to a degree that was almost shocking in its depth. And yet, Grant had signed on for this. And he couldn't regret his involvement, because if he had not hired Seraphina, who'd thus unknowingly brought Brendan and his trouble in her wake, he would not have fallen inexplicably in love with her.

He battled absentmindedness through his morning meetings. He met Roper's concerned glance with a slight shake of his head and begged off a golf game that weekend with an old client.

Finally, the lunch hour came, and he strode into Heritage Acres. His mind came awake, as if he'd been in some kind of trance since Seraphina had left his office that morning. Now, synapses were firing once more, and his pace quickened. Until he saw Kathleen, he hadn't realized his intent. He greeted her with the genuine wide smile she inspired. She met it with only a slight rise of her eyebrows. Her new cell phone was grasped in her hands.

Emma happened to be striding down the hallway and past Kathleen's room as Grant stepped to enter it, and she paused to say hi and wave in at Kathleen. "She doesn't go anywhere without that thing," Emma declared, beaming her approval. "And you might not guess it, but your mom is one of the most popular ladies around. She had a line of folks visiting to get her number, and now she's a veritable social butterfly." She grinned indulgently at Grant, as if they were two proud parents gushing over a prodigal child, and squeezed his arm affectionately. "It was a wonderful gift."

"Thanks," he replied lamely as she walked away. He only felt worse that Seraphina had thought of it before he had. "Hey, Mom." He lowered himself into his seat at the table and nodded appreciatively at today's spread. "The cooks have outdone themselves again."

Summer squash cooked down with milk and onions nestled next to a loaded baked potato generously adorned with sprinkles of bacon, cheddar, and chives, and dollops of butter and sour cream. A thick cut slice of ham covered the other half of his plate. Kathleen's potatoes had been removed from the skin and mashed with sour cream and chives. She'd forgone the ham in favor of a small filet of flaky white fish. She nodded her agreement and used her thumbs to tap out a message.

Grant pulled his phone from his breast pocket in anticipation. He wasn't disappointed. A few seconds later, an incoming text buzzed. Are you okay?

He glanced up at her over the rim of his phone, held aloft. He bit his lip and decided it wasn't worth asking how she'd known something was off. He considered himself adept at keeping his emotions under wrap, but if anyone could see beneath the veneer, it would be his mother.

He sighed and lowered his phone. He scratched his chin and pushed his plate away so he could rest his elbows on the table. Most days, he came for lunch. Today, he'd been driven to Kathleen's side by a desire for someone to help him shed light on Seraphina's decision to turn her back on the bright, tender thing growing between them. "Seraphina doesn't want to see me anymore."

The disappointment in Kathleen's gaze was a prod to the open wound. She tapped furiously, and he was impressed with her speed. So much for old people and new tricks, he thought wryly. Did she say why?

Grant couldn't explain everything. So he wove through the parts he could. "Well, if I eliminate the trust issue as something that can be repaired later—a story I promise to fill you in on at the first available opportunity—and boil everything she said down to the kernel at the center, I can surmise she's scared."

Kathleen nodded.

"I don't blame her." He shrugged. "I don't think she's cowardly or stupid. Hell, that's what makes her appeal so frustrating. I get it. I understand backing out when things start to get uncomfortably real. I've done the same with other women. When they got too cozy." He stopped suddenly, realizing who he was speaking to. He cleared his throat. "That's, uh, more than I intended to share."

Kathleen bent over her phone. She took her time, so Grant cut a corner from his ham and chewed thoughtfully. He was halfway through his baked potato when his phone finally sounded. He wiped his fingers with a napkin and read. Seraphina makes you feel differently? Be sure, Grant. Don't ask her for something you yourself aren't sure you want.

Grant caught himself smiling. "You must enjoy the autocorrect. No more shorthand."

She typed a quick reply with a wide smile. Love it! Then she set the phone aside and began poking at her fish with her fork.

Effectively, she left Grant alone with his thoughts. He rubbed his hands together, then made slow work of ferrying squash from the plate to his mouth. Very slow. His mind churned over the past few weeks.

The tense moments, the companionable silences, and the little details shared; it didn't seem to matter how much he learned about Seraphina, he craved more. They'd danced together in a crowded bar, snuggled deep into thick covers on a Sunday morning, gave and demanded intimate touches, and told secrets and jokes. They'd shared coffee and quick, wry exchanges on a Monday morning at the office, and weary strides to the elevator at the end of a long week. In every capacity, she made him curious and thoughtful, made his very soul hum with her presence.

His phone went off. He realized he'd been staring into space and murmured an apology to Kathleen. The message received wasn't from her, though, but from an unknown local number, but he made a pretty clean guess at the sender.

Word is Saturday is going to be lovely. You and Seraphina should take a long ride out to Lake Pickthorne and see the sights. -O

Grant had no idea if the summons boded well or not. But his heart skipped a beat at the chance to talk to Oliver and Seraphina together. It might finally be time for him to get his chance to come clean, and not a moment too soon. He was convinced if Seraphina knew he was trustworthy, the rest of her concerns about their relationship could easily be put to rest.

A message from Kathleen popped up. Good news or bad? Your face can't seem to decide.

He glanced up with a wry smile. "Maybe a little of both." He put new verve into finishing his meal. "Thanks, Mom. I'm glad you had me ask myself that question. About Seraphina. I realize now I haven't asked her for what I want at all."

* * * *

Kay and Neve bent their heads together and stared at Seraphina with matching smirks. Seraphina rolled her eyes. "Please, stop. Slap-stick comedy is not a tool of persuasion."

Neve picked up her Budweiser. "It's never been properly employed."

"Don't ever tell Neve she can't use something as a weapon," Kay warned.

Seraphina wanted to leave. The bar was nice. Quiet. The drinks were well-made, sweet and not too strong. But she wasn't in the mood for Kay's well-meaning interference. And she definitely wasn't prepared to deal with Neve. She wondered how she'd ever thought the woman was anything like Grant. The two of them couldn't be more different. She almost said as much, but decided it wasn't worth extending the conversation to explain.

The quickest way out was through. She took a fortifying sip of her cranberry vodka and gave Kay a humorless smile. "I appreciate you. I do. You're one of the most important people in my life. But you have to understand that in order to work out my feelings for Grant, I have to go through the fire myself. You can't convince me he's my one true love, and you can't undermine the concerns I've dredged in questioning the relationship. Things with Grant will work out, or they won't, Kay. I know you care about me, you want me to find love and to be happy. But there's only so much a pep talk can do, babe."

She sipped gingerly at her drink while she awaited Neve's soliloquy that inevitably followed anyone's opinion. Even Kay's gaze had shifted to Neve, to see what her response would be. It was as irritating as it was fascinating to witness the pull and magnetism Neve effortlessly wielded.

She shocked Seraphina into dropping her jaw when she shrugged and told Kay, "She's not lying."

Kay blinked slowly a few times. "But...but what if it's love? And she won't even give the guy a chance because of daddy issues?"

"Hey," Seraphina cut in firmly. "I can use that term. When you say it, it's just rude."

"Sorry." Kay lowered her gaze, but only for a fraction of a second. Then her hazel eyes were drilling into Seraphina's. "But—"

"Come on, Kay." Neve patted her hand comfortingly. "It's the reality of relationships. For me and Duke, it was really obvious that I was afraid of the vulnerability that sort of closeness demands. I needed time. Did I really want Duke, or was I just settling for the first man who could stand me, only to get stomped on later when he'd had his fun and wanted to move on? I'm awful. We all know it. I feared he'd eventually want the things he would never find in me. And," she added more kindly, with a knowing look at Seraphina, "When you're not in your early twenties anymore, you lose a bit of that blind, youthful, arrogant belief that you'll always be attractive and alluring. It fades, without warning. One day you wake up and realize you can't count on your fresh face and perky tits to get attention. Naturally, you begin to wonder if what else you've got is enough."

"Exactly." Seraphina's quiet reply seemed to cast them all into somber moods. "I never considered it that way, but I recall the moments I realized I wasn't 'young' anymore. Men's gazes don't linger the way they used to. If something clever doesn't come out of your mouth in the boardroom, they're moving on without a second glance."

"You guys. You're not ancient. Is your age really the problem?"

Kay was incredulous and Seraphina didn't blame her. "No. Not really. But it might have something to do with my waning confidence."

Neve waved her away and took a deep pull from her beer bottle. "It's temporary. There's power in age. A different kind of power than the kind a woman finds in youth." She grinned devilishly. "More potent."

Seraphina believed her and answered with a slight smile. "I'm only a couple years behind you. Good to know it gets better. I just want to be sure I'm going in with my eyes wide open. Not only to be certain that Grant really wants to get involved, because in some respects I think he's surer of this than I am. But we need to go in with the right expectations and for the right reasons."

"And that's wise," Neve said. "I finally realized it wasn't some whim on Duke's part. He'd seen the worst of me and still loved me. Only then could I convince myself to take the leap. Once I decided I wanted in, I couldn't get hitched fast enough. Now the fucker is trapped and going nowhere."

Seraphina sniffed. "As if he wants to." Inexplicably, sweet, earnest Duke Kennicot was hopelessly enthralled by Neve.

"I'm still pretty raw about your eloping." Kay swung her glance between Seraphina and Neve. "This is so weird, but I think you guys are totally clicking right now. Should I leave and let you bond, or do you still need me?"

Neve groaned and Seraphina laughed softly. Her cell phone pinged, the special little noise that she'd chosen to be Grant's notification sound putting a skip in her pulse as she rooted for her phone inside her clutch. She was able to ditch the big bag since she no longer had cause to haul a camera around with her. Her nerves sang as she opened the message.

Mandatory meeting tomorrow. Dress for a picnic.

Short, to the point. Concise. Proper. Everything that was Grant, and yet nothing of the man she'd come to know. If it weren't for their conversation this morning, she could have expected something extra. He might've asked if she'd like to bring a white wine along to make a real date out of the trip. Another message came through. How does one dress for a picnic?

She laughed softly. A wash of fondness swept over her. She missed him. Not because they'd been long parted, more a simple longing for his presence. If she could trade him in for the two women gossiping to each other on the other side of the table, she would. The silliest thought occurred to her then. She could, actually. She was moments away from being at his side, if she wanted it. And she did. Despite every last objection she'd come up with, and even she had to admit some of them were dubious concerns at best.

She bit her lip, argued with herself for what seemed an eternity, and finally replied. Depends. This is a business outing?

His reply seemed long in coming. It is. But not an office matter.

She was confused. So...not tricking me into a date?

No. Related to Tanbee House. I can tell you more when I pick you up.

She was only more confused. Why did they need to leave the city to discuss Tanbee House? But as Grant's messages were short and thin on details, she decided not to push. And if he really wanted her opinion... Those Levi's that fit snug on your hips would be very suitable for a picnic.

Oh God, was she being a tease? She was dismayed and amused by the idea. She'd never considered herself much of a flirt. Or even someone who inspired flirtatiousness in another. Grant made her feel like the sort of woman who was both. His reply was quicker than hers had been. Then might I suggest the blue sundress? Seems picnick-y to me.

A smile stretched her lips. She knew the one. It was almost promiscuously short, with a full, flouncy ruffled skirt and fitted T-shirt style bodice with a scoop-neck. Not exactly a sundress, but she'd ruin the fun by being pedantic.

"Well, now that's a smile."

Seraphina glanced up sharply at Neve's almost predatory grin. She'd almost forgotten where she was. Kay shrugged and nudged Neve. They both looked at Seraphina with mockingly innocent expressions, but spoke as if she weren't there at all. "Do you think she knows?"

Neve nodded. "Classic denial."

Seraphina rolled her eyes. More than ever, she'd like to kick them both to the curb and have Grant in their stead. "Ha-ha, you're hilarious. Two minutes ago, you agreed with me, Neve."

She held up a slender finger. "No. I offered you my understanding. I get it. In no way does that mean I agree with your scaredy-cat tactics. I was a scaredy-cat once. Huge waste of everyone's time."

"I thought we were finally going to get through one drink without you being completely insufferable."

She shrugged, and her brilliant amber gaze didn't waver even a little at Seraphina's thin insult couched in a joke. "I'm a Scorpio. I was born this way."

Seraphina snorted. "I could've guessed if you hadn't told me. Pisces. No wonder we don't jive."

"Right?" Kay concurred. "I'm a Libra. I have no business hanging out with either of you."

"Well, then, allow me to take some small measure to correct the issue." Seraphina slid a pile of bills onto the table. "Drinks on me, ladies. Thanks for coming out and commiserating with me, but I should go. Turns out I have plans tomorrow, and I'd like to get my film developed so they're available when Oliver gets around to asking for them." She frowned. "Or rather, prints off my SD card. You know, I appreciate advances in technology, but there's no elegance in the language."

Kay's pleading gaze turned somber. "I was about to beg you to stay, but that's a good reason to scuttle away, I guess. Not that I'd blame you for bolting because we're overbearing, annoying know-it-alls, desperate to tell you how to live your life." She off-set the remark with a brilliant smile Seraphina couldn't help but return.

"I'll appreciate your meddling eventually. Maybe not tonight, but one of these days."

Neve's grin was as malicious as it was playful. "And I'll accept your apologies and praise of my greater, insufferable wisdom."

"No doubt," Seraphina agreed dryly. God, she hated when that woman was right, but then had to admit Neve filled a niche in her life. Sometimes, it was nice to be around someone who seemed to have all the answers.

Chapter 16

It took all of Grant's self-control not to grin like an idiot when Seraphina stepped off the sidewalk in front of her apartment and slid into the passenger seat. Her dress matched the royal blue paint of the BMW near perfect. As he navigated the city streets and interstates, Seraphina rode silently beside him. Her hands were demure in her lap, her gaze held by scenery flashing by the window.

Once he picked up I-40 East and set the cruise control, she turned to face him. "So, what's this really about?"

She had no idea he had any connection to Oliver, and Grant wasn't ready to reveal that secret. He cursed himself a coward. He wanted backup when Seraphina learned the truth. "Tanbee House. We're going to meet someone who can shed some light on a few of the mysteries we've unearthed. I'll say no more than that."

Her lips were pressed together. The amusement he'd caught in her eyes as she'd folded herself into the car disappeared behind a cautious, intent stare. "I shouldn't go anywhere with you." Her voice was grave and resigned, as if she never had any choice in the matter. She said no more but turned back to the window.

Grant didn't reply because he didn't know what he could say. He hoped Oliver would.

Holland Bottoms State Wildlife Management Area was a well-known area a little more than half an hour from central Little Rock, just on the other side of Jacksonville. It was hemmed in on the western side by Pickthorne Lake, a popular fishing destination, and the Southern Oaks Country Club. The lake had gathered a good crowd for a late Saturday morning. Boats were on the water. Several cars were parked in the lot. Grant drove a slow, fruitless circuit of the parking area, searching for evidence of Oliver, to no avail. Oliver would have to find them.

He parked and met Seraphina's dubious glare. "This isn't much of a picnic area," she noted.

"Oh, I have no intention of having a picnic here. But this is—"

A rap of knuckles across the window at her back made Seraphina jump. Oliver bent down and grinned at them, then waved for them to step outside. Seraphina met Grant's eyes in one quick, shocked moment before she angrily shoved the door open without a word.

Oliver greeted her stony veneer with a friendly hug. "There it is! The face I expected. Good to know I've still got a knack for reading people. Just wait. You don't even know why you're pissed off yet." He swung to Grant as he walked around the car, offering his hand.

Grant shook it with a frown. "There are better places to meet."

Oliver shrugged. He gave the area a quick, disinterested perusal. "We're out of town, not somewhere you'd expect to be found, or be likely to run into anyone you know. I followed you to make sure you weren't followed, so we're good to go. This'll be quick."

Before he could ask, Seraphina yanked the strap of her purse off her arm, rooted inside, and retrieved a white glossy envelope. She held it aloft as if deciding whether she'd prefer to keep the evidence. Her gaze was sharp and biting, pivoting between Oliver and himself. Grant parked his hands on his hips and glared at Oliver with raised eyebrows. The detective could sort out his own mess.

Oliver scratched the back of his neck, mimicked Grant's stance, and gave Seraphina an apologetic glance beneath his lashes. He seemed genuinely contrite. "Yeah. About that. A team is moving on Brendan right now. He's being taken into custody, based on the circumstantial clues that earned us the search warrant. If we don't find anything, we can't hold him. It's a risk, but Cappy Don—that's my captain," he explained in a quick aside to Grant, "decided we might give him time to move evidence if we waited."

Seraphina's glare held steady. "Go on."

Oliver cleared his throat. "Grant. The city. The historical society." He paused, giving the implications time to soak in. "All of them were in on the sting. And you, Seraphina, are the steadfast mare we hitched our wagons to. Sorry for the terrible metaphor."

She didn't flinch. Her eyes didn't seek Grant, and he wondered if it was a good sign or a bad one. Grant gave Oliver an accusing stare as he spoke to Seraphina. "I was told we'd make Brendan suspicious if you and I were seen too often with our heads bent together, or if I accompanied you on your searches of Tanbee House."

She ignored Grant completely, her sights firmly set on Oliver. "Hitched your wagons to. Explain that a little better, Oli."

Oliver grimaced. "You know I hate that name."

"Yes."

Her simple reply didn't invite rejoinder. Oliver gusted out a sigh. "You were maneuvered. A little bit. We knew you were taking a position with Gallagher Interiors, and we knew if we could get Grant's firm to move their latest project to the stash house Brendan used, we could draw him in. We had to get the governor on board, include certain members of the planning commission—"

"Oliver Pierce. I do not give a shit how elaborate and conniving your sting was, nor how painstakingly you pieced it together. What I wish to know is to what extent I was used and lied to, so that I may decide what I will do about it. Seems to me I could've been easily included. You can trust Grant, you can trust a hundred city employees, and yet I was kept in the dark."

"No, you weren't," Grant cut in. Finally, Seraphina's burning stare came his way. For a second, he regretted drawing attention to himself. Then he decided he didn't. If they hashed it out now, the bone of contention couldn't come back to haunt them later. "The only thing you didn't know about was me, and even as I argued with both Oliver and Ophelia, I can't fault their decision. You didn't trust me, Seraphina. Maybe you still don't. And that mistrust would've been noted by Brendan, relaxed him. He might've even seen you as a shield. Anything you threw against him he could've played off as a personal attack. Had you and I shared one secret thought on our faces, he might've seen it. As clever as he is, he might've wondered. Why did I hire him despite his reputation? Why did I so easily accept his bid to work on Tanbee House? On this, we had to be of separate minds."

Oliver nodded. "I counted on you, Sera. I counted on you to be willing to spy for me, to be my eyes and ears. I can't go anywhere near Tanbee House, or Brendan will disappear in a cloud of smoke. Or worse, get a restraining order against me that would taint the entire investigation. Brendan would expect your suspicion, and wouldn't give it a second thought. He did exactly what we expected him to do—keep an eye on you, but not consider you more than an inconvenience. It worked. You can blame me and Ophelia for Grant's part in this. He was upset that you didn't trust him and wanted to tell you he was one of the good guys. We denied the request."

"Ophelia," she murmured. "My supposed assistant."

"One of mine," Oliver offered, with a thin smile. "I can't do inside work anymore. Not after the attention my little operation at Free Leaf Concepts drew. She's my team's new mole."

"So, what's changed? Why now?" She still refused to look at Grant.

He decided he'd take a backseat and observe from here. Oliver had done his best to explain Grant's deceit. Grant could do little more than await her reaction. By the way she ignored him, he surmised she was still deciding how she felt about the day's revelations.

Oliver shrugged, but his expression gave away his anxiety. "Since the warrant is served, Brendan will have guessed he's been watched. He'll know you had some hand in it, Sera. I'd like to keep Grant's part in this quiet. Should we screw this up and get nothing, he'll likely return to work. It's the smartest thing he can do. He needs to stick to his story, and that means sticking to the job as if his professional credentials were ever his only concern. But if the two of you seem like you're on the same team now, he won't be surprised. A little suspicion from Grant would be expected after Brendan's questioning is made public."

For a long minute, silence billowed between the three of them. Grant shifted uneasily. He craved a moment alone with Seraphina. He sensed she held back in front of Oliver.

"Have you had the drugs tested yet?" She shot Grant a look. "No need to fill you in, I presume?"

Oliver ignored her sarcasm and answered in earnest. He laughed breathily, without any humor. "Yeah, actually. The final piece of this big, crappy puzzle has slid into place, and makes for an ugly picture." He grimaced and his gaze fell beyond them, to the lake in the distance. "The lab guys determined the mushrooms we confiscated at Free Leaf Concepts weren't a perfect match to the degraded samples we've gotten from victims that were buyers off the street. Including the ones used on Kay. They were bitter," Oliver went on, his gaze coming back to regard Grant and Seraphina in turn. "Too bitter to be edible. Kay could taste something off after just a few bites. We concluded maybe we'd happened upon a test batch, or perhaps there was a second step to the process. It clicked when the results came back from that little baggie you found. Sugar."

Seraphina's mouth popped open. She closed it abruptly, but her puzzled expression remained. "Sugar?"

"Sugar and a wild concoction of other street drugs, including PCP. The substance is heated to a melting point, and the mushrooms coated. It dries into a hard shell."

Grant tried to get a mental picture in his head. "Candied mushrooms?" He had a hard time imagining sugar improved the taste.

Oliver nodded. "Exactly. It's why overdoses are so common. It's a melting pot of drugs, and the side effects are all over the map."

"God," Seraphina breathed. "That's awful."

"Yeah." Oliver sighed heavily. "It is. But now we know what we're looking for and can run the right tests on the samples we do have. Oh, and the kid they picked up, who came for the stash? They located the drugs, but he's still not talking. We can charge him, though, so we have time to try to convince him to deal with us." Oliver's hand flew to his pocket as a jangle of music burst from it. He laughed lightly. "Cappy Don's ring tone. I better take this. Oh, and could you put in a good word to Kay? She didn't know I'd set her up to enlist you for your help until this morning. Suffice to say, things are tense at home."

While Oliver stepped a few paces away to take his call in privacy, Grant pulled Seraphina aside and pitched his voice for her ears only. "Are we okay?"

For a moment, she peered at him, and her pale blue eyes were unreadable. "No. Not right now." She swiveled to Oliver and waved, heedless of the phone at his ear. "I'm going to need a ride home."

* * * *

Seraphina put fresh eyes on Ophelia as they bent their heads together over the latest batch of updated specs. "Here." Seraphina pointed where the current window existed. The one busted out the night she and Grant had visited Tanbee House, before the beefed-up security measures. "I've had Marc hold off on the repair. I think we should create a side exit."

The other woman nodded. "I can get with the landscaping company and see if they've marked a pathway up this side of the house. Even if it's a cobblestone path, there ought to be something."

If only Roper weren't in the room. Seraphina longed to confront Ophelia. She wanted to ask how the search warrant had panned out. She wanted to ask what she'd done previously to qualify her for this sort of undercover work. Instead, she settled for giving Ophelia pointed glances, which Ophelia ignored.

It wasn't until Brendan Berkley shuffled past Seraphina's office with his head down that she called quits to the meeting. She made a show of checking her watch. "How about that? Time for me to call the electrician."

Roper stretched and stood. "I could use a latté myself." He hadn't done much besides hover, and Seraphina wondered whether he wanted to be helpful, or if Grant had made his wishes plain that Roper stick around.

The dark slash that was Ophelia's brow arched. "I didn't know you were going to speak to the electrician today."

She hadn't either. She almost grinned at the facetious thought. "I want to know if sconces on the brick façade of the fireplace are doable, or if I should keep my plans as they are." This she added for Roper's benefit. She no longer felt compelled to make excuses for Ophelia, who was probably keeping tabs on everything she did. "Besides, I'm getting a crick in my neck."

Ophelia dropped cover long enough to shoot a knowing glare at Seraphina behind Roper's back as he walked toward the office door. The edge of it was softened by the wry ghost of a smile.

Less than a minute later, Seraphina had Oliver on the line. "Brendan Berkley just strode past my office," she declared with feeling. It could only mean the search warrant hadn't provided any viable evidence. She prayed Oliver would give her some other explanation. Maybe they were misleading him on purpose. Just another leg of their long con. "He didn't look like he's having a great day, but I can't believe he's here at all. What happened?"

"Now maybe you understand our need for secrecy. We gave away our advantage, but there's no reason he should puzzle out how deep the sting operation goes. Or went, I guess." He sounded tired and defeated. "They found a candle stick almost exactly like the one you found in Tanbee House in his apartment, but it's not reason enough to hold him. There's no evidence he's ever owned more than just the one, and as such, it's still circumstantial. I can't directly tie them together through anything more than coincidence. They don't match exactly. The details are different."

Seraphina's heart fell in a twist of anxiety. She could tell Oliver was upset and disappointed by the way he babbled. Oliver never babbled. "Surely there's something."

"There isn't!"

She froze with the phone to her ear. She'd never heard Oliver shout. Or sound so hopeless.

He continued, heedless of Seraphina's shock. "Circumstantial. Every link I've got can be explained away. Every last one. The runner he sent to Tanbee House won't talk, we've got no proof he hid the drugs or removed them. It could've been you, Sera, or Marc Curry, if it's a simple matter of access. I mean, we've got evidence. We just need something solid and undeniable linking what we've got to Brendan Berkley. Our experts insist candelabra sets are usually matching. That they aren't exact throws a little too much doubt on their connection. Nor can I come up with a feasible reason he'd stick something he owns in the wall to begin with. Even some of my team are having doubts now, considering perhaps Brendan is being set up. I can't fault their logic. I can't explain why he'd do something that stupid or obvious, either. Why plant something that could be linked to you, even if marginally?"

Seraphina ignored the rhetorical nature of the question. "Um, Oliver…I think I can answer part of that. Recall I mentioned the day Roper confronted me over the amount of time I was spending at Tanbee House? I had to give him something. I told him I thought there was something in Tanbee House. Something valuable and significant."

Oliver made a noise in his throat. "And?"

Seraphina smoothed the file that sat on top of her desk and licked her lips. "When Roper left my office, he bumped into Brendan just outside the door. If he was eavesdropping, he'll have known I expected to find something. It doesn't explain everything, but…."

Silence reigned while Oliver thought. "It does, though," he said. "Brendan was sending you a message, Seraphina. He knows you're onto him. Also, this is another reason we didn't want you and Grant obviously on the same team," Oliver pointed out, almost under his breath. "Imagine what you might've said, even in jest, that that little pecker could've overheard."

"Yeah, well, you made sure that wasn't an issue."

"I did what I thought was right for my investigation. Again, I'm sorry if my methods made for a rough patch in your personal life. A rough patch that's pretty handily corrected, if you can give Grant a break. The man tried. He came here to my home to personally ask that I let him tell you the truth. If you want to be pissed off at someone, I'm your guy, Sera."

The muscle in her jaw worked. Her pride hadn't allowed her to forgive Grant. Not yet. "You're not out of the weeds yet, Oli," she promised. "Anyway, about Brendan. Maybe this was less about sending a message, and more about covering his ass. Once I told Roper, Roper might tell someone else. Maybe it would look funny if nothing ever came of all my searching. Or if someone else thought to start poking around, as well, in hopes of beating me to whatever treasure might be stowed away on the property."

"Maybe." Oliver was silent for a beat. "Also, now you've found the candelabra, you no longer have a reason to poke around Tanbee House. You'll have to come up with a brand new excuse to keep pawning your work off onto Ophelia."

"Pawn? I didn't… Did she complain to you?"

"A little. Don't worry, it's what we wanted."

Seraphina sighed. "I know, Oliver. And I'm glad I could help. But regardless of the reasons and the methods, it's shitty to feel used. Even if you're a tool for good, you're still a tool."

"You're right. I can apologize, but I'm not sorry. You've helped me establish a few possible motives for Brendan to leave behind the candlestick."

"So what happens now?" At least she was in on the plan moving forward.

"Nothing. Brendan wins again. Until we can do better."

That there may no longer be a plan hadn't occurred to her. "So what, we're giving up? This douchebag walks free? After everything? I mean, surely you've got someone looking further into the candelabras, right?"

Oliver's weary sigh almost pulled her down with him. "Nope. I told you, they're just old candlesticks, Seraphina. They aren't all that special or unique. The design is not unheard of. There's no evidence he ever owned more than the one he has. Not a ring of dust around a void where the other candleholder might've sat on the shelf. No photos of his apartment that show both candleholders on the mantel. Someone could be trying to set him up, or it could be the coincidence of a lifetime, but judges don't convict people for coincidences."

Seraphina bit her lip and decided to let Oliver off the hook. She promised to look after Brendan on her end, even as Oliver declared that Cappy Don hadn't totally given up hope. They were looking into other avenues and exploring the details of the search to decide if anything warranted further investigation or prompted a new line of query. She hung up feeling useless and flat, like a balloon slowly deflating.

When Kay rang a few moments later, Seraphina wasn't at all surprised. "Hello, my dear," she greeted her friend. "I bet you think your best friend and handsome lover are both in low spirits and wish to do something to alleviate our gloom?"

Kay's lively snicker made Seraphina smile despite her glumness. "Man, I need to brush up on my mysteriousness or Oliver is going to lose interest."

"Hm. I doubt that. I think your wide-open personality is what he loves most about you."

"That and how I like to force feed people good food when they're in the doldrums," she drawled. "So, yes, please come over for dinner tonight. Not just because I always have the best takeout and stale cookies. Oliver may not have said as much, but he's had his head bent over the photographs they took of Brendan's apartment since before the sun came up this morning. He's a frazzled mess. I figured you're as invested as he is, and it couldn't hurt for a pair of fresh eyes to join him." She paused and her voice lowered. "He's not himself right now. And I don't know how to help him."

Seraphina nodded even though Kay couldn't see her. "I might only get in his way. But I wouldn't mind a look myself." She gave the credit to curiosity, but she had another agenda, as well. Until she was ready to face Grant, she'd take any excuse she could get to avoid him. "I'll see you tonight."

Chapter 17

Seraphina went home and changed at the end of the day. She kept her pale gray slacks, but traded into her peep-toe heels for black canvas tennis shoes, and her white-trimmed blazer for a jean jacket with fat metal buttons. She arrived at Kay's only a few moments after the food. Kay opened the front door, and Seraphina followed her into the kitchen where she began unloading brown paper bags full of white food containers.

Seraphina cocked her head like a dog straining to hear a whistle. "Doesn't smell like Chinese."

Kay gave her a smug smile. "That's because this Southern girl needs stick-to-your-ribs food every once in a while. When's the last time you indulged in some home style fare, my friend? Potato salad, deviled eggs, mac and cheese, barbeque ribs, pulled pork and chicken, baked beans, flaky biscuits…" Her voice grew muffled as she leaned up onto her tip-toes and over to stick her face into one of the bags for a better view. Poor girl was five feet nothing if she was an inch. She cast Seraphina an apologetic glance as she settled back onto the balls of her feet. "Sorry. Not a green vegetable in sight."

Sera usually ate pretty light, but eating with Grant had infected her with a yearning for good food, the homier the better. "I'll live," she promised Kay.

Kay hitched her chin toward the exit. "Oliver's in the parlor."

Sera loaded her plate with potato salad, pulled pork, and two deviled eggs and found her way to the parlor room, where the photographs from Brendan's apartment were spread out across the surface of a low rectangular coffee table. Oliver sat on the sofa with his head pinioned between his palms, the very picture of dejection.

He glanced up as she entered. "Oh. Hey."

Seraphina frowned at him. "Don't be so glum. There's something. There has to be."

In a move most unlike the Oliver she knew, he stood up in a rush, an agitated groan escaping. "No, there isn't." He didn't shout, but close enough to freeze Seraphina mid-step. He ran his hands through his hair. It stuck up at ends. He didn't meet her gaze as he shook his head and stalked past her.

Several bewildered seconds passed before Seraphina could gather herself and look behind her. Oliver was long gone, but Kay stood in the doorway, leaning against the frame. Her arms crossed, and her lips were drawn in an unhappy grimace. "He's been like that since this afternoon. He wasn't able to join in the search. Despite everything, he still has to keep his distance from Brendan. I think he expected to catch something the officers missed."

"I've never seen him so..."

"Angry?" Kay suggested, her brow quirking. "He tries to stay upbeat, but this has been hard for him. He's used to being in the thick of the action, not hiding away like a scared possum. It'd be like sitting on our thumbs while someone else executes our designs."

Seraphina took the warm spot on the couch Oliver had vacated. It was still indented with his shape. "He must've been sitting here for hours."

"Ever since a courier from the department brought the photos by," Kay concurred. "I'm gonna make him a plate and put away leftovers. Feel free." She swept her hand through the air, indicating the piles of pictures.

For a while, Seraphina pecked at her food and glanced through the spread. They'd photographed everything. Kitchen cupboards were all opened and the insides exposed. Other than varying sets of mismatched dishes, she saw nothing of interest. Brendan's fireplace was a narrow column of white brick with a simple yellow pine ledge. And there, the candelabra.

She set aside her plate to dig deeper into the pile until she found a close-up. She sighed. They were different. Not enough that they couldn't, in fact, be a set, though. Both featured little cupids with reaching arms, chubby legs, curly hair, and rosebud mouths. The coloring was different, as well. The one discovered in Tanbee House had a more orange cast to its brassiness. Old as the candelabra might be, the thing was cheap. She bent her head over the photo. Well, if they were antiques, Brendan's would be the less valuable of the two. There was a dent, long and narrow, as if it had fallen from a height and hit the edge of a table or something.

Something about the dent taunted her. The crease wasn't deep or angular enough for brass. The edges of the indentation had an almost rounded quality. She snorted softly. Almost as if the metal were soft.

She froze, her fingers gripping the picture so hard it bent in her grasp. Soft metal.

Something else…something about Brendan tickled the lobes of her brain. She'd felt the sensation once before, back when she'd discovered the candle stick wedged into the wall. But what was it? Some subliminal message from the buried recesses of her mind. While she waited for the idea to surface, she had a firm grasp on another suspicion.

Kay ducked into the room. "Having fun yet?"

Seraphina palmed the picture of Brendan's candelabra. She blinked at the surreptitious action, unsure of her own motives. She had a suspicion, but she wasn't ready to share it just yet. Oliver was in no mind to withstand another disappointment. Until Seraphina was certain, she wouldn't get his hopes up. She stood abruptly. "A blast. Listen, I forgot something. Back at the office. I've got to run, but I'll call you. Later."

Kay's blond brow crinkled. "Are you sure? It's late."

"I've got keys. Besides, there's usually someone hanging around after hours. Young upstarts burning the candle at both ends, janitors, what have you. Sorry, Kay."

She inhaled and sighed. "I understand. At least finish eating, though."

Seraphina was already moving toward the door. "I can't. I'm so sorry. I have to go." She didn't wait for Kay to dismiss her or argue. She bolted for the door and took off at a brisk pace toward town. When she reached a busy enough avenue, she hailed a cab. With her access card, she slipped into Gallagher Interiors and headed straight for the elevator after a curt nod toward the night shift security detail hanging out in the lobby.

It took her five minutes to reach her office. As predicted, she passed a few stragglers. Swiftly, she unlocked her office, stepped inside, and then locked herself inside. In the bottom drawer of the filing cabinet on the far side of her desk, she withdrew the candelabra she'd taken from Tanbee House.

It was only a matter of time before Oliver wanted his evidence. Eventually, he'd break out of his slump and want to attack the potential relation between the two candelabras.

She retrieved her pen knife from her desk and flipped the candle holder over. She placed the tip against the flat bottom and pressed. Then she gave up being delicate about it, and gouged the metal as hard as she could.

Her suspicions were confirmed after the second strike. Brass was tinny, heavy stuff. But the tip of her pen knife pushed into the metal, revealing it as not only soft, but also coated. With her breath held in her throat, she turned the pen over and scraped. A curl of paint peeled away.

She licked her lips. The candelabra wasn't brass at all, but gold. Gold, painted to hide the real value. If the candelabra in Brendan's apartment was also paint-covered gold, would that be enough to declare them a match? How many coincidences were one too many for a judge? This was good, but was it enough?

She was loathe to hand Oliver one more disappointment. Instead, she'd look into it herself, first thing in the morning. Because the answer was simple—as simple as tracking down the appraiser Brendan mentioned that one afternoon in the lounge.

She realized with a start that the flighty feather in the back of her mind had found purchase. The appraiser. Brendan had recommended one to Lucia. Perhaps, he'd let the comment slip without thinking.

If both candelabras were gold, maybe—a strong maybe—she was looking at just another coincidence. But if Seraphina could prove Brendan had the objects appraised together, then hid their worth, well now, that was a solid chain of evidence. That was enough to secure an arrest that would stick, and firmly link Brendan to the drugs at Tanbee House. Whether he'd had the runner who'd nabbed the drugs from Tanbee House leave the candelabra behind, or if he'd snuck into the property himself afterward, she could prove he'd had possession.

Maybe. If, and only if, he'd ever had the antiques appraised. Longer than a long shot, but one she had to take. She groped around in her desk until she found the scarf she'd used to hide her camera. She carefully wrapped the candelabra, and cradled it in the crook of her arm. If someone asked why she was smuggling a bundle out of her office in the evening hours, she'd have to get real clever, real quick. She escaped the building without incident, and paused on the sidewalk in front of the building to withdraw her cell phone and compose a quick text.

In late tomorrow. Helping O.

She hoped that would be enough to keep Grant from bothering her for a few hours. They hadn't spoken since the day at the lake. Even from a distance, far out of sight, she felt linked to him, drawn by a thread of tension that sought relief. She loved him. She knew it, accepted it. But coming to terms with what it might mean for her future—for their future—would take time and consideration. And if she knew him at all, she knew he wouldn't be satisfied leaving things as they were between them for long.

She hailed a cab with her free arm and clutched tight to the swathed candelabra with the other. This was it, perhaps the last chance to bring Brendan Berkley to heel.

* * * *

Grant stared at the text message. He didn't buy it. He sent a quick response, but not to Seraphina. Oliver exposed her false excuse with his reply that he was free in the morning. No plans. No meetings. More scratching his head over results of the search warrant.

Perhaps he deserved Seraphina's deceit. Tit for tat. And if she were anyone else, he'd accept it as his due. But Seraphina wasn't anyone else. She was forthright and unabashed in the face of confrontation. So something else was going on. He stood up, grabbed his keys, and left his apartment. Text messages and phone calls weren't going to cut it.

In less than ten minutes, he was standing outside of Seraphina's building. Her expression at finding him at her door didn't bode well for what happened next. But he refused to leave without trying, at least. "May I?"

She stared at him another few seconds before stepping back, tightlipped. "If you must."

He stepped into the apartment. The lit candles provided an ambient glow.

Suddenly, he felt awkward. Too clumsy and rough for the small, cozy space Seraphina inhabited. He scratched his cheek and tried to recall the singlemindedness that had propelled him here.

He found a grain of it. Just enough to convince the next words to come out of his mouth. "You lied to me. I just wanted to drop by and see for myself if this means we're even now." He met her gaze directly. No chagrin in her pale eyes. Only a sort of wariness that sent a vague sense of alarm through him. "What's going on?"

Seraphina closed the door, brushed past him, and strode into the kitchen with a defiant swagger. She'd been making herself a cup of tea. A fat porcelain mug sat on the counter. She picked up a spoon lying next to the mug and proceeded to swish around the steeping tea bags before meeting his gaze again. "Fine. I'm not going to help Oliver tomorrow morning. But what I'm doing is equally important. I won't take long, I promise. An hour. Two, tops."

He leaned against the other side of the island counter so they could face one another. "We're on the same team. The secret's out. So, why push me away?"

"I'm not pushing anyone," she declared. She stirred her tea. "In fact, there's no momentum to speak of. We are as we've ever been, Grant."

He cocked his head at her. "That's the most false thing I've ever heard you say. I know, as you do, that there's more to your reticence than secrets between us, and this secret wasn't mine to share, after all. I kept Oliver's secret. And I know you, and I know you can't hold that against me for long. So, shall we call this what it really is? I'll happily speak plain."

Her carefully guarded expression slowly hardened, until she might've been made of stone. "Grant, don't."

"Don't?" He stared a challenge at her, daring her lips to form a lie, her eyes to hide the truth. "Don't say out loud that I'm not willing to let you get away this easy? Don't say we both know there's something real and precious between us? Don't accuse you of being too scared to open your heart? Or perhaps you'd tell me don't be offended that you assume all men are like your father? That you suspect I get my kicks from dangling my affection and love just out of your reach, and offer you nothing true?"

Seraphina's eyes were perfectly round and she looked as terrified as a deer caught in the glare of headlights. When she finally blinked, her eyes were lined in unshed tears.

He hated to have caused them. But if he didn't stand his ground, she'd push him so far away he'd never find his way back. "I'm not asking for a chance. I'm not asking you to trust me, or put blind faith in me."

He paused and searched for the courage to say what came next. This seemed easy when it was a matter of Seraphina's vulnerability. But to meet her in the middle, he had to expose his own. He was Grant Gallagher. His reputation revolved around the concept of his immovable will, his life around the illusion of invulnerability. For him to toss all aside was more than simply telling Seraphina how he felt; he was placing a high-stakes bet, and taking a shaky chance on a loss.

He licked his lips, swallowed, and refused to allow himself to glance away, or look anywhere but directly into her eyes. "I'm asking you to tell me you love me. If, in fact, you do. I'm telling you I'm as guarded and distrusting as you are, and I've decided I don't care anymore. If you did break my heart, I can't find any part of me that would ever regret giving it to you. So, it doesn't matter that I love you. It doesn't matter that I'd risk my own ruin and stand vulnerable in front of you, weak and stupid and pleading. It doesn't matter that I've come to regard you as more important than my pride. What love I can give, however short that love may fall, is yours. The only thing that matters now is if you want it."

As they stood staring at one another, Grant thought of great, romantic movie scenes. The heroine and hero look into one another's eyes as they fall into the abyss. Time stands still. Snowflakes fall in gentle swirls.

This wasn't like that at all. This was standing on the precipice of darkness and praying the person you were deadlocked into a staring contest with would reach out to save you before you fell. It was a slow unraveling, a dwindling into the myriad of doubts that rode on the flipside of every word he'd uttered. How many stories were told of men who "knew" what a woman wanted? On the knife's edge of the moment suspended between them, he all but decided her next words would be a gentle letting down. But he'd already offered her his pride. She'd have it, one way or another.

Her hand had traveled up to cover her mouth. Behind it, she drew in a shaky breath. Above it, tears still threatened but held steady on the rims of her lashes, defying the fall. Grant wouldn't put any faith in those. Tears could mean anything, from fear to regret.

He stood there until he was certain the air between them would crack and shatter like glass. His hands seemed to weigh as much as the moon as he reached for her, gently pulled her hand away from her mouth, and took her face between his palms.

He kissed her. Not hard, not soft, but firmly. A promise.

She sucked in a breath and pulled back slightly, so her gaze could scour his face. Grant knew the doubt in the lines around her eyes. She nodded mutely, her lips pressed together. She blinked the moisture from her eyes, and finally uttered, "I do." She bit her lip, as if she still doubted his sincerity. "I do want it."

She kissed him, then. They'd known passion, and they'd been taciturn. They'd spoken of their past hurts, told one another their stories. But in that one kiss, there was a taking and a giving beyond what all they'd shared before. Their careful, singular openness seemed so fragile, Grant was almost afraid to end the contact, or move at all. Like a bubble, the moment could burst.

In the end, it was Seraphina who, after a final deep crush of her mouth on his, stepped away breathless and a little giddy. Maybe he was still reeling from the kiss, but he could swear she bounced on the balls of her feet for a second before planting them firmly. Her eyes were bright and shiny, and they glittered in a different way as she looked at him like she'd never seen him before. Or as if he'd been gone a long time, and she'd missed him dreadfully.

She armed herself with a brilliant smile and pulled his hand toward her. Seraphina didn't smile often or without great cause. But when she did, the curve of her lips moved something deep in his chest. "I'll tell you what I'm up to if you do something for me first."

Grant's mouth twitched into a grin without his consent. He marveled at her smile. "You say that as if I didn't just tell you I'm completely powerless when it comes to you. And certainly, when you look at me like that, I find myself feeling oddly agreeable."

She laughed softly. "The death blow to your reputation. Big, bad Grant Gallagher is a pussy cat," she purred.

He growled, low in his throat. He brought her arm toward him and nipped playfully at the inside of her wrist. "A pussy cat with sharp teeth."

"So you won't mind doing me a favor? There's something I want to show you."

"Oh?"

She took his hand, and he allowed himself to be tugged along toward the back of her apartment.

"Yep. It's in my bedroom. Actually, it's on my bed. Actually, it is my bed."

He grinned. "I've seen your bed before."

She glanced back sexily over her shoulder. "Babe. You haven't seen anything yet."

* * * *

Seraphina couldn't think of a better way to celebrate Grant's confession than to show him just how deeply she appreciated his gift, and gave it back in kind. She laid on her side, draped across his torso in the dark room. Her fingers walked across the span of his chest, the coarse hairs tickling her skin.

A strange, peculiar emotion enthralled her. Here was a place to put her love, if she were strong enough. Her affection. All the things she'd always craved a safe, worthy place for. She had so much to give, and had only ever lacked someone in her life who wanted it and would cherish it. Grant had offered his without strings. A hearth in one hand, and his very heart in the other. A rushing warmth swept through her, and tears pricked her eyes. Not for the first time. Rolling her eyes at her own sentimentality, she blinked back the thick emotion. She'd cry later, whether she wanted to or not. The least she could do was wait until she had a little privacy. She loved Grant, but she had no wish for him to see her undone.

She wanted to wake him up and talk about it. She loved him so much.

She wanted to crawl away and never speak to him again. She loved him too much.

Such a war inside her. Relief and anxiety in equal measures. But she chose, here in the dark, to believe in her own happy ending. For once. Grant had launched himself into her hands, put himself, his pride, and his heart at her mercy. To meet in the middle wasn't enough. And she realized it never would be for either of them. For people like them, inches didn't count. Halfway measures didn't suffice. They gave every bit of themselves to all they did. It only seemed right it would be so in love, as well.

She smiled into the dark. "You're awake, aren't you?"

"Hm." The low, pure maleness of his voice sent a small thrill through her. "Your fingers are waltzing in my chest hair."

"Sorry."

He caught her fingers in his. "Don't be." He paused a beat. "Since we're awake, why don't you catch me up on recent events?"

She sighed. "It irritates me that you can read me."

His chest rumbled with a low chuckle. "I recognize an attempt at subterfuge by someone who is otherwise ill-adept at subterfuge. You're too direct. When you dissemble, it's a fairly obvious departure from the norm."

She grinned despite herself. "I can hardly tell the flattery from the insult."

"No insult intended," he assured her, squeezing her hand lightly.

"Well, since you're here and can't be sidetracked from your mission, I might as well ask your advice." She didn't know if she could keep anything from Grant now. After what passed between them, she didn't know if she had the capacity for secrets. Nor did she want them. A knot inside of her loosened as she realized with that truth came a new one—she could trust Grant. If she asked him to keep her secret, he would. And if he felt he had to tell on her, he'd tell her to her face. "I have a lead. And I'm not sure if I want to involve Oliver yet."

Grant took a few seconds to process what she'd said. The dark kept his expression from her. "Can you explain why? It seems...well, not to seem insulting again, but silly."

"I know. But if you'd seen him going through the pictures from Brendan's search, you wouldn't question my motive. Oliver's stretched tight. He's been fighting against this machine for years now. He's lost a friend, and for a while, his career. This case is a parasite, and it's eating him up. I don't want to give him false hope, because I don't know how much more disappointment he can take. He's cut off from the investigation. He's angry and frustrated. He hides it, but I saw the lines on Kay's face. Oliver's known for playing fast and loose with the rulebook. And his career might not survive another one of his little scandals. This case definitely won't if Oliver gets pushed too far."

Again, Grant was silent for a beat, considering. "You may have a point. I saw it on his face when I went to speak to him about you. He has a lot of anger brewing inside him. I think perhaps he's got a higher boiling point than we might be inclined to give him credit for. But I agree it'd be disastrous if his patience bottomed out."

"Exactly." Seraphina breathed a sigh of relief. "And more to the point, I could be wrong. It's a long shot. I discovered something about the candelabras, but I need more time. If I tell Oliver what I know, he'll take mine that came from Tanbee House. Just for a few hours in the morning. If my suspicion pans out, it might break the case. If it doesn't, then no harm done."

"What can I do?"

Seraphina smiled into the darkness. "Um, well, I guess if anything happens to me, you should tell Oliver that the candelabra is gold. Not brass. The outside is painted to hide the real worth. From the photograph I took of the similar candle holder in Brendan's possession, I think it's likewise disguised. Now, Oliver says two brass candlesticks do not hard evidence make. But if they're both made of gold and camouflaged in a similar manner, maybe that's enough. And certainly, Oliver will want to take the one I have and get the paint tested, then subpoena to have Brendan's tested, as well. I don't know, but maybe they can match the paint or something."

"Wow," Grant breathed. "Why not just take this information to Oliver now?"

"Because I might be able to do better than that. I just need a few hours."

"Okay. I'll make sure you get them. Anything else?"

Seraphina swallowed a strange lump of emotion. She still wasn't used to this feeling of uniformity. She and Grant were on the same side. How strange and wonderful. She couldn't recall that she'd ever had a sense of someone so firmly in her corner. "Just trust me."

Chapter 18

I'm not going to jail. I'm not going to jail.

Technically, Seraphina was not part of the "official" investigation. She prayed that small detail would be enough to protect her if things went south. Otherwise, she'd have to answer some pretty uncomfortable questions about carting around the evidence of an active investigation inside a canvas sack all around town, not to mention the tampering.

The entrance to Swift Appraisal and Pawn was an unassuming wooden door. Old and paint-chipped, she checked the name painted on the glass window a second time. Yep. This was the place. A bell overhead greeted her with a cheery jingle, in direct contrast with the gloomy lighting, muffled silence, and musty smell. "Hello?"

She wavered there. The place seemed deserted. She called out again and waited. Narrow corridors split off in several different directions. She headed straight toward the back. The aisle was crowded on either side by glass counters with poorly lit displays inside, and stacks of books and random gadgets haphazardly piled on the surface. The aisle ended at a simple wooden counter where a skinny old man puzzled over an old-fashioned cash register.

He glanced up through tortoiseshell frames and smiled. His lips seemed to stretch from ear-to-ear. "Hello, hello. I'm Dr. Paul. What can I do for you, darling?"

She caught her expression before she unintentionally exposed her doubt. She was able to say, "Doctor?" with more curiosity than ambiguity.

"Why, sure." He stood up straight and hooked his thumbs on lemon yellow suspenders. "I used to teach an antiquities class at the university, but that was ages and ages ago. I'm a collector these days. Were you looking for something special? I'm pretty good at tracking down the rare and unique."

"Um, no, actually." She approached the counter and reached for the canvas tote slung around her shoulder. "I'm looking for the man who sold this to me. He mentioned you'd appraised the piece for him, and I want to speak to you myself before I take further action." The candelabra landed with a thunk on the counter.

"Oh?" Over the rim of his glasses, Dr. Paul's fuzzy white eyebrows gathered in puzzled fascination as he peered down at the candlestick. "Hm. Yes, yes. I know this. Only last time I seen it, there wasn't none of this..." He flapped his hands and scowled.

"Paint?" she offered. It took everything she had not to whoop and holler. Her instincts had led her true. "It'd be a shame to get robbed on my way here. Now, the gentleman who sold me this said you had appraised this piece." She flipped the piece over and showed him the dent in the side; the one she'd made herself. She'd done her best to make it look like the one Brendan had in his apartment.

She'd done her due diligence and had photographed documentation of the process. As long as Oliver didn't mind claiming this was all his idea, everything would pan out, and she wouldn't go to jail for evidence tampering.

She fingered the dent. "In the photograph I was shown before purchase, this wasn't there. I came to ask if this changes the value significantly before I hunt down the son of a bitch and get my money back. This thing cost a fortune."

Dr. Paul's eyebrows hitched. "Oh, indeed. I'm sure it must have, if he asked close to what I told him he might." He shook his head and pressed his lips together regretfully. "Now, I can give you two possible things, dear. Because I stand by my appraisals. One, you were fleeced. See, this is part of a set of two. He may have shown you the undamaged candelabra, and gave you this one instead. Or could be, he made an honest mistake."

Seraphina gusted out a frustrated sigh. "Well, have you at least got some documentation I could take to him? Someone is going to answer for this."

He bobbed his head. "Oh, yes. Yes, yes. Of course I do. Give me just a minute, I'll fish you out the ticket. Should be enough to prove you ended up with the dented one, so long as you held on to your own receipt."

"Of course I did," she muttered.

He disappeared into the back of the shop. He came tottering back several minutes later, waving a yellow slip of paper. "It's here. Right here." He slapped it onto the counter. "See there? Two in the set. I marked the damage on one. That there's the amount I appraised for both. Now, I striked through Mr. Berkley's contact information," Dr. Paul said apologetically. "Sorry, I won't give out personal information, but that there is his name."

He's a long-time customer of mine, and I've only ever had good dealings with him. If I were to guess, I'd say it was an honest mistake, Miss... I didn't catch your name?"

She snatched the slip from the counter and hefted the candle holder. "You certainly did not. Thanks, Dr. Paul."

He scratched his head but watched her go without further remark. She stopped at the door to return the candelabra to her sack. Her heart thudded in her chest. She couldn't believe her luck. She tucked the yellow ticket into her purse and pulled the door open. A light breeze swirled past her, and she smiled.

She hadn't dared hope that the seemingly inconsequential snippet of conversation she'd heard would pay off. Not to this degree. She'd hoped to prove the candlesticks were possibly a set. Perhaps get enough information to convince Oliver to formally question the proprietor of the appraisal shop. Instead, she had an established link connecting Brendan directly to them. She fairly vibrated with anticipation as she began a brisk walk toward Gallagher Interiors. As a bonus, she was only a few blocks from the office. She didn't even need to bother with cab fare.

The side street was quiet and practically barren. At this time, most people were squirreled away in their offices, clucking over e-mails, sighing over meetings gone too long, and hiding yawns behind third and fourth cups of coffee.

She heard scuffs behind her seconds before something sharp jabbed into her right side. On her left, an arm hooked around her shoulder, pinning her against a hard body at her back. She froze, her mouth open and her heart in her throat.

"This was a departure from your usual good sense." Brendan's husky voice rumbled in her ear.

She jerked violently, trying to tear herself free. He easily snapped her back against him and held her. "Dr. Paul is an old, old friend. He sent me a quick text the second you stepped inside his shop. He sold me out to buy himself time to get the hell out of town before you bring the entire police department down on his head. Thanks for screwing that up for me."

"Get off me," she demanded through gritted teeth. She calmed her nerves. She guessed the pointy thing jabbing into her back was the barrel of a small caliber weapon. He probably didn't expect a fight from her. That pissed her off enough to chase away lingering doubt. To hell with going along with the helpless girl act. "Or I'm going to knock your nuts into your throat."

He laughed and gripped her harder. "You're tough. And smart. And that's a damn shame. I knew you might try to tie me to the candlestick. See, I tried to give you an easy out. You found something valuable in Tanbee House. You could've just let me go. Instead, you called in your cop buddies and got my apartment ransacked."

Seraphina took a deep breath and carefully recalled everything she'd ever learned in her self-defense classes. She poised her body, readied it for action, but she had one last question. "So, you've been watching me, have you?"

"Closely." His breath on her ear was hot. Nausea swirled in her gut. She grimaced and held tight to her concentration. "But without Oliver, you're not much better than a kid playing dress-up. The candelabra was a message, Seraphina. I wanted you to know I was listening and watching."

"I've got a message for you, too, Brendan." She knew he'd be expecting another witty comment. Instead, she acted, taking advantage of those precious few seconds. She threw her elbow back as hard as she could. Immense satisfaction flooded her as Brendan's breath leaped from his mouth in a strangled, guttural moan. She pitched her head backward, catching him in the face.

He released her as he stumbled backward. Seraphina didn't hesitate to utter some scathing quip, or pause to soak in the pain that blossomed on the back of her head, but kicked him square in the groin. His hands went from his bloody nose to his crotch as he dropped to his knees. For a beat, he appeared to struggle to his feet. Instead, he gagged and fell into himself, almost like a caving soufflé. There was no gun. A metal rod less than a foot long clanged to the pavement and rolled a few inches.

She reached for her phone and dialed Grant while she stood over Brendan. He was curled onto his side, moaning, hands at six and twelve. The back of her head throbbed where it had made contact with his face.

"Seraphina." Grant answered in record time, his tone worried and a pitch higher than usual. "Ophelia just came to tell me Brendan took off in a hurry not ten minutes ago. She sent a tail after him, but they're five minutes behind. I have a feeling you've got something to do with this."

Seraphina's breathing was labored, but she managed a coherent explanation. "Swift Appraisal and Pawn. Tell Ophelia she'll need some guys to track down the proprietor of the shop, too. He tipped off Brendan the second I stepped inside." She cast a glance at Brendan, still pitifully prone on the ground. He obviously didn't fight very often. Maybe he usually had thugs to do his dirty work for him. Had he employed them today, this all might've had a far less happy ending. She hadn't expected Brendan to go down so easily, and was glad she hadn't had to test her mettle against someone with more experience. "And you'd better tell Oliver we need an ambulance."

* * * *

Grant beat Oliver's brigade to the scene. Seraphina was no longer alone, but standing with two other men dressed like they were late for an important board meeting. She smiled at them when she saw Grant coming. "Hey. These guys passed by, and I had to tell them I was waiting for Brendan to be arrested. They offered to hang out in case he caught his second wind."

Grant couldn't decide what to stare at. He went from Brendan's prone form to Seraphina's slight grimace until he was almost dizzy. "What... what happened? What'd they do to him?"

"They?" She laughed and rubbed the back of her head. "They didn't do anything, thank you very much."

"You did that to him?"

She shot him an annoyed glance. "I'm a single woman. I don't have a man or a dog to protect me. So, I learned to protect myself. Years ago, I was assaulted after a party on campus one night. I fought and got away, but I didn't want to count on being so lucky next time. Don't stare," she chided him. "Kay carries a gun. Go gawp at her."

"Sorry. Sorry. I just...no, you're right. Wow. I mean, you're okay, though? He didn't touch you?"

"He regrets it now."

He ran a hand through his hair and tried to stop feeling so shocked. He wasn't truly surprised a woman like Seraphina could handle herself, but there was a pretty stark difference between knowing she could and seeing the evidence up close. Brendan cupped his groin, and blood leaked from his nose. Grant covered his mouth. "Jesus."

Hours later, Seraphina sat ready to pay the piper.

They met at Oliver and Kay's, where a very somber Kay admitted them. "He's in the parlor." She said nothing more, and didn't even offer her customary bright smile. For the first time, Grant worried for Seraphina. The three of them filed into the parlor and sat on the sofa near a crumbling marble fireplace. And waited.

Oliver paced angrily back and forth in front of them. His hands moved, emphasizing words he couldn't quite articulate. No one had to ask who he was speaking to. "You... I cannot believe...you just. I mean, evidence. It's evidence! And you... I just..."

Seraphina, for her part, seemed unperturbed as she snuggled next to Grant on the sofa. Kay sat on her other side, casting Oliver annoyed glances but keeping silent. Grant figured Oliver had to get it out of his system.

"I still can't quite believe you."

"I wasn't exactly expecting my little adventure to go down that way, Oliver. I had a hunch, okay? Brendan mentioned the appraiser off-hand. It was a long shot that he'd have taken the candelabras there."

"You're asking for a lot."

"I know," she conceded. She wasn't immune to guilt, but she'd explained to Grant on the way over that everything she'd done had been in the interest of catching Brendan. And if she hadn't, he would've kept pumping his noxious drugs into the city and beyond. "If you want me to come forward, I will. I was given care of the candelabra, so I'm naturally legally responsible for the damage I did, and the fact that I used said evidence without knowledge of the investigators. If I've got to face those charges, I will. I accepted that risk. But I also know that there's a case against Brendan no matter what, and that I could not sit here and say the same had you been the one in that shop. It couldn't have been you, Oliver, and everybody here knows that. Brendan had no idea I was working with you. He thought I was on my own. If he'd known, he wouldn't have come after me. But he did. And he admitted to taking the drugs and planting the candlestick in their place. And I've still got the ticket. I expect Dr. Paul thought Brendan would shortly relieve me of the evidence. But do you think he would've ever given that information up to you? Or still had the ticket in the shop by the time you secured a warrant?"

Oliver stared at her. "Goddamn. Just join the attorney general's office already, will you? With a mouth like yours leading the trial, no one's getting away with shit." The compliment was a rough one, delivered in a dark tone.

Seraphina glared back at Oliver while Grant beamed. Later, he'd find a way to privately express the fierce pride he felt for her. His ass-kicking, case-breaking...girlfriend? No, no. That didn't cut mustard at all.

Kay stood suddenly. She crossed her arms, and her expression matched Seraphina's as she regarded Oliver. "She didn't do anything you wouldn't have done in the same circumstances. You passed along your authority to Seraphina the second you asked her to be your eyes and ears inside Tanbee House. In that capacity, she's done nothing illegal and nothing to jeopardize your case. In fact, she solved it for you. Now, say thank you and let these poor people go home. It's late. It's been a long day, everyone's exhausted, and Seraphina will have to go through all of this again when she's questioned at the precinct." In a quick aside, she murmured an apology to Seraphina. "You'll be talking to Cappy Don. He jumped on a red eye the second Oliver called. He's gruff but kind."

There was tense silence as Oliver considered. His face was carefully blank as he looked at Kay. It softened suddenly. "I love you. You make me crazy, but I love you."

Then he turned to Seraphina. "You scare me. You always have. If it weren't for the bruises on your arm where Brendan gripped you, I don't think we could claim self-defense. You messed the guy up pretty bad. Broken nose, busted top lip, and I hear he's been walking with a limp."

Seraphina shrugged.

Oliver sighed. "But you brought this home. You ended it. And Kay's right. You did exactly what I probably would've done. Now I know why it drives the captain nuts. You realize that if I take credit, that's exactly what I'll get? You were the one who finally nailed Brendan, but it'll be me the press claims was the mastermind. The other way, you might face charges, but there's still a solid case, like you said. And in the end, you'd get credit for what you did today."

Sera laughed uncomfortably and scooted a little closer to Grant's side. After what he'd seen she could do, he felt almost honored to realize she sought him for protection. He dropped his arm around her shoulders and gave her a reassuring squeeze. "I just wanted to help, Oliver. Do you even know who you are without this case eating you alive? You carry it off well, but you're a tortured soul. And whether you realize it or not, you're dragging Kay down with you. You've made this her life, too."

Kay frowned. "Oh, gee. I hadn't thought of that. What if he's only interesting when he's tortured?"

Oliver cast her a narrowed glance, but a smile ghosted across his lips. "I'll show you torture. Later." He gave one last long-suffering sigh, and offered his hand to Seraphina. "Seraphina Fawkes, I'd like to officially thank you for carrying out my careful orders. At great risk to yourself, you followed instructions I passed along. The city owes you a debt." His expression was a sober one.

Grant gathered that while Oliver often juggled the rules, he seldom broke them outright. But in the interest of protecting Seraphina and allowing important evidence to be used in Brendan's trial, Grant personally had no reservations about their decision. It was a matter of red tape versus the right thing. And getting Brendan off the streets and dismantling the drug ring was the right thing.

Seraphina's shoulders squared. She sat up a little straighter. "I'd rather the city not even know my name. And you're welcome, Oliver." Then she turned to face Grant. His heart swelled to see the love in her eyes and to know it was for him. "A debt is owed to you if one is owed to me. Thank you for trusting me, even though I know you didn't approve."

He fought the urge to sweep her up into his arms. The occasion wasn't quite right. He'd make up for it later. "You never need my approval, Seraphina. You have my love, and that's enough to allow for any differences." He grinned. "Besides, had I known you were going to kick Brendan's ass, I'd have merely asked to ride along."

Epilogue

Neve narrowed her eyes. "You know what it is? She's a millennial." Neve seemed too sharp for the delicate pale peach dress she wore, but with some skillfully applied makeup, and her hair styled into a crown of braids, she almost looked soft and feminine in the draping fabric belted high on her waist with a white sash.

Kay rolled her eyes and picked up Seraphina's train. Of course, she looked adorable in the peach frock. "So what if my age is the reason I won't marry Oliver yet? We're young. We both have careers. What's the rush, anyway?"

"None, of course." Neve crushed the bouquet of pale pink tiger lilies into Seraphina's silk gloved hands. "You're just contributing to the breakdown of our society."

Kay cast Seraphina a sidelong glance. "Says the lady who doesn't want kids."

Seraphina sniffed. "Well, that's not fair. None of us want kids."

"Well, sure. But they'll happen. Eventually. Are you ready?"

Seraphina took a deep breath and turned toward the long gilded mirror. The dress was everything she ever dreamed it would be, studded with cubic zirconia and silver beads. She glittered like some fairy princess in the shaft of light that angled down from one of the high windows. The skirt was full, the bodice fitted. She'd skipped the veil. Instead, she wore a simple tiara nestled into the red curls artfully arranged on top of her head. "I think so."

Kay's eyes went wide. "Think? You think you're ready to become Mrs. Gallagher?"

From the mirror, Neve's reflection over her shoulder offered a sly grin. "In case you're not, I have a car waiting." Seraphina couldn't see whatever look Kay threw Neve's way, but guessed it was scathing. As was typical of Neve, she shrugged. "Who am I to deny her an escape route? I tried to bail on Duke twice before he actually got me in front of an altar."

"Still trying to figure out what bet he lost," Kay mumbled under her breath.

Seraphina coughed to hide her smile. Her gaze kept coming back to the image in the mirror. It could easily be someone else in the white gown, being fussed and fawned over by her closest friends.

And someone else marrying Grant Gallagher. Perish the thought.

He was enough in his own right, but through Grant, Seraphina would have the kind of family she'd always wanted. Kathleen had cried at Grant's surprise proposal. Which, true to his style, he had executed during lunch in Kathleen's room at Heritage Acres one day. Kathleen had been as emotional as Seraphina. Through tears she'd sent Seraphina a lengthy text message—as Seraphina had sat there gaping, utterly awestruck at a marriage proposal—and promised Seraphina that no matter what she said, yes or no, Kathleen considered her a daughter.

No matter what. No matter what, she had a family. She blinked back tears so they wouldn't ruin her painstakingly applied makeup. Kay would be furious.

She hadn't given Grant an answer that day. He'd turned a brilliant red, and the rest of the meal was strained. She'd gone home alone that night but not slept. She spent the night alone and in a complete stupor. The next morning, Grant arrived on her doorstep. His expression was thunderous. He'd demanded and begged for an explanation in turn. Seraphina finally came to her senses and dragged him to the bedroom, where she spent the rest of the day assuaging any doubts from Grant's mind.

And now, here she was, rich in ways beyond her most cherished dreams. She laughed softly, delicately wiping moisture from beneath her lashes. "You're right, Kay. I don't think I'm ready to be Mrs. Gallagher. I've been waiting my entire life for it."

THE END

Men Like This

Rumor has it, she can't resist . . .

A Long Shot Romance
by Roxanne Smith

Can she trust a man who pretends for a living?

Horror author Quinn Buzzly knows all about the dark side, but when she meets actor Jack Decker, she's moved to explore something completely different—at least on paper. With his sexy good looks, intriguing manner, and charming Irish-tinged English accent, Jack is the perfect model for her next hero. Quinn decides to spend one year in London writing a historical romance inspired by him. Until real life butts in . . .

Jack's jealous ex-fiancée sparks a media storm when she accuses him and Quinn of having an affair. But Jack knows how to play this game. At his insistence, Quinn agrees to go along with the faux romance until the chatter subsides. Then they'll stage a quiet breakup and go their separate ways. Yet Jack is a shameless—and irresistibly convincing—flirt, and Quinn has to remind herself it's an act. Or is it? If Jack means business, he'll have to find the words to convince a wordsmith that their love is the real thing . . .

Chapter 1

Quinn gaped at Richard as if he'd grown an extra appendage in front of her eyes. He might as well have. He was alien to her, despite having known him for many years. "I'm giving you about three seconds to explain."

He had the nerve to smile. It showed off the large glaringly white teeth inside his too-perfect mouth on his too-perfect face. "You don't like it?" His dark gaze wandered, his approval apparent. "I really thought you would."

They were at a nightclub called Sabini's in Hollywood—Quinn deplored Hollywood. A small treasure of a private bar hid deep in the bowels of the rowdy club: quiet, classy, and far from the maddening *wump-wump-wump* of the dance floor down the hall. Yes, she liked it.

No, she wasn't going to admit it.

She crossed her bare arms, partly from the chill but mostly to show Richard she meant business. "Our relationship demands trust. Why would you lie to me, Richard?"

He spared a quick glance at her defensive posture. "Cold?" When she didn't respond, he waved off her concern. "All I've done is taken you out. Is that so bad?"

A jolt of agitation shot through her. Had he lost his mind? Had one too many cocktails earlier? "Yes, I'd say it was! You dragged me across a nasty dance floor wearing a silk ball gown and diamond brooch worth more than your house. You said my sister planned this. I want an explanation, and I want it now."

Richard continued to scan the bar, unruffled by her outburst. "I brought you through the front because I left my key to the private entrance at home. I apologize." He sat on one of the backless cowhide bar stools and lifted a hand for the bartender. "Bottle of champagne, please. Two glasses."

The busty young woman who could've still been driving on a learner's permit smiled. Her gaze roamed freely over Richard before she dashed off to fulfill his glamorous request.

Quinn fought the urge to stick her finger down her throat. Champagne? Who was he kidding?

He turned back to her and patted the seat beside him as if beckoning her to join him like she were some wayward, spoiled child. "Your feet must hurt." His eyes were kind, and his smile knowing. "Angie has excellent fashion sense, but you shouldn't have let her talk you into those heels."

He spoke the truth.

Quinn's feet throbbed from the towering stilettos she had no business wearing. She planned to set fire to the outrageous instruments of torture the very day they lifted the burn ban in L.A. and fight harder for the ballet flats next time.

She scowled at Richard for being right but sat anyway. The blood rushing back into her feet made her woozy with relief. With some effort, she refocused on Richard. "Quit stalling and tell me what we're doing here, or I'm walking out. If I have to call a cab to get home, I swear, I'm taking my next project to someone else."

Richard's dark and impeccably shaped eyebrows shot up. His mouth fell open. Finally, a dent in his smooth surface. "You wouldn't."

He didn't sound so certain.

Quinn smiled at having the upper hand. "I damn sure would. Like I said, this is a trust thing. It was odd when you told me Emily wanted to get together in Hollywood, but I told myself you wouldn't do anything weird. Then you go and order champagne. It keeps getting weirder, and you refuse to tell me what's really going on. You don't own a white windowless van, do you? Or have duct tape in your suit pocket?"

He didn't appear amused. In fact, he managed to appear unaffected, his impenetrable feathers were back in place. Her show of humor must've left him with the incorrect impression she'd be easily managed.

"You're overthinking this. We had a successful night at the fund-raiser. You're gorgeous. I wanted to have an after-party drink with my favorite client. There's nothing *weird* about wanting to prolong a nice evening with a friend."

He couldn't have mocked her any clearer.

She couldn't have cared any less. "Except for your conniving, I'd agree. Why didn't you simply ask?"

"I wanted to surprise you." He smiled his horse-toothed smile. It ruined everything he had going for his face. "Surprise."

The champagne arrived. He handed her a dainty flute. "Drink this." The sweet condescension in his voice nearly undid the frail threads holding Quinn's temper in check, but she kept her grip on the reins—until she glanced at her glass.

It practically brimmed over with the sparkly wine. A sudden burst of insight hit her. "You're trying to get me drunk."

"Now, Quinn—"

"You used my sister to lure me here knowing I'd never come willingly. Real classy." Quinn came out of her seat, disgusted and angry. She growled at the sharp jabs of pain shooting through the soles of her feet.

Richard must've taken the growl as meant for him. "Quinn, calm down, please. Yes, I'm attracted to you. Yes, I thought this was the only way I'd ever get a date with you."

"This is not a date!" Despite her pain, she stamped her foot. The small *click* of her heel failed to make the desired impact.

Richard placed a hand on her arm. "Obviously."

Her fingernails dug into her palms as her hands formed angry little fists at her sides.

Richard didn't notice. His primary concern seemed to have shifted from her to their audience. "You're causing a scene. You asked for an explanation, now allow me to give one before you get us kicked out."

Quinn seethed but didn't interrupt this time. A lift of her brow invited him to continue.

He cleared his throat and straightened his black silk bowtie. Since they'd come from the prestigious city fund-raiser, he was in a tuxedo jacket and slacks.

They'd been a striking pair. Quinn wore a black strapless gown and styled her long blond hair into an elegant chignon that displayed the diamond drops in her lobes. They matched the cluster pinned to the front of her gown.

In this casual setting, they looked like a bad joke. Overdressed and ill behaved. "You have to understand, Quinn. We work together closely. We talk every day. It's not strange I'm attracted to you. Asking you out seemed unprofessional."

Quinn nearly choked on her unspoken reply. This *wasn't* unprofessional? Her jaw practically unhinged at Richard's startling lack of self-awareness.

"I figured if we went out casually and had a few drinks, things might take their natural course."

A shrug accompanied the statement to show how big of a deal it wasn't, but Quinn saw red. She jabbed at his shoulder with an accusing finger. "I'm not stupid, Richard. You celebrate with a glass of champagne. There are completely different motives at play when you order an entire bottle. You weren't hoping for slightly tipsy. You were going for totally sloshed. Then what? You'd take me back to your place and pretend it got out of hand?"

"No, I'd never—"

Quinn turned away. She braced her hands against the bar in an effort to stay on her bruised feet and tried to breathe. "You sure as hell would. After what Blake did, there's nothing I'd put past a man."

He had the audacity to scoff. "Blake is an idiot."

The comment acted like flame to tinder—instant ignition.

She whirled on him. He was no better. He was probably no worse, but at the least, he and Blake were exactly the same. "Oh, and you're some genius? Do you even realize what you've done? I should fire you." She shook her head to dislodge some of her anger, but it wasn't going anywhere. She trembled. "Get away from me. Leave, now."

"Leave?" He repeated the word slowly. "I'm not going anywhere. I brought you here. I'm responsible for you."

Quinn pinned him with every ounce of fire in her green eyes. They flashed when she was angry. They must be crackling like hot coals now. "Do you really expect me to get back in your car? I'll take a cab home. I don't need your protection. What I need is for someone to protect me from *you*."

He looked like he might refuse again.

She hit him with the final blow. "Our contract is riding on how fast you can get away from me. I mean it, Richard."

Their surroundings seemed to come back to them simultaneously. Everyone stared at Richard as they waited in dead silence for his reaction. Even the bartender watched their exchange with rapt attention. Richard's face flushed a dull red. He stood in a deliberate fashion as if it were his idea to leave. "This is foolish."

His clenched jaw and piercing glare labeled him furious, but Quinn had her own store of ire to draw from. She slipped into the most condescending tone she possessed. "You need to go home and think about what you've done."

He recoiled like she'd slapped him, but she'd wager his reaction was nothing more than embarrassment at getting dressed down in a room full of strangers. Maybe now he'd understand how she felt—mortified and belittled. He'd tricked her into coming here and attempted to ply her with drink for the sake of getting her in bed. She couldn't have done anything more insulting than that.

Richard stormed toward the exit. She hoped the staring eyes of the audience, hers included, burned holes in his back as he went.

Her shoulders fell the moment he disappeared from sight. Her rage fled. She wasn't built for dramatics. She frowned at the two untouched glass flutes on the bar. One sat empty while the other comically full. She'd never much cared for champagne hangovers.

Quinn wiggled her fingers in a girlish wave at the bartender still watching her with round eyes. "Can I get a beer?"

Quinn waited until she almost finished her first drink to call Angie, her best friend, the same demon responsible for her miserable, dejected feet. She plucked her cell phone from the hidden pocket inside the bodice of her gown. She wasn't totally stupid. She'd have never let Richard leave without a backup plan up her sleeve.

Or down her dress, as it were.

Angie answered on the first ring. She sounded unfazed, like she'd expected Quinn's late-night call. "How did the fund-raiser go?"

Oh, that's right. She'd done something fun tonight. "I had a great time. In fact, I wish we were still there."

"Oh, I'm sure you'll have others." Angie sounded slightly distracted. Quinn imagined her painting her toenails or watching television. "What time did you get home?"

Quinn cleared her throat. It wasn't her fault. She shouldn't feel stupid, but for whatever reason she did. Must be some kind of male superpower. "Would it be weird if Richard wanted to sleep with me?"

"Of course not. It'd be weird if he didn't." Angie didn't seem distracted anymore. "Did something happen? Oh my God, did you go home with him?" Her voice dropped to a dramatic whisper. "Did you guys do it? Are you calling in secret from the bathroom? Was he good?"

Richard had inspired an intense lack of charitable feelings, but leave it to Angie to smooth Quinn's angry wrinkles mere seconds into the conversation. "No, nothing like that, but he did bring me to a Hollywood nightclub. Shows a little spark, doesn't it?"

"Hollywood? Does he know you?" The disdain in her best friend's voice was welcome commiseration. "Where are you?"

"A place called Sabini's." Quinn appraised the room once more. Large round bulbs suspended from the ceiling hung low and cast their warm glow over the bar, thus creating quite the snug little atmosphere. "I'm pained to admit it, but the private bar is sort of nice. It's the mosh pit of sweaty, spastic idiots in the dance room next door who frighten me. I can't believe that passes for dancing these days. I thought the first guy I saw was having a seizure. He's lucky I didn't shove my brooch in his mouth to stop him from swallowing his tongue."

Angie snorted. "A creative way to divest yourself of a fortune. I've been to Sabini's before. Your Richard's a classy one. Are you two having a good time?"

"Not exactly." Quinn explained in painful detail how her night had gone so topsy-turvy.

She waited in silence for Angie's reply. She imagined her friend working through the scenario in her mind.

Finally, a response. "Well, okay. I guess my question is why you're still there."

Quinn loved easy questions. She sucked the last drop of beer from the long-neck bottle and smacked her lips for emphasis. "To get drunk. Why does anyone sit at a bar and order booze?"

"Nice. Tomorrow you'll wake up not only divorced and homeless but with a hangover cherry on top. Way to take your power back, honey."

"I'm not homeless. I'm staying at a hotel."

"Homeless isn't synonymous with cardboard box. You don't have a home. You're homeless."

Quinn waved to the bartender. Time for another drink. "Shut up and tell me what I'm supposed to do. Am I overreacting?"

Angie clucked her tongue. "Had he taken you out for kung pao chicken, I'd say yes, but this is kind of a big deal. He dragged you to some shady Hollywood club wearing a thousand-dollar ball gown and million-dollar diamonds. Not just ignorant, mind you. Potentially dangerous. This is L.A., not Friendly, Texas. Letting him leave you there was even dumber, by the way."

"Probably." Quinn tried for a deep breath. It escaped as a depressed groan. "What do I do? Fire him?"

The mere suggestion made her stomach pitch. She mustered up a weak smile for Busty the Barkeep, who promptly deposited Quinn's second beer in front of her.

"There's only one thing you can do." Angie sounded apologetic but remained firm. "You have to kill him."

Quinn pressed the phone closer to her ear. The spectacle had ceased, and people were back to their regularly scheduled partying. "Like it's ever that easy."

Angie scoffed. "You have no problem scalping a sweet, vulnerable, and ruggedly handsome pediatrician with a chainsaw, but you can't kill Richard? You even murdered the poor doctor on the very same night he finally worked up the courage to ask that cute barista out on a date. It took a lot of courage for him to step out of his comfort zone. The guy had issues."

Quinn rested one elbow on the bar and said what she always said. "You're taking it too personally, Ang. You've got to quit falling in love with my subjects."

"What in the hell is a barista doing with a chainsaw in the first place, huh? Does she moonlight as a lumberjack?"

Quinn wanted to roll her eyes at Angie's protest but couldn't. She was too pleased with herself. Her life's work revolved around inspiring heartfelt emotion in others. More's the better if the emotions were dark ones like grief and loss.

They were sort of her calling card. "Look, if I wrote Richard into a story to give him a grisly death, I'm afraid he'd notice. He *is* my agent. And you'd understand why the barista had a chainsaw if you'd bother to finish the book."

"I can't, Quinn, I just can't." Her best friend sniffed. "You kill everyone I love."

"I'm sorry. I'll write you a happy ending one day. Promise."

Angie went from sniveling to haughty in the space of a single sentence. "The only happy endings these days are in massage parlors."

Quinn was still laughing when she ended the call and returned the slim black cell phone to the hidden confines of her ball gown.

Her silk strapless Carolina Herrera ball gown.

Every bit of good humor conjured disappeared. Quinn remembered where she sat and how she got there.

Richard, Richard, Richard. He'd really screwed up tonight. Angie's solution, while amusing, wasn't pragmatic and wouldn't solve anything. Quinn nervously rolled the beer bottle between her hands.

The idea of confronting Richard in his office made her queasy. He'd downplay the entire scene and make her out to be a dramatic prude. The smoothness she counted on for publishing negotiations would come back to bite her when she found herself looking down the barrel of it rather than grinning smugly from behind it, but what were her choices?

She had to make a stand. She needed to put him in his place, be the iron fist of the feminine movement.

Then again, there wasn't much determined avoidance couldn't patch up. Key West was fabulous this time of year. Cabanas, boat drinks, palm trees, and pool boys.

When had she last gone on vacation? Disneyland three years ago. With Blake. Quinn didn't want to think about that. She wanted to daydream about pool boys. For research, of course. She was far too old for a pool boy.

She'd need a pool *man*.

"You don't match."

For an instant, the deep voice coming from behind stunned her. Since she sat virtually alone on her side of the L-shaped bar, she had no choice but to accept the man—a pool man if her luck had improved any—intended the words for her. Some drunken fool trying to succeed where Richard failed. What had she been thinking staying here? She should've picked up a bottle of tequila and moved this pity party to the privacy of her hotel room.

He had an accent, although she couldn't place the dialect. Definitely European. Rather than turn around right away to face her new visitor, she took a long, hard look at the beer bottle in her hand. Too soon to order her third? She wanted fuzzy, not pickled.

She'd put it off long enough. Quinn swung around on the tail end of an eye roll to greet Bachelor Number Two. The smart reply she had ready died on her lips.

Meet the Author

A Florida native, **Roxanne Smith** has called everywhere from Houston to Cheyenne home. Currently residing in Asheville, North Carolina, she's an avid reader of every genre, a cat lover, pit bull advocate, and semi-geek. She loves video games, Doctor Who, and her dashing husband. Her two kids are the light of her life. Visit her website at roxannesmith.net, and her blog at smithrox.blogspot.com.